Tempting F...

They were so close she could smell the trace of cologne he was wearing, smell the raw maleness of his skin. She thought she had never wanted anyone so badly.

He briefly closed his eyes, trying to keep himself together. "I'm your teacher. We can't have this conversation." The rote phrases were the only thing keeping him from stepping over the precipice.

"So if you weren't my teacher...?" The question hung in the air.

"Juliet..." He couldn't answer. He couldn't lie convincingly and to admit the truth was impossible.

"Do you want me?" She was leaning even closer, millimetres from his body. Pretty much any other guy in the bar would kill to be in this position.

"More than anything." He could hardly believe he had admitted it. She had him transfixed. "Right now, being this close to you is like torture. But it's wrong and nothing is going to happen. Even if you weren't my student, I'm far too old for you."

TEMPTING HER TEACHER

by

Noël Cades

First Printing, 2016

ISBN: 0-9925017-9-2
ISBN-13: 978-0-9925017-9-2

To Georgette Gray

I. The bet

"Juliet Martin, are you wearing lipstick?"

Oh no. The first day of term and already Miss Villiers was on her case.

"Go and wash your face immediately. And don't be late for class."

Juliet dragged herself off into the nearest cloakroom. Her best friend Margot was in there, sitting up on the washbasins and leaning against the mirror, her eyes half closed. She was listening to music and showed no intention of going to class. Several of her braids had escaped her ponytail and she hadn't taken her second ear studs out, as you were supposed to.

"Villiers?" she asked, seeing Juliet wiping her mouth with a tissue.

"She's always on my case."

Margot, like Juliet, wore as much make up as she could get away with. Even though St Gillian's was a girls-only Catholic school, appearances mattered. Plus there could always be some random event like half a dozen hot paratroopers accidentally landing in the school yard.

This had never happened, but they lived in hope.

"You're going to be late," Juliet said, tying her own blonde hair back neatly in case the teacher was still lurking outside. She got in enough trouble as it was, she didn't need any more on the first day. She and Margot both had the same Latin class to get to so they headed there together.

Margot looked at her through heavily mascaraed lashes that definitely wouldn't have passed Miss Villiers' inspection, any more than her multiple earrings. "Tell me again why the hell I ever decided to take Latin?"

The answer to this was quite simple. Old Mr Bryan, who taught Latin, was considered to be a soft touch and his classes were very laid back.

Truth be told, Juliet had secretly grown to love the Roman poetry they translated. Even more than the Romantic poets they studied in English. But she kept this quiet from her friends who might have mocked her.

"It's stupid, all these rules. We're eighteen now, legal adults, and we're still treated like little kids," Margot said as they walked down the corridor together.

They arrived and went to take their seats at the back as usual. It was such a small class that there was plenty of choice where to sit, though no one ever dared sit on the back row. It was established as Juliet's and Margot's territory.

"Oh look, what joy, it's the charity case foster slut and her sidekick."

It was Cynthia, their nemesis, scowling one of her usual greetings.

Juliet stiffened but Margot wasn't going to give Cynthia the satisfaction of seeing Juliet upset.

"I think you have chocolate on your chin, bitch. Oh wait no, it's just the shit that comes out of your mouth."

Without giving Cynthia a chance to respond she brushed past her desk, pushing Juliet along with her so she didn't try to retaliate as well. Cynthia always managed to make trouble for Juliet.

They took their places and got ready for the class. Margot still had her earbuds in as she figured Mr Bryan wouldn't notice.

The class was kept waiting for a few minutes for the Latin teacher to arrive. The conversation level rose as students relaxed and chatted, even though they were supposed to keep quiet.

Suddenly the room fell silent.

"Ave Caesar, what do we have here?" Margot suddenly murmured.

Juliet had been buried in her exercise book, doodling while she awaited Mr Bryan. She looked up.

Wow.

Whoever this was, it wasn't Mr Bryan.

A young man - and not just that, an incredibly good looking young man - was arranging some books and papers on Mr Bryan's desk. He was tall, with dark brown hair and greenish hazel eyes.

He immediately had their full and undivided attention, although he didn't realise it. When he was ready, he stood up before them.

"Good morning, I'm Mr Spencer and I'll be taking you for Latin this term."

He assumed a confident air yet Juliet wasn't entirely sure that it was solid. Facing a classroom of girls as new teacher was always going to be nerve-wracking. Or in any social situation where you were a stranger introducing yourself to a roomful of people, she thought.

"Where's Mr Bryan?"

"Is Mr Bryan coming back?"

"Is he dead?"

The new teacher smiled at this one. "No, he's very much alive and well. He's just taken a sabbatical and I'm filling in."

There was silence while people digested this.

What everyone wanted to know was who he was, where he was from, how old he was - Juliet guessed mid twenties - and whether he would be a pushover like Mr Bryan. Hopefully so, since he didn't look too strict.

They couldn't directly ask this last question of course, but they did manage to extract that he was twenty-seven, had previously taught at a private boys' school, and had studied in the United Kingdom at St Stephen's House, Oxford.

"St Stephen's?" one girl said. "Isn't that for priests? Our neighbours' pastor went there."

"It is a theological foundation, but not all students are ordinands. Studying for ordination I mean," he explained.

"So you're not a priest?"

"No, I'm not."

"But you could have been?" This came from Margot. She was merciless when she wanted to be.

"It isn't my immediate plan."

So was that his plan in future? Was this super hot, super fit guy going to end up ordained and celibate? He looked more like he should be modelling outdoor clothing for some mountain gear catalogue.

"So what are you into?" Juliet asked.

Mr Spencer looked disconcerted. "Excuse me?"

Juliet gave one of her sweet but suggestive smiles that from experience, completely unnerved most men. "What Latin writers are your favourites, I mean?"

It had the desired effect. He almost blushed. "Much of my study has been in mediaeval Latin, though this year we'll be doing Vergil and Cicero." It wasn't really an answer.

"Doing Vergil?" Margot said, putting innuendo on the first word. A few people snickered.

Mr Spencer either didn't notice or ignored this. "Cicero's Pro Catiline and the Aeneid, Book IV. Now if you could hand round these worksheets, starting with..." he looked questioningly at Cynthia on the front row.

Mr Bryan had made the grave error of letting the class know that "Cynthia" was pronounced "Koontia" by the Ancient Greeks, so Juliet and Margot had taken to pronouncing it that way to annoy her, as it sounded like the C-word.

"Koontia," Margot helpfully supplied.

"...Koontia," he repeated, looking at Cynthia and frowning slightly.

"It's Cynthia!" She swung her head around to glare at Margot and Juliet. In her irritation Cynthia managed to make her name sound even more like a snake's hiss than ever.

Margot's face was the picture of innocence, as much as Margot could look innocent anyway. Juliet was trying not to laugh. She briefly caught the new teacher's eye and he did look flushed and confused.

She almost felt bad. But he was a new teacher, and temporary. Being put through the wringer was expected.

As Mr Spencer turned back to write something on the whiteboard, Juliet noticed how strong and broad his back was. His hands were really masculine and strong as well. She found herself imagining what they might feel like on her body: undoing her clothes, pushing them off. Firmly, maybe a little bit rough.

She squirmed in her seat, just thinking about it. Maybe he hadn't had sex for a while and would be really pent up. Locking the door when everyone else had left he classroom, pinning her down, not taking no for an answer. His lips on her neck. Sliding his hands between her thighs…

Juliet shook herself out of the daydream. What the hell had come over her? She found herself blushing when he turned around. He caught her eye momentarily and for a moment she freaked out that he could read her thoughts. She should be concentrating on the Latin text.

* * *

Afterwards they walked back through the courtyard together.

"Well that was a dead loss," Margot said.

Juliet asked what she meant.

"All that hot male talent and it's practically wearing a dog collar. Not that it matters, he's not my type."

"Isn't he?" Juliet thought a man that attractive would be anyone's type, particularly in the Great Man Desert that was St Gillian's.

"Too much of a Gilbert. As in Gilbert Blythe, Anne of Green Gables. Wholesome boy next door. I guess he's okay for a white guy."

Juliet nearly choked. "For a white guy? What does that mean? Your last three boyfriends were white."

"Yeah, and look where that got me. I think it's time to switch back. Mr Spencer is all yours, if that bitch doesn't get him first." She meant Cynthia, who had been making obvious eyes at the new Latin teacher all class.

"Well thank you kindly, ma'am, for leaving at least one specimen for me," Juliet said, her tone mock-sarcastic.

Margot shrugged. "He looks like the sort of guy who'd rather go for a bike ride and picnic than get down and dirty. The type of boy your parents would love you to date. If he wasn't your teacher, obviously. The kind of man who…"

11

"Okay, I get the picture!" Juliet said. "What makes you sure he wouldn't get down and dirty? He might have a whole secret life going on."

"Yeah, you just think that if you want to. Honestly, look at the guy. He actually had a bible on his desk. He's so much of a virgin that he makes the Pope look like a stud."

For some reason this annoyed Juliet. "I bet I could change that."

"I bet you could not."

"He's just a guy. He must have urges," Juliet said. "He probably had girlfriends at university, all students screw around."

Margot shot her a wicked glance. "Fifty bucks says he's a virgin and will still have his V-card by the end of the year."

"A hundred bucks says he won't."

Margot started laughing. "Girl, are we seriously betting on whether you can seduce our new Latin teacher?"

Juliet wavered for a moment, then felt resolute. "Yes. Why not?"

"I can think of a million reasons but they're all as sensible as hell. This actually sounds amusing. I'll even help you."

"You're not going to have a go yourself?"

"Jesus no," Margot said. "As I said he's not my type. I mean I wouldn't kick him out if I was feeling bored and horny, but the effort of seducing someone like that, no thanks. Not worth it. Imagine how useless he'd be in bed, the first time. All fumbling."

Margot was a lot more sexually experienced than Juliet. Even so, Juliet wasn't going to take her word for it.

"You never know. Some guys are naturally gifted." She had personally thought that Mr Spencer looked very capable.

"I can assure you he won't be. But if you want that hundred dollars so badly, I guess you'll find out one way or another."

* * *

It was a sunny day so they ate their lunch on the grass with their other friend, Fhemie, who didn't do Latin with them.

"So I heard Mr Bryan got fired and has a hot new replacement," Fhemie said. "What's he like?"

12

Fhemie was even more boy crazy than both Juliet and Margot combined. This was despite the fact her grandmother wanted her to become a nun.

"Hot enough that you'll wish you'll did Latin once you see him," Juliet said.

Fhemie laughed, biting into a brownie. "Never!" she said, her mouth full of chocolate.

"I never know how you can eat all that and stay so skinny," Juliet said. Fhemie's first course had been two bags of chips. "You're addicted to junk."

"It's all the dancing. I burn it off. I really can't be doing with that quinoa shit you eat, it looks gross."

Margot, who only ever ate fruit for lunch, lay back in the sun. "Once you stop dancing you'll balloon up like a fat bag of dough. I saw it happen to Ashley Neiman when she did her knee in and couldn't do athletics any more."

"I will never stop dancing." Fhemie's only ambition, despite her family's opposition, was to become a dancer. They regarded it as an immodest profession. Her grandmother had never forgiven her father for dropping out of seminary in Manila to marry Fhemie's mother. She saw Fhemie entering a convent as compensation, not that Fhemie was having any of it.

Juliet envied Fhemie her single-mindedness. She still had no idea what she wanted to do when they finished school. She was looking at getting loans for college but it would be a struggle.

She stretched out her legs in the September sun, enjoying the contrast of the warm rays on top and the cool grass beneath her skin. Her skirt was riding up but she didn't care.

"You're practically showing your va-jay," Margot said.

"So?"

"Look who's walking past."

Juliet sat up with a jerk, causing her skirt to fall right back and momentarily flash her underwear. Only to see Mr Spencer walking past them at that exact moment. He clearly saw what she had on display, but turned his head away abruptly.

Margot laughed. "I swear he's crossing himself mentally at the sight of such temptation. He'll be off to bathe in holy water."

"Is that him?" Fhemie said. "Wow. That has to be the hottest teacher I've ever seen. Including in TV shows or movies. Maybe he'll hold detention and I can get myself in trouble."

"Hands off, because he's Juliet's. She's going to seduce him by the end of term. Otherwise I win a hundred bucks."

Fhemie rolled her eyes. "Like a hundred bucks matters to you, you're such a little rich girl." Fhemie's family were also wealthy - you had to be to afford the fees at St Gillian's - but her grandmother kept a tight hold on the purse strings.

Juliet had been given a subsidised place, something Cynthia constantly taunted her about. Margot and Fhemie couldn't have cared less whether Juliet's family were bankrupt or billionaires, which was why they were such great friends. All they cared about was having fun, and getting away with breaking as many rules as possible.

There was no bigger rule to break than having an affair with a teacher, Juliet thought. She would totally be expelled if she was ever found out.

* * *

Juliet might have given up on the bet as a stupid joke or whim, except she found herself dreaming of Mr Spencer that night.

It started all weird and twisted about all over the place, as dreams do. All her friends were waving goodbye to her, going on a school trip to the moon in the school bus. "They've put wings on it!" Fhemie was saying.

But Juliet was left behind because she had forgotten her shoes. She was desperately trying to find them but the others were getting further and further way. She had to have shoes because it was going to be very rocky. Where were they?

She was going through every classroom searching for them, and then she was in the Latin classroom.

"You don't have your shoes Juliet. You'll have to stay and do more Latin," Mr Spencer was saying. For some reason he was dressed as a priest with a black shirt and a white collar.

In her dream Juliet felt really torn between wanting to go to the moon with her friends and staying behind in Latin. Mr Spencer was looking at her with searing eyes.

Then suddenly she was lying over his desk and he was pinning her down.

"This is how you need to learn Latin. Here..." Mr Spencer's hand had slipped beneath her underwear and he was teasing her, bringing her to the brink.

His lips hovered over hers... so close... she could feel the air move between his face and hers but he wouldn't bring his lips down on her or press hard enough with his hands. His fingers were circling around her sensitive flesh, tormenting, driving her nerves wild.

She was writhing up against him, trying to get him to give her the pressure she needed.

"Please, please..." she was crying out, but Mr Spencer was telling her it was forbidden to go any further. Then suddenly everything was sucked away and she was naked and freezing cold and alone and he was gone.

Juliet woke up with a start. She had kicked her quilt off and was lying there in nothing but her thin nightgown: no wonder she was freezing in her dream. She rarely ever had dreams this vivid or about actual people. What could it mean?

II. Raising the stakes

Juliet honestly wasn't sure why she had agreed on this stupid bet. But now she had, she wasn't backing out.

Mr Spencer was extremely sexy, and the purity thing gave it an extra edge, she thought. And after all, it wasn't like he was a Roman Catholic priest who wasn't allowed to marry, regardless of how he had appeared in her dream. She probably wouldn't go to hell for this. Probably.

She started Mission: Seduce Spencer in the most obvious way: flirting outrageously with him in class. Or as outrageously as she could get away with. She wasn't the only one fluttering her eyelashes and giving him suggestive smiles though. Half the class had crushes on the new Latin teacher.

Every day before his class she would slip to the bathroom and put on extra make-up, trying to get from there to his classroom without Miss Villiers or another teacher spotting her.

Margot couldn't stop laughing at her. "You need a booth like Wonderwoman. He might actually notice if you showed up in a bikini."

So far Juliet didn't seem to be getting any reaction. But she was undeterred. She was certain that at least once she had caught his eye while they were supposed to be working on a translation, and he had quickly looked away.

It was just a flicker: but it was enough. Enough to encourage her to continue. It was more about proving a point to Margot really, than the money.

They had been discussing Vestal Virgins in class: Roman women appointed as priestesses who had to remain celibate until they retired. Margot thought it sounded awful. Juliet rather liked the idea of it as the women were considered very powerful.

"Well you couldn't be one anyway," Margot said.

"I could if I wanted to."

"Too late for that, girl. But I know someone who can." Margot shot a glance at Mr Spencer and the two girls dissolved into giggles which they had to suppress as coughs when the Latin teacher looked over at them.

"Anything you'd like to ask?" he asked them.

Margot grinned. "We were just discussing becoming Vestal Virgins, Sir."

Mr Spencer went slightly red, which wasn't helped by Cynthia chiming in.

"I think you'll find they don't take sluts," she muttered, looking pointedly at Juliet.

"What was that, Cynthia?" Mr Spencer asked.

"Nothing," Cynthia said.

"She was just talking to herself," Margot told him. "She does that a lot." When he had turned back to the whiteboard she turned to Cynthia and mouthed "slut" back at her.

It was very hard trying to flirt with Mr Spencer because he seemed to get all the more serious the more Juliet tried. He was so good looking, she loved the way his hair looked kind of tousled on top. His lips were firm and well moulded and he had a strong, beautifully sculpted bone structure.

"Where do you go to mass, Sir?" someone asked, trying to delay the return to their Latin study.

Mr Spencer looked awkward. "I don't go to mass."

"You don't go to church?" This caused some shocked murmurs as usually all the teachers at St Gillian's were really devout.

"I didn't say that. I don't go to mass, because I'm not a Catholic. I go to a baptist church," he told them.

There was an even greater murmur of interest at this. "I thought you had to be Catholic to teach here," Juliet said.

"Usually, perhaps. But there aren't so many Latin teachers to go around, so they made an exception. Which is how I'm lucky enough to have become your teacher," Mr Spencer said, giving them a broad smile.

He was devastating when he smiled, it made Juliet's stomach flip. Like a sexy, macho angel. He caught Juliet's eye and she wondered if he was teasing them.

She also wondered if she was falling for him. That wasn't in her plan at all.

* * *

Margot came back to Juliet's house after school, supposedly to do homework. The reality was that they just wanted to hang out but Juliet wasn't supposed go to the mall or anywhere else after school. Her Aunt Mary, whom she lived with, was very strict.

She was actually a distant cousin of Juliet's father but it had seemed weird to call her "Cousin Mary", so "Aunt" had stuck.

"Where's your aunt tonight?" Margot asked.

"Out at her bible study thing. She won't be back until this evening." Aunt Mary was very devout which was why she had insisted on Juliet going to Catholic school.

Margot yawned. "As soon as I finish at St Gillian's I'm throwing every bible away."

Juliet was shocked. "You can't do that, they're like sacred objects."

"Not to me." Margot bit into a cookie. "These are great, did you make these or did Aunt Marilla?" She had nicknamed Juliet's aunt after Marilla in Anne of Green Gables.

"I did," Juliet said. "You'll end up calling her that name to her face one day if you're not careful."

"It fits so well. She's just like her, taking on a poor orphan girl and being all strict and proper about everything," Margot said.

Juliet really didn't get Margot's obsession with the book or the TV series, which Margot owned on DVD.

"We're just like them," Margot insisted. "I mean you haven't got red hair and Diana wasn't black I guess, but other that that the parallels are eerie."

"We're not even Canadian. So who does that make Fhemie?"

"Ruby, the hot flirtatious one, naturally," Margot said.

18

"Doesn't she die?"

Margot looked a little wistful. "Yeah, I love that scene. It's so sad."

Juliet had hated it. "It's like she has to die because she's flirty and fun loving. Ruby I mean, not Fhemie. Like the wages of sin are death or whatever."

"You're the good little Catholic girl, so you would know."

Then they both laughed. Neither of them could be described as "good", they were known at St Gillian's for being hell raisers. In the past couple of years Juliet had tried to behave better but it got so boring.

* * *

Juliet decided to get bolder. She wore her skirt as short as possible to Latin, looked at Mr Spencer from lowered eyelashes, pouted and chewed her lip.

If she had tried this with Mr Bryan he would have probably had a heart attack. But she was getting nowhere with the new Latin teacher so far. If anything it felt like he was being more distant to her.

She put her hand up. "Sir, are you married?"

He wasn't wearing a ring but you never knew. The rest of the class waited avidly for his answer as it was something that nearly everyone else wanted to know as well.

"I'm not, no."

Before he could elaborate, Margot chimed in. "Why not?"

"I'm engaged."

This took the wind out a few sails. Including Juliet's, who figured the bet was now off.

Nonetheless there was a volley of questions. Everyone was curious about the new teacher.

"When are you getting married?"

"What does she do?"

"How did you meet?"

Mr Spencer gave a half-smile. "I think we're getting diverted from Vergil. Cynthia, will you scan line twenty-seven please."

19

Cynthia always made a big mess of this and Margot rolled her eyes in impatience waiting for her to struggle through it. Juliet also felt frustrated. The rhythm of the Latin verse came easily to her and it was horrible hearing it butchered by Cynthia.

At one point Cynthia managed to mispronounce a Latin word and made it sound obscene in English. Juliet and Margot couldn't stop giggling and Mr Spencer noticed.

"Just a moment, Cynthia." He looked at them. "Would you care to explain what is so amusing?"

Margot, expecting to disconcert him, explained the joke. But the Latin teacher was unruffled.

"Do you really think it's appropriate to use such disgusting language?" he asked. "What would your parents think if they they could hear you?"

Juliet's laughter dried up at this and her face clouded over. "My parents are dead," she told him. She was surprised he didn't know this as all her background was in her student file.

Mr Spencer now looked very disconcerted. "I'm sorry." There was an awkward pause. "Let's just get back to the text."

The class continued and when the bell finally went for recess, Mr Spencer called Juliet to stay behind.

She approached his desk feeling oddly nervous, clutching her folders against her chest.

"About before," he began. "I didn't know about your parents, otherwise…"

"It's okay." She tried to reassure him. "It was a long time ago. Years ago." Very long, very horrible years. She still missed them and felt panic from time to time that she was forgetting what memories she did have.

"Regardless, I wouldn't have mentioned it if I had known. I'm sorry if it caused you pain."

The look in his eyes was truly sincere and for the first time Juliet met his gaze, both of them serious. She had caught his eye many times with the flirting and the messing around in class, but in this moment everything had shifted.

"Truly, I'm fine."

They were both silent for a moment. She looked at his strong shoulders and wondered what it would be like to have his arms around her. She wondered what he was thinking.

He broke the silence. "I'll see you tomorrow in class then."

Juliet went towards the door but before exiting she turned to ask him something. "Wasn't it in my student file, about my family history?"

"I never read those," he told her. "Not at the start anyway. I prefer to make my own conclusions."

"I see. I hope the ones you made of me aren't too bad."

Mr Spencer smiled. "You have a lot of talent for Latin. It's up to you whether you waste that or not."

* * *

"So that's that then," Juliet said afterwards to Margot.

"That's what?"

"The end of the bet. He has a fiancée."

Margot gave her a wicked smile. "Oh not it's not girl. Everything just got a whole lot more interesting. And easier, maybe. Every man wants a final fling, right? To make sure they're choosing the right woman."

Juliet wasn't sure about this. It felt kind of wrong, trying to seduce someone in a relationship. Also Mr Spencer had been so kind and apologetic after class. "It doesn't seem very nice to his fiancée."

"I bet she's not all that," Margot said. "Did you see his face when he spoke of her? It didn't exactly light up."

"What would you expect? We were in class. He's hardly going to start singing a love song."

Margot shrugged. "It's a feeling I have. Anyway, you're going to have to change strategies. The full on flirting thing is getting nowhere."

Juliet had to agree. "So what do I do?"

"We should track him down outside school. Find his church maybe, and start going there," Margot suggested.

"But it's a Baptist thing." Juliet's aunt expected her to attend Catholic mass on Sundays.

"I don't mean Sunday. Those people, they go to church like every day. We'll go one evening. Tell your aunt it's a multi-faith prayer meeting or something."

It might be interesting to see what it was like, if nothing else. "Maybe." Juliet really wasn't sure if her aunt would see it that way. She took religion seriously.

Satisfied that Juliet agreed, Margot changed the subject the weekend. "Can you stay over Friday? We can use our fake ID and go to a bar. My parents have a dinner date so they won't know."

Juliet and Fhemie only ever managed to stay out late if they were sleeping over at Margot's place. "Sure, if my aunt doesn't throw up some objection."

If truth be told, Juliet didn't want to give up on Mr Spencer just yet. She didn't want to admit it but she was getting a genuine crush on the Latin teacher. Having erotic dreams about him had been really confusing.

III. Conflicted feelings

It was Carl Spencer's rule to switch off from school thoughts when he went home each day, at least for a couple of hours. Later in the evening he often had marking to attend to, and he felt at least couple of hours mental break were healthy.

Today though St Gillian's and its students remained on his mind. In particular one student: Juliet Martin.

Carl found himself thinking of the blonde schoolgirl more often than he would have liked. There was something about her that had struck him on the first day. She was a beautiful girl but she looked troubled.

"You're zoning out again, honey, I need you to give me an opinion on these wedding invitations."

His fiancée Rebecca was round at his place, going over their wedding plans. They didn't live together of course, as both were waiting until marriage to move in together.

"Do you like the gold edged ones better or the ones with the silver scrolling?"

Carl tried to feel an interest in the different pieces of card. Really, the details of the wedding didn't overly interest him. He just wanted to get it done: start his married life, have a family and all the other things he had in his life plan.

Rebecca smoothed down her long skirt. Her hair fell down over her shoulder as she looked at the invitations, trying to decide between them. She had long, dark, straight hair, held off her face with a couple of clips.

"The ivory ones have little gold crosses on them. It think that's kind of nice, don't you?" she said. "Appropriate".

Carl and Rebecca had met through their church. The pace of their courtship had been quite rapid, but then that was often the way if you didn't spend months or years having a test run by cohabiting, as Carl thought of it. There was no reason to drag it out.

Seeing Rebecca's dark hair he had a flashback to Juliet's blonde hair. She also pinned hers back, as was the requirement at St Gillian's, but a strand would often escape and she would play with it in class. It was an unconscious habit but Carl found it strangely distracting.

He was feeling particularly guilty that evening. Partly for his lack of tact in mentioning Juliet's parents and upsetting her. But also because he had felt the strongest urge to put his arms around her when she had stood there after his class, looking so sad and trying to act as though everything was okay.

"You're daydreaming again." Rebecca's voice broke through his reverie.

Carl tried to erase his memories of the day by thinking back to his relationship with Rebecca. He remembered the first time they had held hands, on a church picnic when they were officially dating. Their first kiss - awkward, but that was presumably always the way - after a date at an Italian restaurant.

"Sorry. I'm happy with any of them. The ivory ones seems nice," he said, saying it only because he thought Rebecca liked them.

Rebecca looked pleased. "Ivory it is then. I think they're more solemn, don't you? After all it is about sanctifying our future life together."

She was also working on the guest list which was predominantly their families and people from church. Carl had thought they might invite friends from college, even a couple of guys from his home town, but Rebecca was concerned about keeping numbers tight.

It was probably wise. There was no point starting married life with huge debts from a blowout wedding.

"You know we could just fly to Vegas one weekend," he joked.

Rebecca turned to him, shocked. "Are you serious? Starting our marriage in a city of sin, gambling and…" She couldn't bring herself to say "prostitution".

"Relax, I was only joking. Of course we'll do it the correct way. Even though it's hard waiting to be with you properly as my wife."

Even as he said this it felt kind of hollow. The celibacy had actually been easier than he had thought. He figured it was thanks to prayer, though he remembered how his friend Daniel had been practically climbing the walls ahead of his own wedding night, and his fiancée - now wife - as well.

No wonder that Dan and Jenny were pregnant just weeks after the honeymoon. But Carl himself didn't find the waiting as hard as he had imagined it might be.

The zeal and the joy with with Dan and Jenny had approached their wedding was one of the things that had encouraged him to propose to Rebecca. He and Rebecca hadn't been dating that long: they had fallen into it partly due to being two single young people in church. Everything was easier as a couple, you could double date with other couples, do social activities.

Carl had admired Rebecca's devotion to her faith. He was at an age himself where he was starting to think of having a family and making a life with someone. Rebecca was a good person, attractive, she was both church and career minded. It had made almost perfect sense. They seemed entirely compatible.

Rebecca stood up, gathering the invitation samples together and putting them in her bag. "I have to get going, I have some work to catch up on tonight." Rebecca worked in a bank and was studying towards a financial qualification.

"Don't forget that we have marriage class tomorrow night after church," she reminded him.

As if Carl could forget. The marriage classes were held at their church for engaged couples and he and Rebecca had faithfully attended every one. They wanted to do all they could to ensure they started married life properly.

Rebecca gathered her things together and tilted her head for Carl's kiss. Chaste kissing was considered appropriate, but the pastor who led the marriage classes continually warned of the dangers of going further, even when one was engaged. "A marriage based on lust is a union that won't go the distance," he had said.

Rebecca had taken the pastor's teachings very much to heart, taking on the responsibility to keep her Carl at arm's length from her until their union was properly sanctified. It wasn't hard for either of them as they'd both been committed to chastity since teenagerhood. After a while you got used to it.

As Rebecca left, Carl wondered if it was healthy or not that he didn't feel much desire to break the rules. Maybe a switch would flick on once they were confirmed as man and wife. It wasn't that he didn't have urges or sexual thoughts, but whenever he did they were rarely triggered by Rebecca. Perhaps that was a good thing, because he respected her so much.

Despite himself he found his mind wandering to St Gillian's and the sultry look that Juliet had given him as she read out a line of Latin love poetry. He realised he had grown hard just remembering it.

This wouldn't do. He was a teacher, his students were completely forbidden fruit to even fantasise about. He would need to pray about this.

* * *

"I looked up Baptist churches. It must be one of these two." Margot showed Juliet the locations on a street directory.

They were at Margot's house, getting ready to go out. She was lucky that she didn't have to babysit her younger siblings very often as her parents had a housekeeper who lived with them.

Vanessa, a cute five-year-old, bounced into the room.

"Can you come and play with my dolls? Can I try on your make up? Can you do my nail varnish?"

Margot rolled her eyes and reached into a drawer, where she kept some old make up just for this purpose.

"Here you go. Here's the special pink sparkly powder. But you keep quiet."

Vanessa started applying it like face paint, all over her cheeks and forehead.

Juliet laughed. "Here, you're supposed to put it on your eyelids. Close your eyes." Vanessa obeyed while Juliet applied it properly for her. "There, you look super sophisticated."

"Do I look like a princess? Can I come out with you to the ball? Can I wear my Cinderella dress?"

"Yes and no. We're not going to a ball, and you'd find it super boring," Margot told her.

They were meeting Fhemie in town, having told their respective parents and Juliet's Aunt Mary that they were going to the movies.

It was a warm evening so Juliet was wearing skinny black jeans and a silver crop top showing off her midriff, which was still tanned from summer. She kept outfits like this at Margot's house because her aunt would have burnt them and called for the priest to do an exorcism if she ever discovered them. Margot was wearing a skirt that barely covered her thong, with high heels. Her legs looked endless.

"You look like a Victoria's Secret model," Juliet said, admiring her friend.

"Except for the hair. They wouldn't let me on the catwalk with these," Margot said, arranging her braids.

"That's their loss."

They drove down to the city in Margot's car. Fhemie met them in the the usual place. "See this?" she said, showing them her arm which had a big scribbled line on it. "A tattoo thanks to Eunice. With a Sharpie so it won't come off. My god, Juliet, you are so lucky you don't have annoying little sisters."

Juliet, who would have loved to have had siblings, said nothing. Having lost both her parents and spending most of her childhood in a series of foster homes, she often felt very alone in the world. But she didn't like to talk about it with the others.

"So where are we going?" Fhemie asked.

"The Green Room," Margot told her, naming a popular bar that got busy without being crowded to the point of bursting.

"Awesome. Did you track down that hot Latin teacher yet?" Fhemie was fascinated by the bet between Juliet and Margot.

Juliet told her that they were still working on it. "Margot reckons we should try either the church on New Street or the one in Kennedy Avenue."

Fhemie wasn't impressed. "Why don't you just follow him home from school? I'll do it for you if you like. He doesn't know who I am, and I'm small. I can hide behind bushes."

They all burst out laughing at the idea of Fhemie stalking Mr Spencer.

"You might just ask him outright what church he goes to," Fhemie suggested.

Juliet was worried that this would be too obvious.

"Too obvious? Girl, you've practically been hanging off him in class for the last two weeks," Margot said.

"You know what I mean. If we ask him where he goes, and then we just show up there, it seems kind of stalkerish."

They would just have to try both churches and keep visiting until they managed to encounter him there.

* * *

As they entered the bar Fhemie groaned. "Oh shit, they have karaoke night. Let's go elsewhere."

"No, let's stay," Margot said, having already spotted a cute guy by the bar.

"You know I hate karaoke." Fhemie was tone deaf, which meant she hadn't been roped into singing in the school choir like Margot and Juliet had been.

There was a large girl on the small stage trying to sing Mariah Carey and sounding like she was being murdered. "You couldn't do worse than her," Margot pointed out. "You could just rap something."

This presumed they were all going to sign up. Juliet had only done karaoke once before at someone's birthday party, when everyone had sung in a big group and she had been nowhere near the microphone. Other than that she only sang in the choir, but never got solos because Cynthia was the choir teacher's pet. Even though Cynthia frequently sang off-key on the high notes.

Margot went to get them some song slips while Juliet bought drinks for the three of them. As expected, Margot had chosen Rihanna and Beyoncé for herself.

"You'll never sing that," Fhemie said, looking at her choices. "It's really tricky."

"Like you would know." Margot dismissed her concerns. "What about you?" she asked Juliet.

Juliet skimmed through the song sheet. She had a thing for older songs, and picked Heart of Glass by Blondie much to Fhemie's disgust. "What the hell is that? That's like from before you were born. Sing something from this century at least."

"It's classic," Juliet said.

As the slips were handed in to the karaoke host Juliet suddenly felt her stomach turn into a ball of nerves. What the hell had she done? She suddenly realised she might actually have to stand up in front of a bar full of drunken people and sing something by herself. She nudged Margot. "I don't think I can do this. Will you go up with me if they call me?"

Margot refused and Fhemie was no help either. "I don't sing that shit. I don't sing, if you remember."

The sexy guy that had been giving Margot the eye approached them with his friend and started chatting them up. Juliet had guessed they were college students but as it turned out, neither of them had been to college. Terrance, the one who liked Margot, had a landscaping business. His friend Jayson managed a sportswear store owned by his uncle.

Jayson was clearly trying to chat Juliet up which was awkward as she wasn't interested in him, and it was leaving Fhemie out in the cold. Suddenly Juliet heard her name called by the host.

She panicked. She tugged Margot's arm. "Let's get out of here, go somewhere else. I really don't want to do this."

Margot shook her off. "I'm not leaving. Just go and hide in the bathroom."

Juliet was about to do this when the karaoke host called her name one more time and Fhemie gave her a hard shove towards the stage. This meant the host spotted her so there was no escape.

Her hand shaking as she took the microphone, Juliet closed her eyes as the backing track started. She tried to pretend she was in her bedroom. The song started on a C sharp which was a higher note and she felt like she squeaked it out.

But after the first line suddenly everything fell into place. Even when she opened her eyes the room had kind of dissolved and it was just her and the music. She couldn't tell if she was singing well but her voice didn't seem to waver and she found she loved it. Singing alone was so different to choir.

As the song finished and the karaoke host led a round of applause - which every singer received, though Juliet's was noticeably louder and longer than some of the other participants - the spell broke. She suddenly felt mortified with embarrassment and slunk back to join Margot and Fhemie, trying not to meet anyone's eye.

"That was awesome!" Margot told her. "I knew you could sing choir songs but I didn't know you could sing like that."

Juliet mumbled something about it being an easy song.

Margot was up next singing one of Rihanna's recent tracks. It wasn't American Idol but she made a good effort and got some applause.

"I'm just about done here," Fhemie told them when Margot came back. "Now you two have done your diva thing, can we go somewhere else?"

Terrance and Jayson suggested another bar and they agreed to try it.

On her way out, Juliet was stopped by a guy at the other end of the bar. "Hey, are you leaving? I heard you sing, you have a really beautiful voice."

Juliet assumed this was a chat up attempt and made to leave but the guy managed to stop her.

He had light brown hair that fell partly over his face and light grey eyes. He was medium tall and thin. He didn't look like a psycho, but you never knew.

"I'm in a band, we're looking for a singer. You should try out. I think you'd be great." He scribbled down an email address on the back of a receipt. "Here. Get in touch if you're interested."

Juliet folded the piece of paper and put it in her pocket, running to catch up with the others who were already out of the door.

IV. Church quest

Margot and Fhemie had been scathing about the guy who allegedly wanted Juliet to audition for his band.

"It's the oldest trick in the book," Fhemie said. "I'm surprised he didn't try and tell you he was a big shot record company exec and try to get you to his private studio."

"Which would be some dungeon that he'd tie you up in. Probably a cabin in the woods. No one would ever find you," Margot continued for her.

Juliet, who had felt flattered, now felt deflated. But she couldn't bring herself to throw the piece of paper away. The guy had just seemed like a regular person not a serial killer.

Tonight though her mind was on other things. She and Margot were making their first trip to one of the two baptist churches that they thought Mr Spencer might attend. Fhemie had to babysit her little sisters and couldn't come.

"You need to dress like a good Christian girl," Margot told her. "Like for church on Sunday."

Juliet had a special wardrobe for this: conservative clothes that she wore to appease Aunt Mary. In the first years of staying at her aunt's house she had fiercely fought against having to attend church every week, but Aunt Mary had made it a condition of Juliet living with her.

"You too then," Juliet said. "Or it will look really weird."

So there they were, dressed like the dowdiest girls in school, heading off to a church service on a weeknight.

Juliet was secretly worried that they were taking things too far and felt uncomfortable about going. So she had made a secret bargain with herself: if he wasn't there, she would persuade Margot to give the whole thing up.

But if he was there, then she would take that as a sign from Fate or whatever that she should stick with this. Juliet didn't really believe in Fate, but it seemed blasphemous to interpret Mr Spencer's presence as a sign from God. She imagined God had more important things to worry about than high school crushes and bets. After all, gambling was a sin, wasn't it?

Two friendly African American women met them at the door. "Welcome!" They didn't ask any probing questions about why Juliet and Margot had shown up to their church but ushered them in and had someone else show them to a seat. Most of the people there were in Sunday-style clothes: the men in dress shirts and slacks.

An old lady handed them both hymn books. "Are you baptised in Jesus Christ my dears?" she asked them.

Juliet wasn't entirely sure if they were or not. "We're actually Catholic," she said.

The woman was all smiles. "All people are welcome here. The love of Christ is for everyone and we're all here to learn from His teachings. We have a meet-and-greet for new folks afterwards, I hope you'll stay and join us."

It was certainly a very different experience to the staid and solemn Sunday morning mass that Juliet attended with her aunt. Did they do the sacrament here as well? she wondered. Would they do it midweek? She had no idea what the rules were.

Margot was looking around the congregation trying to see if she could spot Mr Spencer. Now they were actually there, Juliet didn't dare look. She felt she would be freaked out if he was there and disappointed if he wasn't.

"Target sighted at eleven o'clock. Locked and loaded," Margot said.

Juliet's stomach lurched. "What the hell does eleven o'clock mean?" she hissed.

"Over there by that pillar. I think that's him anyway."

Juliet looked and sure enough, there was the well-sculpted head of Mr Spencer. She had made a thorough study of the back view of his head during all the times he wrote on the whiteboard in class.

"I can't believe we're really doing this. Maybe we should just leave now, while we can."

Margot ignored her. "I wonder who that is next to him." There was a woman with long dark hair seated by Mr Spencer. They couldn't see her face. Juliet found herself burning with curiosity for her to turn around.

The service started. There was a lot of singing: a mix of contemporary and traditional songs. Juliet recognised at least some of them but didn't feel confident enough to sing. Margot was in full Gospel mode with the ones she knew.

* * *

There was no quick escape: they were cornered afterwards by the friendly old lady. "Come and meet our pastor, we're always glad to see new faces."

Feeling like the biggest fraud on earth, Juliet followed Margot to shake hands with Pastor Brown, the head minister of the church. They were offered cups of tea and introduced to other people. They weren't the only first-timers which was something of a relief.

Then across the room Juliet saw Mr Spencer and he saw her. He raised his eyebrows in surprise and she felt her face grow red.

He came over to them. "Juliet, Margot. It's unexpected seeing you both here."

Margot took the lead."We're on a spiritual journey," she said. She had already used this phrase several times, including to the pastor. Juliet was waiting for a lightning strike to come down upon them as Margot didn't even believe in God, or so she said.

"We didn't know it was your church," Juliet said. This wasn't exactly a lie. "We can find somewhere else."

Mr Spencer looked bewildered. "Why would you need to do that? I'm delighted to see you. Everyone is welcome here."

The dark haired girl who had been sitting next to him during the service appeared by his side. Juliet could see her face now: she was pleasant enough but nothing special.

"Care to introduce me?" she said to Mr Spencer.

"These are two of my students from St Gillian's," he told her. "Juliet - Margot - this is Rebecca."

"His fiancée," Rebecca added. Her smile looked fake, Juliet thought. "Aren't you both Catholics, going to that school?" There was a trace of suspicion in her eyes.

Juliet tried to sound convincing. "We're trying out other faiths. It's kind of a spiritual experiment."

"I see. Well I hope you've enjoyed your visit to our church." There was a subtle emphasis on the "our" and she made it sound as though the visit should be a one-off. Rebecca apparently didn't welcome the idea of Mr Spencer's students attending the same church as him.

"We look forward to seeing you again," Mr Spencer said, his eyes meeting Juliet's. Rebecca shot him a glance, she clearly wasn't pleased by him extending the invitation. "And I'll see you both in Latin tomorrow, so I hope you've done your homework."

He smiled and Juliet felt her stomach flip. She really hoped he couldn't read her mind. She couldn't stop thinking about the image of him in her dreams: stripped, muscles rippling, taking her right in his classroom.

Not that it was ever going to happen in real life. Was it?

* * *

They walked back to Margot's car; Juliet both relieved to have left and disappointed to have had no time with Mr Spencer alone.

She mentioned this to Margot. "There's no point going to church to seduce him if his fiancée is also going to be there."

Margot rolled her eyes. "Girl, you're not going to jump his bones in church! You're going to play good-little-Christian girl and get to know him."

If Mr Spencer ever did read her school file, he wasn't going to think she was much of a good Christian girl, Juliet thought.

Margot opened the car door. "Anyhow, this isn't just a bet any more. It's a rescue mission."

"A rescue mission?"

"Rescuing him from that sour faced bitch hanging off him," Margot said.

Juliet felt that this was a bit harsh. They had barely spent a minute in Rebecca's presence.

"I can tell a bitch when I see one. Holy or not," Margot told her.

"I liked the service," Juliet said, changing the subject. "They all seemed so friendly."

"Friendly like a cult. They just want to suck you in," Margot said.

It hadn't felt that way to Juliet. People had seemed genuinely friendly and welcoming, no strings attached. "It's not like they took our names and addresses and tried to sign us up or anything."

"You just wait. I bet it will come."

"So should we go again?" Juliet asked.

"You should, if you want to win this bet. But I'm not wasting my time going to some church on a weeknight, mass is bad enough. Take Fhemie."

Margot pulled up outside Juliet's place. "But you know," she added, "I think it's working. Like when he spoke to you, there was something. Maybe that's why that bitch got so edgy."

This gave Juliet a faintly giddy feeling. "You really think so?"

"Yeah. And why not? I mean you're hot, way more hot than his fiancée." She drew the word out in an exaggerated way. "And that bitch knows it."

* * *

"I really don't think it's appropriate for your students to be turning up at our church."

Rebecca had felt annoyed ever since the two St Gillian's students showed up at the service.

"It's not our church, we don't own it. I'm happy to see them finding their way in their faith," Carl said. He was driving her home as he usually did.

"It's your private life. It's our private life. Can't we keep something separate from your job? It's bad enough you have to take so much work home all the time."

It was the nearest they had come to arguing about something related to faith, and Carl was troubled by it. He couldn't understand Rebecca's resistance.

"You have your study too. My work gives me something to do while you're busy with that." He tried to defuse the tension, make a joke out of it.

But Rebecca didn't agree. "My study is temporary. Once I've completed my qualification I won't be working in the evenings. But when will you stop bringing work home?"

Carl had thought that Rebecca understood that for a teacher, the work didn't stop when the bell rang. There was always marking, reports, lesson planning. He didn't mind because he loved his work.

He tried to reassure her. "We'll still have time for us. You know that. If it ever takes over… well, we can have a discussion if and when that happens. But it's never an unreasonable amount of work."

He was surprised by the strength of her reaction. Rebecca had made remarks a few times about how it might be a good career path for Carl to become a pastor, and he'd given it some serious thought. After all he had come close to taking orders during his studies in Oxford.

But it hadn't been right then and it wasn't now. It couldn't be a choice: it had to be a vocation. And teaching was his vocation, it was what he loved. He felt that he was doing something really worthwhile when he taught his classes. He had hoped that Rebecca would understand this.

Rebecca was silent. She couldn't admit even to herself that she had felt a flash of jealousy at the two girls, and the warmth of Carl's greeting towards them. She had been much happier when he was working at the boys' school. Teenage girls could be so precocious.

Carl was feeling a twinge of discomfort himself. Juliet had looked so pretty earlier and he had felt genuinely glad to see her. He wasn't sure if this was an appropriate emotion or not.

She had such a beautiful smile but there was always a sadness in her eyes that made his heart tighten. Not to mention his loins.

He would have to be careful in class because she was starting to get to him.

* * *

Aunt Mary was in the living room when Juliet entered, with her bible and another religious book next to her. She often did devotional reading in the evening. Juliet sometimes wondered why she hadn't become a nun.

"How was your prayer group?" she asked.

"It was fine. Nice people," Juliet said, grabbing a banana from the kitchen and heading upstairs. She needed a little space and solitary time. Her head was rushing around with different thoughts.

She lay on her bed for a while, trying to zone out. But her head wouldn't clear, so she decided to clear her room. There was a heap of clothes that needed to go to the laundry. As she picked them up to dump them in a basket, a piece of paper fluttered down.

Juliet picked it up, only just glancing at it before she was about to crumple it and toss it. Then she saw that it was the email address the guy in the bar had given her.

At the time Fhemie and Margot had talked her out of doing anything about it. Now, though she wondered. What did she have to lose? She was kind of curious anyway, even if it was a pick up attempt.

Mainly though she needed something to distract her from the images of Mr Spencer swirling around and around in her mind.

So she got out her laptop. Aunt Mary had finally allowed her to have a computer and internet access in her bedroom the previous year, since Juliet needed it for study. On the one hand Aunt Mary had heard a lot of scare stories about sinful content online. On the other hand she had very little technical knowledge so couldn't have investigated Juliet's files and browsing history even if she had wanted to.

Hello, you gave me your email address the other day in The Green Room. My name is Juliet.

She pressed send, wondering when she would get a reply, and then started working on a history assignment she had.

The little chime and email symbol arrived about half an hour later.

Thanks for getting in touch, I'm Drew. If you're interested, come down 11am on Saturday to 15 Dover Avenue. Sing whatever you like, the Blondie was awesome.

Dover Avenue didn't sound like a cabin in the woods. It was only a few streets away from school. Still, it would be safer to take Margot or Fhemie along with her if she did go as you never knew.

But Juliet was torn. She thought her friends might tease her or try to talk her out of it.

I'll be there. J.

Now at least she had something else to think about other than her growing obsession with Mr Spencer.

V. Getting closer

Fhemie outright refused to accompany Juliet to Mr Spencer's Baptist church the next week.

"No way. I would rather do extra homework than extra church. You go but leave me out of it. If you want to stalk him at a bar, then I'm your girl."

Juliet didn't have the impression that Mr Spencer would frequent bars. She tried to get Margot to go with her but Margot was resolute.

"I've already got a date," she told Juliet.

"Who with?"

"Terrance, the guy from the other night."

Juliet couldn't blame her. "I guess I'm going it alone then."

"I guess you are."

After school Juliet went home to once again choose a "church outfit". She wondered what would happen if she showed up in a super short skirt. Or a low cut top. Mr Spencer had only ever seen her in school uniform and the modest clothing she had worn last time. She wanted an opportunity to really make him notice her.

Now though, was not the time. She brushed her hair and put on subtle lipgloss and eyeliner. After all, God didn't forbid make-up, did He? Unlike Miss Villiers. She'd probably try and run heaven like a military camp if she ever made it there.

Juliet hadn't got a car so she had to walk to the church. It was only a couple of miles and she liked walking. Even in urban areas there were always curious little things to see, bits of nature. You took in more of the environment at a slower pace.

Once again she was greeted warmly and given a hymn book. "Is your friend not with you tonight, my dear?" the same old lady as last time asked her.

"No. Her aunt was visiting," Juliet lied as she didn't think ditching church for a date would go down very well here. Ironic that the only reason she was coming to church was to get a date.

She was one of the later people to arrive and could see that Mr Spencer was already there, seated a few rows in front. Juliet shifted so that a woman with a large hat blocked her from his view. She couldn't see his fiancée: perhaps she was late or seated elsewhere.

There was a lot about "witnessing" that evening. Various members of the congregation were called up to talk about how they had "borne witness to the Lord Jesus Christ" or something similar. It wasn't really Juliet's cup of tea. She was relieved that Mr Spencer wasn't one of the people up there, practically sobbing about their religious experience. It all seemed a bit ostentatious.

After the service she stayed for the meet-and-greet, hoping that he would notice her without her having to notice him first.

Which, fortunately, he did.

"Juliet. You came back. And Margot?"

She was suddenly nervous. He looked so attractive tonight, with his broad shoulders looking even more angular and masculine in a well tailored jacket, and his clear eyes set above chiselled cheekbones. Juliet looked around, wondering where his fiancée was.

"Margot had another engagement. I'm here by myself."

Was it her imagination or was there a flicker in his eyes at this. "I'm glad you came."

"How about you?" Juliet asked.

"Me?" Mr Spencer looked confused.

"I mean did you… are you with…?" Here by yourself, she wanted to ask, but couldn't quite say it. She also couldn't bring herself to say his fiancée's name.

"Oh, I'm also here alone tonight. Rebecca has a class. She's studying for some financial exams."

Great. Her rival was some super qualified career woman type, and Juliet hadn't even graduated high school. Yet, anyway.

There was an awkward pause. "It's good to see you," he said, repeating himself. "How do you find our style of worship?"

"Very different from school and mass," Juliet said. "But once you get used to it, it's kind of fun. More alive."

Mr Spencer smiled. "I've always felt that. But I think all forms of worship have their place. They're just different paths leading us to the same Lord."

There was silence between them again. Both gazing at one another, not knowing what to say. Juliet wanted to stand closer to him, to breathe in his aroma. She wanted to see what it would feel like to run her hands through his hair. To have his lips on hers.

He seemed so kind of shining when he talked about religion. On one hand it made Juliet feel almost reverential towards him.

On the other, it made her want to seduce him and turn him on until he was begging for her, demanding her flesh. She wondered what he would do if she went up to him and kissed him.

For a split second Juliet felt like Mr Spencer was leaning in closer to her and she couldn't breathe for a moment, then the tension was suddenly broken when Pastor Brown came up.

"Good evening and welcome." He screwed up his forehead. "It's Juliet, isn't it?"

She was surprised he remembered. "Yes."

"And one of Carl's students, if I also remember correctly?"

"That's right." Mr Spencer was looking strangely uncomfortable and Juliet wondered why. Surely he couldn't have guessed what was going through her mind? If he had the first notion of what she felt when she was around him it would be super embarrassing.

The last thing she wanted was for him to realise she had a crush on him. He would just think she was some foolish high school student. She wanted to impress him, surprise him.

But she had no idea how she was going to manage that. Somehow, she needed to get him alone.

Even as the pastor left that opportunity was denied her. The friendly old lady who had greeted Juliet before the service came up. "Carl. Is Rebecca not with you? Many happy returns anyway." She handed him a card.

"Is it your birthday?" Juliet asked.

"Tomorrow," he told her.

"Oh, well happy birthday then."

"Thank you." He smiled, looking directly into her eyes. The he turned to the old lady. "Thank you so much, Agnes."

"You have a lovely day, young man." She left, and Juliet giggled.

Mr Spencer looked confused. "Something amusing?"

"Just you being called young man," she explained.

He looked mock-hurt. "I'm not that old."

"I guess not." Juliet looked at him suggestively as she said this. "Not too old at all."

Once again the tension was like a knife edge between them. Mr Spencer took a breath, and Juliet decided she had done all she could for that evening. She had unsettled him at least. Part of her felt triumph in starting to achieve her aim. But the other part felt a kind of guilt, because she couldn't help really liking him. He was such a nice guy, as well as being devastatingly attractive.

"I'd better get going, I have schoolwork for tomorrow," she told him.

"I'll see you in class then." They shared a last look, that lingered a little longer than it should have done between student and teacher, and Juliet left.

* * *

"Happy birthday, Sir. These are for you."

Juliet put the plate of home-made cookies on Mr Spencer's desk. They were oatmeal chocolate chip and she had got up early in the morning to bake them fresh.

Mr Spencer looked pleased and embarrassed. "You didn't need to do this, but it's very kind of you. Now everyone is going to know I'm getting old."

He was joking to defuse the tension. Juliet slipped off to her desk. Margot was late that morning.

The aroma of the cookies permeated the room, causing other girls to notice. Cooking was one thing that Juliet had become really good at. She had suffered years of awful food in foster homes, often not even being given enough food and going hungry, and being yelled at and even punished physically if she had tried to get something for herself.

When she had finally been taken in by Aunt Mary, just being given free rein in the kitchen had been an amazing luxury. It turned out that Aunt Mary wasn't particularly keen on cooking. It was just a necessary chore for her. So gradually Juliet had taken over, starting with simple recipes and using cookbooks and magazines to learn more advanced techniques, with Aunt Mary quite happy for it to become her responsibility.

Aunt Mary still cooked, but it was mainly Juliet's job now. The only thing Juliet regretted was that her aunt had quite simple tastes. Juliet longed to try and create fancier dishes but her aunt liked the "plain and wholesome food the good Lord provided".

So Juliet just concentrated on making basic recipes as awesome as she could. As such she was pretty confident that her oatmeal cookies would blow Mr Spencer away. She had seen him accept a cookie after church, so she figured he wasn't diabetic or on a low carb diet.

Not that he needed to low carb. He was super slim and fit. She longed to get an even closer view of those hard, fit muscles beneath his clothing. She wondered enviously how much access Rebecca had to them.

* * *

Carl Spencer felt dizzy with the thought of Juliet and the aroma of the cookies. She was winding her way into his senses. Against all his self-discipline he had found himself more than happy to see her at church last night. He had also felt glad to be able to speak with her alone, a gladness he now he felt very conflicted and guilty about.

He was a grown man, he shouldn't be so affected by a high school student like this.

He still hadn't read Juliet's file. From several things she had said, and a couple of comments from other teachers, there was clearly some trouble in her past. But as curious as he was growing about her, he couldn't bring himself to snoop.

It felt like a violation: it had always been Carl's rule to take students as he found them. If there was a serious current issue, such as a family crisis or significant disciplinary issues, the head teacher would have briefed him anyway.

But it was more than that. He felt that reading about Juliet's past would be falling further down the rabbit hole. He needed to get a grip because he was starting to get obsessed with this girl and it was wrong and terribly unfair to Rebecca.

Rebecca. He must think of her: focus his thoughts on their wedding and their future together.

But every time he tried to picture Rebecca the sweet, sexy image of Juliet Martin came into his head instead. After church last night he had lain in bed alone unable to sleep, he was so turned on by the thought of her. While he didn't believe the doctrine that self-relief made you blind or was the worst of sins, he knew it would be a sin and a betrayal to fantasise about his student in that way.

So he had tossed and turned, tried reading some bible passages, and didn't manage to fall asleep until the early hours.

Now he had to get through an entire Latin class trying not to be distracted by her. But even when he tried not looking at her, and giving his attention to other students, the sweet, delicious smell of the cookies were a constant reminder.

* * *

"Any more progress?" Fhemie asked as they sat outside, eating lunch. She had become more interested in the bet between Juliet and Margot over time.

"She made him cookies," Margot said. "Like the ultimate teacher's pet."

Fhemie crunched on her chips. Once again there was a complete absence of any fruit or vegetables in her lunch. "Well you know what they say," she said, licking her fingers. "The way to a man's heart is through his stomach."

"Biologically speaking, the way to anyone's heart is through their stomach. Or their ribs at least," Juliet pointed out.

"You know that's not what I meant. So did it work? Did Mr Spencer make a move? Ask you out?" Fhemie asked.

Hardly. It was way too early for that. Juliet shrugged. "I think he liked them."

Margot groaned. "His face literally lit up," she told Fhemie. "And he can't stop looking at her in class, though he tries so hard not to."

This was news to Juliet. "Does he?"

"I can't believe you haven't noticed. Though he's trying to avoid you noticing, but I see everything that's going on."

Juliet wondered if Cynthia had noticed. Their enemy had a huge crush on their Latin teacher herself and might make trouble if she sensed he preferred Juliet.

They were walking down the corridor to history class, past the main noticeboard. There were the usual announcements about school events and clubs. They didn't change too frequently, so a large, printed notice in the middle of the board caught everyone's eye.

St Gillian's Choir Trip: Paris, Winter Break - those interested in attending please sign up below. Parental permission required.

There was also a little image of the Eiffel Tower with a few musical notes floating around it, making clear that it was definitely a European trip, not Paris, Texas.

"Oh my god, why do I have to be tone deaf?" Fhemie lamented. "Paris! They went to lame old Vancouver last year."

"It wasn't that lame," Margot said. "There were some super hot Canadian boys."

Juliet didn't say anything. She hadn't been able to go last year because the trip had been too expensive. It would be even more so this year.

"So you'll go on the Paris one?" Fhemie asked Margot.

"Maybe." Margot cast a glance at Juliet and tried to change the subject. "It depends on my parents and whatever. Anyway I need to borrow your notes from Biology because Terrance kept texting me and I lost track. I just know that bitch is going to pop quiz us tomorrow."

VI. The audition

Feeling half foolish, half nervous, Juliet made her way to Dover Avenue on Saturday morning. She told Aunt Mary she was going for a walk to get some fresh air. Aunt Mary was the kind of person who thought that fresh air was a wholesome thing.

It was a bright, sunny day though not overly warm. Being October, the summer was decidedly over with the last heat of September slipping away, but it made for good walking weather.

Fifteen Dover Avenue was a house much like any of the other houses on the street. Nervously Juliet approached the front door and pressed the bell.

A short guy with dark spiky hair and thick dark eyebrows answered it. "Hey."

"Hello," Juliet replied. She had no idea how these things were supposed to go. "Drew mentioned I should drop by?" She was trying to appear cool but inside she was twisted up in knots.

"Ah yeah. Auditions." He opened the door to let her through. She followed him down a hallway through a kitchen, then down into a basement where there was a group of people and a load of musical equipment.

Juliet felt horribly out of place. She was relieved to recognise Drew who smiled in a friendly way. "Hi. Glad you could make it. This is the band."

There were five of them including Drew, who made all the introductions. Lead guitar, second guitar, keyboards, bass, drums. Plus two girls who weren't members: one had red hair, the other was small and dark.

Juliet thought they must be auditioning as well. But it turned out that the girl with dyed auburn hair was dating the bassist. The other was the sister of the keyboardist, Jax, whose house it was. He was the dark haired guy who had opened the front door.

It was a lot to take in: a lot of names to remember. Not that she would probably need to remember them after today. She would probably never see any of these people ever again.

Someone offered her a beer, which she sipped tentatively. It wasn't her favourite drink but anything might calm her nerves.

There was some discussion involving the guitarists about an amp and feedback, much of which was going over Juliet's head.

"So what happened to your previous singer?" she asked.

"There wasn't one. It's mainly split between me and Jax, but we wanted a female vocalist for a new direction we're taking," Drew told her. "It's kind of an experiment, like trip hop with some punk and new wave. It's Jax's baby, he's the musical genius."

Jax seemed to be a guy of few words. "You sing Blondie, right? Can you do Rapture?"

Juliet wasn't sure. She had some idea of the first lines. "Not all the rap sections though." It was really long, from memory.

"That's okay," Drew said. "It's just to give us an idea."

Somehow it felt a thousand times harder singing in front of these few people than in front of a crowded bar the other week. But Juliet steeled herself. She wasn't sure where she got the courage but deep inside she had a burning desire to do this.

The microphone was on a stand though she would have preferred to hold it. To grip onto something, for dear life. She wasn't sure what to expect in terms of accompaniment but the band clearly knew this one, as the drummer started playing and then the rest of them joined in.

Juliet closed her eyes and simply sang. Her voice winding and snaking around the high, melodic notes. She found that she remembered the start of the rap section from some long buried memory. In her nervousness her voice was huskier than usual but she could see images in her mind as she spoke, like her own music video.

When she finished, forgetting the lyrics and having to stop, smiling to cover her embarrassment, the band applauded her. "That was, like, flawless," the bassist said.

He looked over at Jax, at did Drew, expectantly. Jax, whose expression gave nothing away, simply nodded. "Yeah. It will work," he said.

And that was that. Somehow Juliet had passed some test, and they wanted her to sing with them. She had imagined a huge string of people auditioning but it seemed they were happy enough with her.

"So we rehearse Tuesdays, Thursdays, Saturdays," Drew told her. "Can you make that?"

For now she could.

"Do you write music at all?" one of the other band members asked her.

Juliet didn't. She had never had the opportunity to learn an instrument, have lessons, anything like that. "Not really. Just lyrics, sometimes." Lyrics were poetry after all. She could write poems.

"That could be useful," Drew said. "I'll email you anyway." They also exchanged mobile numbers and Juliet left, in something of a daze. There was no way she could tell Aunt Mary anything about this. She was going to have to come up with some other reason to explain her new absences to her aunt.

* * *

The sky had clouded over by the time Juliet left, and a sudden downpour took her by suprise. She had no raincoat or umbrella and there were no suitable trees to shelter under.

So she kept going. She was going to be soaked by the time she got home.

As she walked along, feeling her mascara streaking down her face and her top clinging wet to her body, she heard a car draw up alongside her.

First assuming it was a kidnapper or something she quickened her step.

But a voice called out: "Juliet?"

It was Mr Spencer.

Oh god, how could he see her like this? was her first thought. She stopped, wishing that lightning could just strike down and have done with it. He leaned over and pushed the passenger door open for her from the inside. "Get in, you must be drenched."

She obeyed.

"You went out without a raincoat?" he asked.

"I didn't see the weather reports," Juliet mumbled, embarrassed "It was sunny when I left earlier."

She was painfully conscious of her proximity to the Latin teacher and the intimacy of being in a car with him. It should have been the perfect seduction opportunity, if she had planned it, but she felt like a drowned rat. What must he think of her?

"Are you heading home? Where can I take you?" Mr Spencer asked her.

"It's not far, I could walk, honestly."

"Not in this rainstorm. I'm in no rush, just tell me where you need to go."

Juliet gave him the directions to her aunt's house. She found herself wishing it was further away, to prolong her time with him. Mr Spencer's hands looked strong and firm on the steering wheel. His thighs were muscular in his jeans. If she put her hand on his leg, where might it lead?

But she didn't dare.

Maybe if she had been less bedraggled. Maybe if she had been less caught off-guard.

"So do you live near here as well?" she asked.

"Just a few blocks away. Aspen Drive," he told her.

She vaguely knew it. She wondered if he lived there with Rebecca. Would they live together before marriage?

All too soon Mr Spencer was pulling up outside her aunt's house and parking the car.

He turned to her.

Their eyes locked and he spoke her name. "Juliet..."

He was about to say something or ask her something but he didn't continue. The two of them just sat there for what seemed like minutes, though it was probably only seconds.

Then Mr Spencer suddenly straightened and became formal. "Well I guess I'll see you at school on Monday."

She wanted to stay with him in his car forever. "I guess so. Thank you so much for the ride, I hope I didn't get your car damp."

He smiled. "Don't worry about that."

As he drove off, Juliet noticed that his numberplate contained her lucky number. Seventy-seven. She told herself that it was just a coincidence, not a sign. If it was her entire birthdate, that might have been a sign.

Her aunt had seen the car dropping Juliet off and questioned her the moment she stepped into the house. "Who was that giving you a lift?" Her tone was curious but not overly suspicious.

"It was a teacher from school. He saw me walking in the rain, I guess it was really nice of him to stop." She prayed her face wouldn't betray her emotions, which were in turmoil.

"I hope you thanked him. It was very foolish, going out without an umbrella. This time of year can be very changeable," her aunt chided.

"I know. I'm sorry." Juliet fled to the privacy of her room, to lie down and try to sort out her whirling, tangled rush of feelings.

VII. Feeling blue

Cynthia was as smug as anything at choir practice on Monday. She had gathered a little group of cronies and sycophants around her.

"Of course, I'll probably get upgraded as I have gold frequent flyer membership. My parents take me overseas so often that I have more air miles than I can use," Cynthia was saying.

Spoilt rich bitch, Juliet thought. At least Margot never bragged about her wealth. She had so much more class than Cynthia.

"I hope we get to stay in a decent hotel. We always stay at five star hotels in Europe, but I guess on a school trip some people might not be able to afford that." She cast a look at Juliet.

"Oh I'm sorry," Cynthia continued, feigning sympathy. "We shouldn't be talking about this in front of the poor foster slut. You couldn't even afford a bus ride to Vegas and two nights at a cheap hooker motel, could you? Though if you could, I'm sure it would be so much more your scene."

She smiled with fake sweetness, meaning Juliet couldn't slap her because as their choir conductor entered, it would look to her as though Cynthia was being nice.

Miss Mead was a sweet woman but as blind as a bat where Cynthia was concerned. She was short and plump with pink cheeks and hair that forever escaped its pins. In her long patterned skirts and frill-necked blouses she reminded Juliet of a nervous hedgehog. She looked perennially flustered.

"Good afternoon, girls," she greeted them. "Now where is Margot?" She looked expectantly at Juliet as they were friends.

Juliet had no idea where Margot was. She hadn't seen her since morning classes. Margot had skipped lunch.

Suddenly the door burst open and Margot arrived. "Sorry for being late, I got held up," she said.

Juliet saw Cynthia rolling her eyes at her friend and mouthing what Juliet was pretty sure was a racist remark. Cynthia couldn't bear the fact that Margot's family were even richer than hers.

Miss Mead, who was always a little intimidated by Margot, let it go. "Please be prompt next time, dear. Now we have the end of term concert to rehearse for, and we're already behind, so let's get started. We'll be using some of these songs for the choir trip this winter. I expect you've already seen that we're going to Paris this year."

Everyone had, and everyone except Juliet was pretty excited about it.

The choir sang every Sunday during Mass as well as performing a Christmas concert for the community. This involved several solos which Miss Mead tried to share out, despite her preference for Cynthia. Cynthia had already been given the entire first verse of Once In Royal David's City, which was the main one.

"Juliet, let's hear how you sound on the Coventry Carol," Miss Mead requested.

Feeling a little more confident after her experience at the audition, Juliet gave it her best attempt. Even she was surprised how well it went, and this was confirmed by Cynthia's jealous scowl. She muttered to the girl next to her something that was obviously unpleasant about Juliet.

"That was very impressive, Juliet," Miss Mead said. "You don't take lessons, do you dear?"

Juliet didn't. Her aunt couldn't afford them, and wouldn't have seen them as necessary. Singing was something you did in church for the Lord, not something you needed to get fancy about.

"Well perhaps we should arrange some tuition. Those were some quite beautiful notes. I think we'll have you take the solo in that one for the concert."

The practice continued, Cynthia shooting daggers at Juliet throughout. She was even more furious when Juliet's row was given the descants to do. Miss Mead even swapped a couple of girls into the descant group who were particularly strong on the higher notes. Cynthia was not among them and she was seething with fury.

I'll end up paying for this somehow, Juliet thought.

"We'll get that bitch," Margot murmured, reading her mind.

After the practice ended Miss Mead called Juliet to stay behind. She heard Cynthia make another remark about "foster slut" and then there was a yell and a crash as Cynthia tripped over a line of chairs, landing in a sprawl with her things flying everywhere.

"She tripped me! That bitch" - Juliet could tell that Cynthia had only just suppressed a racist term here - "deliberately tripped me!"

Cynthia indicated Margot who stood there with an air as innocent as the Virgin Mary combined with the Angel Gabriel.

"That's enough, Cynthia. There's no need for such language."

Cynthia's mouth fell open, shocked to be be told off by the choir teacher. She gathered her things and marched out of the room, her eyes glaring in fury, doubtless already planning revenge.

Miss Mead waited until everyone had left before turning to Juliet. She looked slightly nervous.

"As you know, dear, the choir trip this winter is to Paris. Now I know that you haven't been able to attend previous trips, perhaps due to… circumstances." Miss Mead was too embarrassed to say the word "financial".

"However," she continued, looking more and more uncomfortable with every word, "there is a special fund available for special circumstances." She practically whispered the word "fund". Juliet's poverty was a greater embarrassment to Miss Mead than obscenity.

"A fund?" Juliet wasn't entirely sure where this was heading, due to all the tip-toeing around.

"What I mean, my dear, is that the school would be able to cover the costs of your trip, if your family agreed to you attending."

Juliet's heart did a wild flip. Paris! It was like a golden ticket being dangled before her. She needed to snatch it before Aunt Mary could find some reason to blow it away.

"I'll ask my aunt. Thank you." It seemed inadequate, faced with such a huge offer, but she wasn't sure what else to say. "I would really love to go, if possible."

"And we would be more than delighted to have you join us, my dear."

There was sympathy in the choir teacher's eyes that brought a lump to Juliet's throat and made her eyes blur. It was times like this that she was reminded how different her life and her childhood had been to that of most other girls. They had mothers, fathers - even if divorced, though there weren't so many divorces among Catholics of course - and brothers and sisters. Often lots of other relatives. Homes. Memories.

All Juliet had was Aunt Mary. She knew she should be grateful for that at least, but there was a huge, gnawing ache in her heart for what she had lost and what she could never have.

Unwittingly Miss Mead, with her well-meaning kindness and concern, had just ripped the bandage off.

* * *

After finally escaping Miss Mead, Juliet didn't feel like rejoining her friends. She wanted to be alone, to lick her wounds for a bit.

Latin was the next class but there was still some time before the bell went for afternoon lessons. So she headed to the bathroom that was nearest to the Latin room.

Damn. It was locked and out of order for some reason, with a notice instructing people to use another facility at the far end of the building.

Juliet didn't want to trudge all that way. It increased the chance of bumping into people and she simply wanted solitude. So she went and sat at the top of some stairs that led to a fire escape, which were separate from the main staircase. No one ever used them.

She closed her eyes and for a while tried to wish the world away. Tried to wish away the last ten or so years and return to a time when she was a normal girl, with a normal family. Three people.

Three people who loved one another.

"Juliet? Are you okay?"

Startled, she opened her eyes and sat up from leaning against the wall.

Mr Spencer, having seen her through the glass of the fire door while on the way to his classroom, was holding it open in concern.

Juliet felt embarrassed because she knew her cheeks were wet. "I'm fine."

He frowned. "Do you want to come and sit in my classroom until class starts? It doesn't look very comfortable here."

There was no reason not to accept the offer and every reason to take it up. So she followed him. "Thanks."

Inside she went to straight to the back row, her usual seat.

Then they were both awkward, neither knowing what to do. Juliet wanted to put her head on her arms and close her eyes, sleep for a few minutes even. But she couldn't do that with someone else there.

Mr Spencer, who had brought some class preparation to do, seemed reluctant to just ignore her as she seemed distressed.

He came and stood by her desk, looking at her intently. "Is something wrong?"

"No. Yes. I was just remembering some stuff."

"If you want me to get the school counsellor...?" He tailed off, not really knowing how to proceed.

Kindness always made her cry at a time like this. She felt the tears well over but dug her fingernails into her palms hard to stop herself from actually crying.

Tentatively - he knew he wasn't supposed to touch a student, but human instinct won over - he put a hand on her shoulder. His touch burned through the fabric of her clothing, far more than its mere warmth should have done.

"If you ever need to talk about it… or if you need me to find you someone you feel comfortable talking with…" Once again he was struggling to know what to say.

Juliet brushed her eyes with her hand and tried to force a brighter expression. She turned her head to look up at him. "Really, I'm fine. I was just being silly, it's very long past."

He wasn't convinced. "Is it something to do with your family? Your parents?"

Juliet smiled weakly. "I know I should be over it. Just sometimes it gets to me still. You know how it is, or you probably don't. I hope you don't," she said.

Mr Spencer pulled a chair across and sat down next to her. "I can't imagine it's something one ever gets over, no matter how long ago. I doubt I would get over it, even if it happened now, in adulthood."

He looked so strong as he said this, so sincere, that Juliet was moved.

Her hands were on the desk and he had put his hand on the side of the desk as he sat down. Their fingers were only inches apart. Juliet felt as though there was a magnetic field there.

Slowly, still looking into her eyes, he moved his fingers over hers, to rest his hand on her hand. It was a gesture of comfort, but it was also a forbidden gesture.

It was more than a hand on her shoulder: his skin was touching hers. It was sending shockwaves through her arm and body.

Juliet had been with so many guys before, far more intimately, why did she feel so nervous? She could hardly breathe. She ran her tongue over her lips which seemed dry.

She had an urge to say his first name. She knew it was Carl.

But she didn't dare.

Instead they remained looking at one another, his hand still on hers. Making her skin tingle. His eyes looked almost golden in this light. His lips were firm and masculine but beautifully carved, like a Greek statue.

Oh god how she wanted him to kiss her...

For a fraction of a second she imagined he was just leaning in a little closer. She could smell his skin. She wanted his lips on hers...

For a moment... nearly... if they just leaned in a little further...

Juliet's heart was hammering in her chest and the palms of her hands felt damp.

Suddenly, just as they teetered near the point of no return, there was a noise in the doorway.

Mr Spencer instantly took his hand off Juliet's and jumped back, standing up, trying not to look guilty.

It was just two other girls in the class who had also arrived early. Probably deliberately to flirt with him, judging by the dirty expressions they shot Juliet. Still, at least it wasn't Cynthia.

"We just wanted to read over our notes before class, Sir," one of them said.

Suck-up, Juliet thought. Still, it wouldn't hurt her to check over her own homework. So she pretended to be poring over hers, as though she had come there for the same reason.

* * *

"What happened to you after choir? What did Miss Mead want?" Margot asked Juliet as they walked together after Latin.

"Just something about the choir trip. There's a fund or something," Juliet told her.

Margot looked puzzled. "A fund? For what?"

"Apparently for me, if I get my aunt's permission."

Margot whirled around. "That's awesome. It will be so much more fun with you there!" She had even tried to offer to pay Juliet's ticket as the cost was nothing to her parents, but Aunt Mary would never have allowed outright charity.

However a special school fund might be a different matter. Juliet hoped so, anyway.

Fhemie caught up with them on the way to History. "So any progress with that hot Latin pastor guy?"

"He's not a pastor," Juliet said. She was strangely reluctant to tell them about being alone with Mr Spencer in the classroom before. The brief time they had shared seemed kind of special. Private.

"There was something up though, wasn't there?" Margot said. "There was like a vibe," she told Fhemie.

"I'm thinking maybe I should give it all up," Juliet said.

"If you're not getting anywhere, then I guess so," Margot agreed. "You lose a hundred bucks though."

Juliet didn't really care about the bet money. She knew Margot wouldn't actually expect her to pay, nor would she have taken any money from Margot.

But this time it was Fhemie who was looking at her with a suspicious gaze. "You're hiding something," she said to Juliet. "I know that look. It's the same one you had after you made out with Nathan at Sue-Anne's party."

Juliet wanted to forget that episode. She had been very drunk, Nathan was Sue-Anne's ex, and Sue-Anne had been hoping to reconcile with him. His making out with Juliet had made it the worst birthday ever. Making it even more regrettable, Juliet didn't even like Nathan and wouldn't have gone near him when sober.

"Guilt then," Margot said.

Juliet said nothing. They both rounded on her. "Confess or else!"

"Really, it was nothing. I just got there early, and we talked, and he kind of held my hand. Or put his hand on my hand I mean." When she actually described it, it really didn't sound like very much at all. But what she had felt during it - the tension between them - was huge.

Fhemie rolled her eyes. "That is the lamest thing I ever heard."

"Or the most repressed and hot thing ever," Margot said. "Like maybe that's the furthest he's ever gone with a girl. I mean you saw that fiancée of his. She looks like she washes her va-jay with holy water and keeps it pure for Jesus."

They all laughed at this.

"Seriously, girl, you gotta step it up," Margot told her. "Go for the kill."

VIII. In turmoil

What the hell was he going to do? Carl even thought the word "hell" in his head, which was a blasphemy. But what was happening was throwing him into turmoil.

He had been inches - seconds - away from leaning in and kissing a student. What the hell was wrong with him?

Just touching her hand, the softness of her skin, had been electric.

He remembered the tip of her tongue passing over her lips, and the way it had taken all his strength not to put his hands on her head, tilt her face towards him, and bring his lips down upon hers.

He had wanted to press her against him, to drink her in. To feel her soft body moulded against his. But she was a student! Someone who was absolutely forbidden fruit, over whom he was in a position of authority. To abuse that would be unthinkable.

Maybe he should confess and get it off his chest. For a moment he envied the Catholic confessional, where you could tell everything to a priest who would keep it sacrosanct. His church didn't exactly work like that. Things were more open, more communal. The pastor would probably try to get him to confess it all to Rebecca and talk it through with her. Carl did not think she would take it well at all.

Maybe the problem was that he and Rebecca were being too formal with one another. They barely even held hands. Carl decided he would try and encourage a little more physical affection between them.

He must stop thinking of Juliet. Even being alone with her in his classroom was playing with fire.

Resolving to get better control of himself, Carl got up when he heard the doorbell go. Rebecca was supposed to be coming over for more wedding planning.

"Hello." He went to kiss her but she coyly turned her head so his lips met her cheek. In fairness they had been advised to keep the "wedding kiss" special.

Rebecca came in, carrying a large bag which Carl knew would contain various magazines and brochures related to weddings and marriage. She set the bag down, hung up her coat, and drew out a DVD. "I thought we could watch this together. Ruth recommended it." Ruth was a mutual friend at their church.

The DVD was titled: "Sacred Respect: A Couple's Guide to Marriage in Christ". Carl doubted it could offer much more than the marriage classes they already went to but he was happy to watch it for Rebecca's sake. There was a documentary on Caesar and Rome that he had hoped to watch, but he could record that.

Carl fetched Rebecca a drink and slid the DVD into the player. He sat next to her on the couch and they watched as the video started. As it got underway he sat a little closer to her and reached for her hand, but Rebecca withdrew it.

"We're supposed to be watching this. It's really important for our future," she told him.

"I only wanted to hold your hand." He tried to be light-hearted about it.

Rebecca turned to him. "You know where that stuff leads. And we both want to wait, right?"

"I think I can control myself, Rebecca. We don't have to keep distance between us all the time."

But his fiancée seemed unwilling to risk closer physical contact, so Carl suppressed a sigh and continued watching the marriage video. He was trying to imagine how it would be when they were finally married. Relaxing on the couch together, in one another's arms, being affectionate and sharing a joke. Sharing a bed…

The problem was not simply that he couldn't imagine it. After all, this was a good thing: he had been praying hard to keep those kinds of thoughts out of his head. Why stir up sexual frustration unnecessarily? All that, as Rebecca said, could wait.

No, the problem was that he didn't particularly want to imagine it. It just didn't seem to hold much appeal. Maybe it was because Rebecca was being so rigid now that it wasn't easy to create an image of her being the opposite.

Carl took a swig of his drink, a soda.

He was lying to himself, of course, and he knew it.

The real reason he couldn't imagine Rebecca lying in his arms, and didn't even want to try to envision it, was because he couldn't stop thinking of holding Juliet instead. Feeling her soft, slender curves and the warmth of her body against him.

Carl wasn't nearly so confident that he would be able to control himself around her if she was next to him on the sofa. His mind wandered from the Christian couples talking about their vows on the television, wondering what Juliet was up to.

* * *

Aunt Mary was satisfied with Juliet watching the documentary on Caesar and Rome because it was educational. She had studied Latin herself as a girl and was pleased to see Juliet showing an interest.

They sat and watched the show together. Juliet hadn't yet broached the subject of the choir trip as she was waiting for a time when her relative might be most receptive. Now seemed as good a time as any.

"There's going to be a choir trip at school, and there's a fund available to help with the costs," she began.

Aunt Mary put down her knitting. "St Gillian's has already been very generous to you, providing you with a free place. I don't think it would do to seek further charity."

Juliet had feared something like this. "I didn't ask, Miss Mead - the choir mistress - told me about it. I think she wants me to attend because I'm doing some solos."

"There must be many other girls with good voices, Juliet. I hope that being singled out is not leading to vanity." Aunt Mary's tone was very disapproving.

"It's not that at all, truly." How was she going to make her aunt understand? "Maybe if you spoke with Miss Mead…?"

Having completed another row of knitting, Aunt Mary adjusted her wool. "I'll consider it. Where is this trip to?"

"To Paris."

"Paris!" Aunt Mary dropped several stitches. "Why on earth would they be going somewhere so remote and so expensive?"

"It's also a cultural trip," Juliet said. "We'll be seeing other things, such as - " she scoured her brain for French religious sites " - Notre Dame cathedral, and Lourdes."

This was something of a trump card as Aunt Mary had often mentioned Lourdes. Several of her friends had made pilgrimages there, and one even claimed to have been cured from arthritis after praying at the holy grotto.

Even Aunt Mary had been sceptical of this miracle as the woman in question continued to take various medications, but it remained a place she was interested in.

Fortunately her geography wasn't much better than Juliet's when it came to mainland Europe. The five hundred mile distance between Paris and Lourdes made it highly unlikely the choir would get to take a day trip there. But for now she was mollified.

Juliet was a step closer to taking her first ever trip overseas.

IX. Trick or treat?

If Aunt Mary had seen Juliet now she would have clutched her rosary, crossed herself and fallen on her knees in prayer. And probably tried to have Juliet committed to a nunnery.

Juliet had got dressed for Hallowe'en earlier that evening at Fhemie's house, along with Margot. Two slutty witches and a slutty witch's cat, since Fhemie with her dancer's physique looked awesome in a skin tight leotard. She wore a little pair of cat ears and had a tail swishing from her butt.

Juliet's costume was made of black and purple satin low cut in the neckline above a fitted bodice. Shredded strips of satin and gauze formed the skirt, going all the way up her thighs. She was worried that it was a bit too much.

"Everything is practically hanging out everywhere," she complained.

"Yeah, that's why it's Slutty Witch," Fhemie said. "It's like bad luck not to look slutty on Hallowe'en. It keeps ghosts away."

She waved goodbye to her mother, who was talking on the phone to Fhemie's grandmother in Tagalog. Fhemie grinned, translating for them. "She's just reassuring Granny that I'm doing well and attending to my Bible studies."

"Thank God it's not a video call or you'd give your grandmother a stroke, wearing that," Margot said.

The three of them were going to a party being held not far from Dover Avenue where Juliet's new band rehearsed. It was the usual scene: much drunkenness, people falling into a swimming pool, couples making out all over the place.

"A proper Hallowe'en orgy," Fhemie said, satisfied. She disappeared into a nearby bedroom with a cute Hispanic guy soon after they arrived and the others didn't see her again for hours.

Terrance, the guy Margot was now dating, was interstate that weekend. They weren't officially exclusive but Margot was hoping it might get that way, so she had decided to stay away from other guys that night.

It was hard though: the slutty witch costumes that she and Juliet were wearing attracted a lot of attention.

"There's nothing stopping you," Margot said to Juliet after she had brushed off yet another guy.

"I know. I guess I'm just not in the mood."

Margot looked at her evilly. "And I know why. You can't get a certain someone out of your head, can you?"

Juliet tried to deny it but it was obviously true.

"Never mix business with pleasure. You've made a fatal mistake," Margot told her. "You should have stayed dispassionate. Reeled him in, spat him out, and collected the money."

They had both already had too much of the Hallowe'en Punch and this loosened Juliet's lips. "He lives not far from here," she said.

"What? How the hell do you know that?!"

Juliet shrugged. "He mentioned it once. When he gave me a lift in the rain that time."

"What's the street name?" Margot asked.

"Aspen Drive."

A plan was already ticking over in Margot's head but Juliet was getting too fuzzy to think straight. She wandered off to get them both some more punch and bumped into a guy, sending the drinks flying. "Hey! Sorry." He thought the collision was his fault.

"No problem, it was me who tripped," Juliet told him. He looked vaguely familiar but she couldn't place him. While she was struggling to put a name to the face, he recognised her.

"It's Juliet, right? Under the make-up?"

Of course! It was the bass player from the band.

"It is." She apologised for not recognising him straight away and they chatted for a few moments before Juliet returned to where Margot was, having fetched two new glasses of punch.

Margot's had a slice of apple floating in it, which she took out and licked the juice from.

"So? Who was that guy?"

"Just someone. I bumped into him by accident," Juliet told her.

"It looked like you knew him."

Juliet didn't want to lie outright. "I think I've seen him around somewhere."

The evening drew on and somewhere after eleven o'clock Fhemie appeared, looked a little dishevelled with a wicked smile on her face. "Such a great party!"

"How would you know, you spent the entire night in a bedroom," Juliet said.

Fhemie just grinned. "So where are we going next? Another party? A bar?"

Margot looked mysterious. "We're going for a little walk. To Aspen Drive."

* * *

Juliet had protested all the way. They couldn't just rock up at Mr Spencer's house. He might have company. He'd probably be asleep. She didn't know the actual house number anyway.

"You know his car? If he's in, it will be parked outside," Margot said.

Juliet, as influenced by alcohol as she was, still managed to feel that this was a really bad idea. She even tried arguing that Baptists didn't do Hallowe'en. "It's Satanic or blasphemous or something to them."

"So? We're the ones celebrating it, not him," Fhemie said. She loved the idea.

The coolness of the night air was sobering Juliet up and she was feeling worse and worse about this plan. But no one would pay any attention to her concerns. To numb her nerves, she had thrown down a couple more glasses of punch before Margot and Fhemie practically frogmarched her down the road.

Once there, they walked down and Juliet felt her insides melting when she recognised his car. Remembering the brief ride

65

she had taken in it. Knowing he'd be inside the house right now - there was a glow from a downstairs window still on, so hopefully he was still up. She really didn't want to wake him up.

They walked up the driveway to the front porch.

"Go on then," Fhemie said. "Knock on his door."

The punch had made Juliet feel a lot bolder. She gave a sharp rap and they waited until the door was opened. Mr Spencer stood there, wearing jeans and a casual shirt. They hadn't seen him out of the smarter slacks and tie he wore for school before, as well as at church.

Juliet smiled at him, her eyes glinting. "Trick or treat?"

He was disconcerted. "I've run out of candy, there were so many kids coming round earlier. Isn't it a bit late for you three to be out?"

"It's not midnight yet," Fhemie pointed out.

"So, trick or treat?" Juliet asked him, looking alluringly up at him.

"I guess a trick then, since I'm out of treats. Just don't destroy my car or anything."

Juliet took a step towards him and leaned towards him. She saw his eyes fall on her neckline and back to her face. He looked very uncomfortable. "Or you can have the treat," she whispered.

Mr Spencer froze as she reached up and brushed her lips against his, light as a feather, inhaling his scent. His lips were warm and dry and she wanted to kiss him more deeply but didn't dare.

She could feel the tension in him, he was wound up, tightly coiled. If the others hadn't been there she might have tried to go further. The alcohol had loosened her inhibitions and all she wanted was to be with him, making out with him, having his hands all over her body.

Juliet felt herself tingling, an ache between her legs, just from the brief contact. She was amazed that just kissing him - barely kissing him even - could turn her on so much.

As she gazed back at him, her lips parted from the embrace, his face was frozen. He didn't even speak.

She wondered if he felt anywhere near the same that she did. His body looked so hard and masculine, he was so much taller than her. Had he responded in the same way or was he in complete control, indifferent to her?

"Goodnight then," she said, smiling once more.

Then she left with the others, leaving Carl at his door. Both Fhemie and Margot were silent, suppressing both surprise and laughter, more shocked than they had expected to be. After all, Juliet had just kissed a teacher while drunk.

X. The confessional

Carl had always thought that "taking a cold shower" was just a joke, but this time he actually went to take one.

He was disturbed and aroused and shaken up: he couldn't get the sight of Juliet out of his mind. Or the memory of her lips on his.

Just the taste of her... the scent of her...

He had never seen her out of her school uniform before, or the modest blouse she had worn to his church. Now he couldn't stop thinking of how the curve of her breasts swelled from the low-cut neckline, or the smooth length of her thighs.

Obviously he'd seen women in revealing clothing before, he hadn't lived in a monastery since birth. But this was the first time he had been so closely confronted by the body of a girl whom he not only found arousing, but who was completely off-limits. Someone whom he'd been struggling not to think about for weeks.

Carl felt too guilty to even pray, though he tried. "Lord, if this is some kind of a test, please give me the strength to pass it."

He lay in bed, feeling wired. Trying to superimpose Rebecca's face onto Juliet's, but failing.

In the end he got up and looked at his clock. It was 3am. He pulled on some clothes and went for a jog around the block. Maybe if he exhausted himself physically he'd be able to collapse into a dreamless sleep?

Juliet... Juliet... Juliet... His feet were pounding along the sidewalk, drumming her name into his head.

How was he going to concentrate the next time he taught her Latin class? After what had just happened - when he should have stood back, kept his distance, made the three of them leave. He was equally to blame. Juliet had clearly had alcohol on her breath and wasn't fully in control of herself.

But he had been sober. He was the adult. The one who should have been in control.

The fact was he hadn't stepped back because he hadn't really wanted to. He had wanted to be close to her. He had wanted to breathe her in.

He had been tempted, and he had started to fall.

* * *

Juliet woke with her head pounding. It took her a few moments to remember where she was: at Fhemie's house. She never normally drank that much. What had she been thinking?

Opening her eyes, she looked across the room and saw Margot still asleep on the other guest bed.

Slowly the events of the previous evening were trickling back into her head. They flashed through in stages, like a movie trailer.

The party and the heavily spiked punch.

The cold night air on her skin as they walked through the streets.

Approaching his door…

Juliet could remember exactly how he looked, it was like having taken a photo and stored it in her brain. His obvious surprise combined with calm politeness. No shoes and his shirt a little rumpled, as though he had just got up from the couch. The startled expression in his eyes when she had spoken of a treat.

She had kissed him.

Lying there, her head pounding, she could still feel the tingle and the burn on her lips where they had brushed his. She felt a sick excitement combined with a sense of panic that she had gone too far.

This was something she could get expelled for. Turning up at a teacher's house, drunk, throwing herself at him.

Juliet covered her face with the sheet. What had she done?

Later, they sat around Fhemie's kitchen table, drinking the strongest black coffee possible and analysing the events of the previous night. Both Margot and Fhemie found the whole thing hilarious.

"You don't think he looked really angry?" Juliet asked.

"He looked dazed," Fhemie told her. "In a good way. Not like repulsed or anything."

"If we hadn't been there who knows what might have happened?" Margot said.

Juliet shivered, thinking about it.

"Do you think he'll say anything about it on Monday? Will I get into trouble?"

Margot laughed. "When have you ever cared about getting into trouble, girl? Don't tell me Mr Hot and Holy is actually turning you into a good Christian girl for real."

"If it is, you can take my place as a nun," Fhemie told her.

Seeing that Juliet was looking conflicted, Margot tried to reassure her. "Honestly, I think he's got it bad. He was frozen to the spot but it was in a good way. Like he just got a surprise present."

"Or a strippergram," Fhemie said. She grinned at Juliet's horrified reaction. "Nah, it's all good, you're hooking him in. I've bet Margot that you'll seduce him by Christmas."

* * *

The weekend only got worse for Carl. After a night of fragmented sleep and disturbing dreams, he had another wedding planning session with Rebecca.

It was absolutely the last thing he wanted to do. The whole process seemed interminable. He couldn't summon up a fraction of enthusiasm though he did his best to look cheerful and feign interest.

Rebecca was going over the order of service and Carl was only half listening. It didn't really matter to him how they did it or even what hymns were sung, it was the result that was important to him.

So if Rebecca felt strongly about a certain reading, he was happy to let her have her way.

"I know you wanted your cousin to do the second reading, but I really don't think it's appropriate. I mean given the circumstances I don't think it's right, having him read," Rebecca was saying.

Carl had practically grown up with his cousin Billy, they were like brothers.

"What?"

"Well, you know. I mean it's not like he supports Christian marriage, with his lifestyle," Rebecca said.

Carl wasn't sure if he was hearing correctly. He hadn't been paying full attention before so he was trying to get his head around what his fiancée was saying.

Rebecca pushed one side of her hair back over her shoulder. "I was actually wondering... I mean the guest list is getting so long, and it's important to both of us that all our friends from church are able to attend. And immediate family, of course. I was thinking that maybe it would be best if your cousin... I mean maybe he wouldn't even want to come?"

"You don't want Billy at our wedding?"

"Oh no, I don't mean to to put it in those terms. It's not that I don't like him, of course, I mean he's your cousin. But he lives some distance away, and maybe if we emphasised how it's really a very strongly religious event for both of us..." Rebecca smiled, in a kind of questioning way, anticipating his agreement and approval.

She would get neither. Carl was stunned.

"You want me to uninvite my cousin Billy, because he's gay?"

Rebecca gave a half smile. "I knew you'd understand. It's not like he could really enjoy himself, is it? I mean there won't be any... others like him there, will there?" She practically shuddered while saying the word "others".

Carl wanted space. He wanted to be alone to process this.

"You think I can just call him and tell him he's not welcome at my own wedding? I mean what would you even expect me to say?"

Rebecca frowned.

"I guess it's awkward, with him being your cousin and all."

The phone rang, to Carl's huge relief. He thought had got his point across calmly, with Rebecca having capitulated. As if he could turn his own cousin away! Picking up the phone he heard Dan's voice at the end of the line.

"Jenny's gone to visit her family for a couple of days. One of her old high school friends just had a baby that she has to go and see, you know what it's like with women and babies," Dan joked. Carl didn't yet, but he could imagine. "So if you want to come around for a movie and beers later, we can do a guys' night."

It was the escape he needed. "That was Dan," he said, returning to the living room where Rebecca was making marks against the guest list. "I forgot that he asked me over tonight."

"Oh." Rebecca looked a little disappointed. She and Carl hadn't had concrete plans but they would probably have ended up having dinner together.

Carl was still wondering if he had understood their previous conversation properly. He felt deeply disturbed about everything.

* * *

Drinks. A couch. A mindless action move.

A doctor couldn't have provided a better tonic for the way Carl was feeling right now.

Dan, who was perceptive, could tell something was up. Carl saw the question in his eyes but his friend didn't push it.

Ninety minutes of car chases, people dangling from helicopters and some kind of jewel heist later, he was finally starting to feel normal again. It wasn't his favourite kind of film but it was what he needed right now.

"So," Dan began, flicking Carl a sidelong glance, "all good with the wedding progress?"

"There's more involved than I thought," Carl said.

Dan laughed and handed him another drink. "Tell me about it. I thought it would never end. But I guess this stuff is important to them, so I just let Jenny do her thing."

It had been a wise move, Carl thought, as Dan's and Jenny's wedding had been good fun. Dignified where it mattered, and relaxed and enjoyable for the rest of it.

He was silent, thinking about his own situation.

Dan wasn't going to ask him outright what was wrong. "You must be nearly done with the marriage classes. Jenny and I were pretty over them by the end of it all."

"How do you mean?"

Dan shrugged. "It's all a bit overdone, isn't it? They mean well, but constantly being reminded to save it for the day... well it just increases the pressure, doesn't it?"

Carl frowned. "Did you find that aspect difficult?"

"What do you reckon?! One night we nearly threw it all in and went to Vegas. Jenny was even more up for it than I was."

Vegas. Carl thought of Rebecca's very different reaction to his own joking suggestion.

"What made you stay?" he asked Dan.

"All the money we'd spent. Angry relatives. Mainly the fact that Jenny really wanted to wear the dress, and it was still being fixed up at the bridal shop." Dan took a swig of his drink. "If we'd had it with us, we might well have eloped. The pressure was pretty full on by then, as you can imagine." He gave a wicked grin, assuming Carl was experiencing the same.

Once again Carl was silent. He didn't usually talk about stuff this personal with his friends. Or even his pastor.

"It hasn't really been an issue," he said.

"You mean you're both too well disciplined?"

"I guess. Something like that, maybe." He couldn't hide his troubled expression.

Now Dan looked puzzled and concerned. "What's up?"

So many things. The fact that Carl was constantly aroused by another girl and couldn't stop thinking about her. The fact that he felt no physical attraction towards the woman he was about to commit his entire life to. The fact that after tonight, he wasn't even sure whether he knew her properly. Did they even share the same values?

"Doubts are pretty normal," Dan said, to try to reassure him. "It's about reinforcing to yourself that you're doing the right thing."

"Did you have them?" Carl asked.

"You've met Jenny's mother, right? What do you reckon?" Jenny's mother was something of a battle-axe. Dan set the can down. "I shouldn't say that, she's got a good heart, Barbara. But yeah, I mean everyone has doubts. Or not so much doubts, but 'what ifs'. At the end of the day you're opening more doors than you're closing. Or one much better door, perhaps. Think of it that way."

* * *

Inside the confessional it smelt of wood polish and the dust of ages. The faint smell of incense lingered in the air. It was a very different atmosphere to the modern cheer of Carl's own church, but he had come here because he couldn't think what else to do.

He needed to confess. To seek guidance.

But he couldn't face telling his own pastor.

As he knelt on the hard cushion inside the confessional booth, there was a sliding sound as the shutter drew across. It left only a lattice between Carl and the unseen priest.

Carl waited. He had some idea that he or the priest was supposed to say something, but he wasn't sure what.

Eventually the priest spoke. "Do you wish to confess, my son?"

The first thing Carl needed to confess was that he wasn't a Catholic. "This isn't actually my church, Father. I'm not really sure how to proceed."

The priest's voice was warm. "The house of the Lord is open to all. Why don't you start by telling me what is troubling you?"

Where to begin? "I'm supposed to be getting married, Father…" He trailed off, unsure how to continue. "But I'm having doubts."

"It is not unusual to feel uncertainty at such a time."

Carl wondered what the priest looked like. He sounded patient and wise. "It's more than just uncertainty. I can't stop thinking about someone else. I don't know what to do."

"Have these remained merely thoughts, my son?" the priest asked.

74

You couldn't lie in a confessional. Of all the places in the world, this was the last place you could lie. "Not quite. But nothing much, nothing…" Carl spoke quickly, wondering what the relevant transgression was called by Catholics. A kiss that he hadn't done enough to prevent. "Nothing mortal."

"Can you put distance between yourself and this other person?"

"No, she's…" he stopped himself from saying "one of my students" as it sounded so appalling. "She's at my place of work."

"Then you must do your best to put what distance you can there."

Carl already knew this, though it was painful to think of having to avoid Juliet. "Yes, Father."

"With this person removed from your thoughts, would your doubts be gone?"

This was the crux of it. This was the thing that Carl was trying to establish. Sitting there in the dark and calm, infused with the ancient odour of church, the holy serenity of it all, Carl finally got the clarity he sought.

"No, Father." He and Rebecca were just too different. Their values were too different. He realised that now.

"Perhaps time and distance from both these women will help you find the correct path," the priest said.

When Carl walked back outside from the dark stillness of the church, into the bright wintry sunlight, he felt as though a burden had been lifted from his shoulders. He had been stressed that his attraction towards Juliet and growing feelings for her were interfering with his affection for Rebecca.

Now he realised that regardless of Juliet, he and Rebecca were simply wrong together. He didn't have the appropriate emotional or physical feelings towards her. Despite his revulsion at her attitude towards his cousin, he was reluctant to hurt her more than necessary.

XI. Avoidance

It was all her fault. Mr Spencer was avoiding her, and it was all because she had been stupid and drunk and made an idiot of herself. She had practically thrown herself at him. No wonder Mr Spencer was repulsed.

Juliet felt utterly miserable. Since Hallowe'en the Latin teacher had been studiously avoiding her. He still had to teach her in his classes, but he rarely if ever called on her for an answer, or spoke to her for any purpose if he didn't have to.

He was flawlessly polite and professional, but that was it. She had blown it.

It wasn't even about the bet any longer, if in fact it ever had been. Juliet had completely fallen for Mr Spencer and he didn't want to give her the time of day.

She nursed her misery to herself, trying to avoid the scrutiny of Fhemie and Margot who could sense that something was up.

"Girl, he's really got it bad!" Margot whispered one day in class.

Juliet could have wept. It was during a lesson in which Mr Spencer had literally asked every single girl in the class except Juliet to translate a line, or answer a question about the text. She wasn't convinced, despite Margot's encouragement, that Mr Spencer was deliberately avoiding her because he secretly liked her. It was pretty clear that he was disgusted by her.

He was so good looking. She knew what his skin smelled like close up. The firm warmth of his lips. It had tripped a switch in her, making her all the more desperate for him.

If only she could turn the clock back. But it was too late for that.

* * *

"Everything okay?" Dan asked Carl.

They were having coffee while Jenny and Rebecca shopped for baby things.

"I don't know," Carl said. "They should be."

Dan tore open a small packet of sugar. "Work or home?" he asked.

Carl wished he could just confide in Dan. But he felt it would be a betrayal of Rebecca. "It's home, but it's complicated," he said.

Dan, who had strongly suspected that something was up between Carl and Rebecca, was concerned about his friend. Their conversation a few days earlier had troubled him.

"Cold feet?"

"Something like that." Carl gazed out of the window, wishing he could freeze the world and have a few days by himself just to think about things.

It was killing him. Trying to pretend that Juliet wasn't there, trying to avoid speaking to her in class. Seeing the hurt and confusion in her eyes. It wrenched his heart.

The last image he had of her other than at school was in her sexy Hallowe'en costume. His mind was fixated on the memory of it. The memory of her lips brushing his.

Juliet hadn't even been back to his church since that night. He guessed that she was embarrassed and probably regretted something she would never have done if sober. Once again Carl blamed himself: he had deliberately not moved away from her, wanting her so badly in that one moment of weakness.

"I even tried going to confession," he told Dan.

"What, like Catholic confession? Something hasn't actually happened, has it?" Dan saw the flicker of guilt in Carl's eyes.

"Not exactly."

"Even if it has it's not a disaster." Dan put his coffee down and looked rueful. "If you must know, Jenny and I weren't the greatest at adhering to all of those arm's length rules they go on about in the classes. After all, betrothal used to be the green light for that side of things, in times past."

Carl knew this, although it was against the current teachings of their church.

"It's not that." If only it was. "It's in some ways the opposite."

Dan was puzzled. He remembered his previous conversation with Carl. But lack of sexual feeling wasn't the kind of thing that you needed to go to confession about. Unless… "You don't mean you're having feelings the other way?"

Now Carl was bewildered, then realised what Dan meant. "No, not at all. But not for Rebecca either." He couldn't bring himself to mention that he did have those feelings for another girl.

But Dan was putting two and two together. Confession meant guilt, and that could only mean one thing. "There's someone else?"

"Not as such. Just someone who made me realise what it probably should be, and isn't," Carl told him.

* * *

With Mr Spencer freezing her out, Juliet tried to throw herself into band rehearsals. So far she had managed to conceal the whole band thing from everyone.

Remembering that the best lie is the one that's closest to the truth, she had told Aunt Mary she was going to a music appreciation club on Tuesdays and a poetry circle on Thursdays.

"It's important to have some extracurricular achievements for my college application," Juliet had said.

Anything new she gleaned about music from rehearsals could be dropped into conversation as though it came from music appreciation. Jax in particular was a music nerd and discussed things from all realms of music, including classical.

If Aunt Mary ever asked about the poetry group Juliet could show her the lyrics she was writing for the band. An edited version, anyway.

The best thing of all was having the Paris choir tour to look forward to. Following a letter from Miss Mead, Juliet's aunt had finally consented. Juliet had never been abroad before and it was going to be the trip of a lifetime.

* * *

"Can anyone explain what Vergil is trying to do with this line?"

Carl looked around the room. There were only a couple of hands up, one of them Juliet's. He had already called on the other girl earlier in the class so he had to take Juliet's response this time. "Yes, Juliet?"

Her face brightened when he finally acknowledged her and Carl had to do all he could to keep his own face steady.

"Sibilance, to sound soothing. *Suadentque cadentia sidera somnos.*" Juliet pronounced the phrase flawlessly, emphasising the esses to illustrate her point.

"That's very good." Despite himself Carl smiled at her and she reddened.

If only he could have spoken with her, apologised, made her understand that the kiss had been his fault. But even to reassure her was now forbidden since he was trying to put some distance there.

The problem was that he liked her: it was more than physical attraction. Juliet was highly intelligent, spirited yet vulnerable. Carl admired her courage, having seen how often some of the other girls made spiteful remarks towards her.

Juliet was clearly from a less privileged background than most of her classmates but she didn't let it hold her back. Carl had enjoyed talking with her before the whole Hallowe'en thing happened.

What was he going to do?

* * *

There was only one thing Carl could do. It was one of the hardest conversations he had ever had to have.

Rebecca was furious. Disbelieving and furious. "You can't do this to me! To us! I've done all this preparation towards our wedding, what are we supposed to do with all that?"

If anything, her response vindicated Carl's decision. He had done all he could to soften the blow, even blaming himself as much as possible for "not being ready".

But the cold hard truth was that he simply didn't love her enough. He didn't really love her at all.

"I think we both need to take some time to think about our values, and what we both want," Carl said. Then he immediately regretted it because it left the door ajar. He wanted this to be a final break up. He simply couldn't imagine any future scenario in which he would feel any renewed desire to marry Rebecca.

"I know exactly what my values are," Rebecca told him. "And I wouldn't have been spending so much effort and time planning this wedding if I hadn't known what I wanted."

Carl noted, not for the first time, that Rebecca's focus was on the wedding rather than on him or the two of them as a couple. She could have said "I want you" but she didn't. It had worried him before: once all the planning was done, and the big day came, and they were finally united: what then?

"I'll cover all the expenses we've already run to," he said.

Rebecca stared at him, open mouthed. "I can't believe you're talking like this. You're not thinking straight. You need to speak with Pastor Brown."

"I'll speak with him if you like, but it's not going to change things. I've prayed over this and I've thought about it deeply. It's not right for either of us. We're not where we should be as a couple, and I don't think we ever will be."

She looked furious. "This is about all the physical side, isn't it? Your constant attempts to push for that. It's only a few months that you need to be patient for, I don't understand what your problem is."

There was so much more anger in her than sorrow, so it seemed to him, but perhaps it was her way of dealing with it.

"How do you think that side of things would have gone, after the wedding, Rebecca? People talk of 'chemistry' but do you think it's guaranteed? Because right now I don't think that we have it."

"That's because I've been praying and exercising self control," she snapped. "Besides, people put too much emphasis on that. It shouldn't have to be some kind of obsession."

Carl looked at her. "Have you ever felt it? With me? Have you ever even felt tempted?"

There was a faint flicker of fear and uncertainty in her eyes before she replied. "I can't believe you would ask me something so disgusting, so sinful."

"I don't think it's sinful to talk about it. The couples in the marriage DVDs talk about it quite openly, how they struggled with it ahead of the marriage. It's only a sin if you yield to temptation."

Saying this, Carl got a pang of guilt thinking about Juliet and the kiss. Though he had managed to keep things professional since that devastating encounter.

"Well maybe it's for the best," Rebecca was saying. "You seem to have become some kind of sexual deviant. I'll pray for you, Carl, and I hope you come to your senses."

XII. The Green Room

"Oh my God you'll never guess!" Margot was bursting with excitement.

Fhemie and Juliet were already eating lunch. Juliet had a tuna wrap and Fhemie was eating a chocolate chip muffin, tossing a few crumbs to a small bird that pecked them up from the ground nearby.

"You are correct, I will never guess, so just put us all out of our misery. Or into it," Fhemie said.

Margot wasn't deterred by Fhemie's lack of enthusiasm.

"So you know how Miss Villiers is supposed to be taking the choir trip with Miss Mead?"

They all knew this. Miss Villiers taught modern languages, and since the trip was in France, it made sense for her to go. She was also a much tougher pair of hands than Miss Mead, whom the girls could run riot over.

"Well," Margot continued, "she has something with some relative. So she can't go. So guess who else is going instead?"

"I can't guess." Fhemie refused to play the game.

"Mr Spencer!"

Juliet felt a jolt.

Fhemie was even more envious about the trip now. "He'll be so much more easy going than Villiers. You guys will have a ball."

"And Juliet can finally get some alone time with him," Margot said.

"As if." Juliet wasn't even going to let herself think about that.

Margot and Fhemie exchanged a glance.

"In other news," Margot said, having nearly forgotten, "some guy Terrance knows is having a party this Friday. So you're both invited."

Juliet couldn't make it. "I'm busy Friday."

Margot turned on her. "Busy with what? You're always busy these days. I figure you're not going to that church thing so what are you doing?"

"I bet it's like that book my grandmother sent me. She's secretly doing novitiate classes and she's going to join the convent on the last day of term," Fhemie said.

"That wasn't a book, that was an old film. With Hayley Mills," Margot said.

Fhemie shrugged. "I read it in a book. Most stupid ending ever."

"Whatever. So what exactly are you up to, Juliet?"

Juliet was going to have to tell them sooner or later. She braced herself for the teasing.

"You remember that guy who gave me his contact after the karaoke night?" she said.

"Please tell me you did not call him."

"I did, and I've been singing in this band they have," Juliet told her.

Fhemie picked muffin crumbs from her lap and threw them to the small bird. "But you didn't tell us because it's a shit band, right? We did warn you."

"I don't think so," Juliet said. "I don't mean my singing is all that. But I think they know what they're doing."

Margot raised her eyebrows. "So when do we get to hear this musical marvel?"

"This Friday. At the Green Room. I was going to ask if I could tell my aunt I was staying at your place."

"So where are you actually going to be staying?"

Juliet hadn't entirely figured this out. She had hoped that maybe she could crash with one of the band members. Sneaking into Aunt Mary's house past midnight, possibly reeking of cigarettes and alcohol, wasn't a risk worth taking. Anything like that and her aunt would cancel the Paris trip.

"We'll come and watch you, you can stay at mine," Fhemie offered. Margot was spending the night with Terrance, using Fhemie for a cover.

Juliet flooded with gratitude and remorse for not telling her friends earlier. She should never have doubted them. "What about the party?"

"We can go there afterwards. Bands don't usually play in the Green Room that late. It will all work out."

Fhemie had brought out another large muffin and was starting to eat it to Margot's disgust.

"One I get, but two is like a step away from America's Most Obese," Margot said. "It will catch up with you one day."

Juliet looked at the wrapper. "You know I could bake you something so much nicer than those. Healthier too. The ones you buy are gross."

"Why don't you then?" Fhemie said. "Only if it tastes of bran or some such shit, I won't eat it."

Juliet laughed. "It won't. I'll even add chocolate chips."

She experienced a sudden pang as she remembered the cookies she had baked for Mr Spencer. She imagined his fiancée baking him trays of goodies while the two of them enjoyed a cosy night in, and felt bereft.

* * *

There were so many people. Obviously there would be, since it was a Friday night, but Juliet had secretly been hoping that the place would be half-empty. If she screwed up there would be such a huge crowd to witness it.

Drew was really supportive of her. They'd become firm friends over the weeks of rehearsing and he could see how nervous she was.

She kind of wished Margot and Fhemie weren't coming. It would be all the worse if they witnessed her humiliation.

"You okay?" Drew asked, while they were still setting up.

"I think so." She was as ready as she would ever be.

"You look great," he told her.

Juliet was actually wearing her school uniform, though it had undergone such a transformation that Miss Villiers would have barely recognised it. If she had, she would have had a heart attack.

Juliet's oldest school skirt - now too short to meet regulations - was rolled up at the waist, paired with a white blouse tied to show her midriff below and unbuttoned to show the top of her bra. This was black and lacy, also against regulations which required discreet, neutral underwear. The outfit had been Jax's sister's idea. The band had been amused when they found out Juliet went to St Gillian's, which was a relief as she had worried they might object to her still being at high school.

"Good Catholic girl gone wild. Let's do that," Jax's sister had said.

It certainly made it easier than buying new clothes. Juliet need to save all her money for the Paris trip.

She wasn't sure how she would feel when the performance started. She was fretting that she would get stage fright. Yet when they were finally announced, and the first song started, Juliet found herself going into a kind of trance. She and the band and the stage formed their own world. The audience was there but further away, separate. She wasn't even distracted by trying to see Margot and Fhemie in the crowd.

* * *

Dan had dragged Carl out on the town to drown his sorrows.

"Better to face the world than sit about brooding."

Carl had been reluctant to go out for a drink, since he rarely touched alcohol though Dan was a bit more lapsed his in habits. It felt too much like celebrating something that had been a painful event. The relief he felt at having broken off his engagement only made it more uncomfortable because he felt guilty.

He hadn't even been sure if he should show up to church or not, in case it made things harder for Rebecca. So he had skipped services for the first week, then gone and tried to keep low key. Rebecca had been there, she had given him a tight, formal nod but hadn't otherwise spoken to him.

He wasn't sure if he should have spoken to her. But what could he say. "Hope you're okay?" "No hard feelings?"

It was such an awkward situation.

Dan was right: if Carl stayed at home he would just sit about brooding and getting distracted from his marking by thoughts of a certain student that he was still struggling to forget. So he accepted Dan's invitation.

They ended up in a noisy, crowded bar that Carl had previously walked past but never gone into. He usually preferred quieter places, and Rebecca hadn't even liked to go to bars and pubs at all.

"This looks lively," Dan said as they made their way to the bar. "And there's a band going to play."

A beer in hand, letting the noise of the crowd and the currently playing music wash over him, Carl was starting to feel grounded again.

"You made the right decision," Dan said.

"Really?" Dan's and Jenny's reaction was something that Carl had initially feared, since they had frequently socialised as a foursome.

"If you're not suited, you're not suited," Dan said. "And in all honesty, Jen and I had wondered about you both a few times." This was putting it mildly. Jenny did her absolute best to like Rebecca but the other woman wasn't really her chosen type of friend. Christian forbearance only went so far: there were more than a few occasions when Jenny had vented to her husband after Carl and Rebecca had left, usually about something sanctimonious Rebecca had said.

Deep down Carl knew he had done the right thing. The problem was that it had all got confused and complicated by the Juliet Martin situation. He had also mistakenly thought that finishing with Rebecca would defuse the tensions he felt over his student.

Instead the opposite had happened. He dreamt about her even more, and the dreams were even less appropriate than previously. He would wake up feeling frustrated, aching hard at the image of her and trying to concentrate on other thoughts.

What was the purpose of this temptation? He prayed about it constantly. If it was a test, when would it be over?

Which was why for a moment Carl thought he was hallucinating when he suddenly saw Juliet's face, light shining on her hair like a halo, just across the room. Her face was that of an angel, and her body...

Carl nearly dropped his beer. Just what was she wearing? It was like the sexiest, most illicit parody of St Gillian's school uniform imaginable. It made her Hallowe'en costume look modest. Juliet was singing and she sounded like a sensual angel, the slim curves of her body winding with the music.

He couldn't tear his eyes away.

Dan noticed him looking. "That singer's something, isn't she? Young though. She looks vaguely familiar."

Please don't recognise her, Carl thought. Dan had been there the nights that Juliet had come to their church but they hadn't been introduced.

How could anyone look so angelic and so erotic at the same time? Carl was transfixed. If the crowd suddenly melted away and she came over to him, he wouldn't be able to resist her. He could only imagine how she would feel: soft, pliant, curving and arching against him. Reaching up to him as he crushed her in an embrace.

Enough! He prayed again for strength. He tried recalling a passage of Latin text. He even tried thinking about Rebecca to blot out his ardour for Juliet.

Nothing worked.

How he was going to face her in class, in her school uniform after seeing her like his, he had no idea.

* * *

Fhemie spotted Carl and gave Margot a sharp nudge. It was hard to hold a conversation above the music so she had to gesture towards where their teacher was sitting.

Margot looked over and saw their Latin teacher watching Juliet. To be fair most of the room was watching Juliet given she was on a stage with lights on her, but Mr Spencer looked kind of frozen.

The band were about to take a break for half an hour and as soon as they did, Juliet's friends rushed up to her. "Guess who's here?"

For a moment Juliet had a sense of dread that Aunt Mary had stopped by, then was both thrilled and mortified to realise who they meant. She had looked towards where they were indicating and of course caught his eye immediately.

"You should go and say hi," Margot told her.

"Yeah, maybe give him your autograph," Fhemie said.

Juliet was on something of a high from the singing and couldn't help but notice how incredibly good looking Mr Spencer was, over at the bar. He was queueing to buy drinks.

"Hello." She had felt bold before approaching him but when she got there, she couldn't think of anything to say.

"Juliet." He greeted her. "You sing really well."

"I wouldn't have thought it was your kind of music."

"It's not something I'm very familiar with, but I liked it," he told her.

Juliet was trying to figure out if he was here with his fiancée. She looked around but couldn't see her. "Are you here with people?" she asked him.

"Just a friend," he said.

"Oh." She assumed he meant Rebecca and her heart sank a little.

Carl read the disappointment in her eyes. He knew he was tempting fate, but he couldn't help clarifying. "Dan, whom you may have met at my church."

"Oh!" The light went on in her eyes again and Carl felt his heart flip. "Your fiancée isn't here?" Juliet asked.

This really was playing with fire. The spectre of Rebecca was one of his last defences. "There isn't a fiancée any more. Rebecca and I broke up."

Juliet tried to suppress a spark of joy. "I'm sorry," she told him. As she said it she found that she was genuinely sorry, she didn't like to think of Mr Spencer being hurt.

"It wasn't working," he told her. Out of old loyalty to Rebecca he had wanted to avoid stating who ended it, but Juliet guessed from his tone that he was the one who had finished it.

Her spark of joy turned into a flash of guilt. "This wasn't because of Hallowe'en?" she asked him.

Carl knew what she was referring to. "Nothing to do with that. We simply weren't suited."

"Did you mind?" she asked.

"Mind what?" He was momentarily confused.

"That I kissed you."

Carl had to take a couple of seconds to steady himself. With her words Juliet had brought the whole event rushing back. It didn't help that she was once again standing in front of him with half her breasts showing, her skirt revealing most of her thighs. It took every ounce of his self control not to reach out for her.

"Were you angry?" she asked him. She had thought he was from the way he had seemed to avoid her since that night.

"No." He barely voiced it but she read his lips.

"Would you be angry if I did it again?"

The number of people and the crowd at the bar had pushed the two of them closer, nearly touching. Carl had to work on his breathing to remain still: he was a hair's breadth from being right against her. He couldn't take his eyes off her lips. "We can't, Juliet. It would be totally inappropriate."

She gave him a seductive smile. "But you want me to?" she said, her voice almost a whisper. They were so close she could smell the trace of cologne he was wearing, smell the raw maleness of his skin. She thought she had never wanted anyone so badly.

He briefly closed his eyes, trying to keep himself together. "I'm your teacher. We can't have this conversation." The rote phrases were the only thing keeping him from stepping over the precipice.

"So if you weren't my teacher...?" The question hung in the air.

"Juliet..." He couldn't answer. He couldn't lie convincingly and to admit the truth was impossible.

"Do you want me?" She was leaning even closer, millimetres from his body. Pretty much any other guy in the bar would kill to be in this position. Carl dreaded to think what Dan's reaction must be. He couldn't bring himself to look over.

"More than anything." He could hardly believe he had admitted it. She had him transfixed. "Right now, being this close to you is like torture. But it's wrong and nothing is going to happen. Even if you weren't my student, I'm far too old for you."

As he spoke he managed to get his composure back. To bring himself back down to earth.

"I'm eighteen. I'm above the age of consent."

Just this phrase nearly knocked Carl off balance again. He could only imagine the sweetness of actually taking her. But he was resolved. He picked up the drinks. "It makes no difference." His voice was firm.

Juliet had to get back anyway for the second half of the show. "I'll see you at school then?" She looked directly into his eyes and they held one another's gaze for a moment.

"I'll see you at school." Carl had a feeling this was far from over but he would steel himself into more careful behaviour in future. Juliet slipped off to the band and Carl return to Dan.

Dan looked at him quizzically. "That looked like a cosy chat. Do you know her?"

Carl couldn't lie, Dan might well find out anyway. "She's actually one of my students."

Dan whistled under his breath. "That's some serious jailbait. Are they all like that?"

"She's a good student." Carl found himself defensive of Juliet.

"With a serious teacher crush," Dan countered.

Despite himself Carl felt uplifted at this. After all Juliet was young and beautiful and pretty much every guy in the place would have had his eye on her that night, wearing her outrageous outfit and singing like an angel. Even though it was completely wrong, he was flattered to think that she found him attractive.

Glancing around and seeing other hungry male eyes on her, Carl had to fight his instinct to grab a coat and put it around her.

The guilt would doubtless hit him in the early hours, as he had yet another dream of her, and he would struggle to get through the weekend alternately missing her and trying not to think of her.

XIII. Anticipation

Juliet could barely sleep the night after the gig, she was floating on air. Mr Spencer wanted her. "More than anything" he had said.

It was the admission itself more than the actual words that was significant. For her teacher to actually admit his desire to her was huge.

"Told you he was still into you," Margot said.

"How did you know?" Juliet asked.

"The way he tried not to look at you in class all the time. It was so obvious."

All the misery Juliet had felt at his avoidance of her and formality around her was replaced with a bursting, stomach dissolving joy. She wasn't sure how he would react towards her in Latin the following Monday. But somehow it would happen. It had to happen.

Saturday dragged after she got home from Fhemie's house. Juliet had one thing on her mind. She even thought about walking past his house but chickened out.

Instead she buried herself in homework, and made another batch of muffins to take to school. Fhemie had gone wild for them, and had encouraged Juliet to start a surreptitious trade in home-baked goodies. "I would pay for these."

"You don't have to, they're a gift."

"So sell them to other people," Fhemie suggested.

Juliet had worried about it not being allowed under school rules.

"Jesus, it's not like they're drugs. Give them to me, I'll sort it out."

So Fhemie started selling Juliet's muffins for her, refusing to take anything but free muffins for her commission.

It had solved Juliet's dilemma over spending money for the Paris trip. She wanted to get some really nice souvenirs while she was over there but Aunt Mary didn't like her working during the school semester.

Later she made a couple more batches, thinking of Mr Spencer while she did so, and wondering what he was up to.

* * *

Cold shower. Prayer. Bible.

Rinse, repeat.

It was no good. This was bigger than Carl could deal with. He couldn't get it out of his system no matter what he tried.

He almost regretted breaking up with Rebecca because at least it was an extra barrier between him and Juliet, something else for him to focus on. If he had still been engaged he would never had confessed what he had to her.

Confessed. Confession. Maybe that was where he needed to go. It had given him clarity before, even if he didn't feel his soul was shriven. How could he possibly seek guidance from Pastor Brown about something this damning? He needed anonymity, privacy.

Carl had been surprised by the amount of support from members of his church after his broken engagement became known. He had assumed that people would have rallied around Rebecca and perhaps even kept their distance with him. Instead there was sympathy for both of them.

"I was sorry to hear of your situation, my dear. But you're both young and the Lord has a plan for you, whatever it may be." This was from Agnes. Carl liked her, she was such a kind old woman with her snowy hair and bright eyes.

Carl came to realise that others had recognised the incompatibility for a long time, which was galling. He hoped Rebecca would find happiness elsewhere, but he doubted his own ability to.

He couldn't even look at another woman. The only female in the entire world that he wanted was Juliet Martin.

But I say unto you, That whosoever looketh on a woman to lust after her hath committed adultery with her already in his heart.

His bible brought little comfort. He should be able to deal with this. He was a grown man and a teacher with several years experience. Falling for a student in this way was absurd.

* * *

The bench was hard beneath her and the church was draughty and cold. Juliet sat in Sunday mass next to her aunt, unable to feel any interest in the service. Even the hymns seemed flat.

Her mind wandered to Mr Spencer. Was he at his own church right this moment? What was he doing?

She looked over at the confessional boxes, where she hadn't been in ages. She wasn't even sure if she believed in that stuff any more. Baptists didn't do it, and nor did most other Christian denominations.

If she went, what would she confess first? Impure thoughts, words or deeds?

The thought of Mr Spencer peeling off her clothes and running his strong, firm hands over her body.

Telling Mr Spencer how much she wanted him and what she wanted him to do to her.

Going up to Mr Spencer and putting her lips on his, winding herself around his body, feeling him grow hard against her own body...

She shivered and received a sharp glance from her aunt.

Tomorrow, she would pluck up her courage and approach Mr Spencer. She wasn't yet sure what she would say. But she couldn't go on like this.

* * *

Carl couldn't concentrate on Pastor Brown's sermon. He felt exhausted. He was lying to his friends, his God, even himself. He wasn't okay. He was in turmoil.

He would have to speak with Juliet tomorrow. Try and clear the air. Explain that he still valued and respected her as a student, and hoped that she could forget his words the other night and move past them.

Right now he would have given almost anything just to be with her. He wished he could take a single day out of time and spend it with her.

Jenny came up to him after the service. She was glowing, her stomach visibly larger. "Why don't you come over for dinner later?" she asked Carl.

"Thanks, but I have a stack of marking." In actual fact he wanted to sit at home and brood.

"That's a shame." Jenny grinned. "We were looking forward to finding out more about your sinful desires."

"What?" Carl felt cold. Had Dan guessed about his attraction to Juliet and told his wife?

"I was just joking. I'm afraid Rebecca has been making some insinuations about the reasons for your split. Not that we believe them, knowing Rebecca. I did remind her of Proverbs 11:13 which shut her up."

Carl felt weary. No wonder he'd had a few funny looks from some of the members of the Women's Prayer Group that Rebecca attended.

* * *

Cynthia was being unbearable in Latin. She was crowing about her designer wardrobe and how it would be impossible to choose which outfits to take to Paris. Mr Spencer was a few minutes late and she took the opportunity to hold court among her sycophantic little clique of friends.

"Of course I'm going to need extra suitcase space for the clothes I'll get over there." She started reeling off a long list of European designers she planned to buy.

Margot rolled her eyes. "I don't know where she thinks she's going to get the time to do that. Every second of the day will be spent being dragged around churches and museums, not shopping on the Champs Elysées."

Juliet didn't care what they were made to do overseas, she was just so excited about getting to go in the first place.

"French boys are so much more sophisticated," Cynthia was saying. "When we were on holiday on the Côte d'Azur - that's the French Riviera, you know - and we were staying in Cannes in the presidential suite…"

"The shit that comes of your mouth," Margot said.

Before a furious Cynthia could retaliate Mr Spencer arrived so conversation had to end.

He looked so handsome today. His clear-cut features, the intelligence and sincerity in his gaze. Juliet had worried he would avoid her again but his eyes met hers briefly. His expression was neutral but there was something there, as though he was trying to read her reaction to him.

The class proceeded. Mr Spencer focused the class on scansion that day: how to work out the rhythms of Vergil's lines. He explained that it would help them interpret the meaning. They went round the class, each girl reading a few lines in Latin and English. Juliet got the verse where the hero meets the ghost of his dead wife.

"Three times I tried to embrace her, three times she slipped away," she translated, looking directly into Mr Spencer's eyes.

They both knew what each other was thinking of on the word "embrace". The air in the classroom felt charged with electricity to Juliet, she prayed that no one else noticed.

At the end of the class Mr Spencer asked her to remain behind. "Juliet, if you could just stay back for a moment."

She feigned a look of surprise as though she didn't know what it was he wanted.

Cynthia, who couldn't imagine in a million years that Mr Spencer might prefer someone like Juliet over someone like herself, assumed Juliet was in for a telling off. "Guess the foster slut fucked up again," she said to Juliet under her breath as she left.

"What was that, Cynthia?" Mr Spencer asked.

Cynthia ignored him and left. She had failed all semester to ingratiate herself with the Latin teacher but she wasn't afraid of him either. Her father was so rich and influential that what Cynthia wanted, Cynthia got. She always managed to get out of detention or have her grades moved upwards.

When Cynthia had finally gone and everyone else had left the room, Margot shooting Juliet a sly grin as she exited, Juliet went up to Mr Spencer's desk. She stood there, hugging her pile of folders against her chest.

They were both lost for words. But something needed to be said. She let him take the lead, after all he was the one that had summoned her.

Mr Spencer began. "About Friday night, what I said…"

Juliet feared he was going to try and retract it.

"We both know that I shouldn't have said it," he continued.

"But it was true?"

Mr Spencer sighed. "Juliet, we can't go through this again. That's what I needed to tell you. Conversations like that are off limits."

"But you can't take it back."

"I know." He looked contrite.

"And I can't forget hearing it."

"But you need to, Juliet. We both do." His expression was serious but also sad.

She was near enough to feel the magnetism of him, drawing her in.

"I can't. And you know I feel the same," she told him.

"You're so young, it's not uncommon for someone your age…"

Juliet felt a flash of anger and broke in. "It's not because I'm young. It's not as though I'm inexperienced."

Her words hung in the air between them. She immediately regretted them: now he must be thinking that Cynthia's insults about her were true.

"I know. But these feelings, when they're not appropriate, they're sent to test us," Mr Spencer said.

"Why?"

Why? It was the question that Carl Spencer had asked himself and his God again and again. It was the question he had been agonising over. What was the purpose of him struggling with these feelings for his student? If only she were less beautiful, less intelligent, less desirable. He felt the heat rise between them again.

Juliet was weak with wanting him. Just for him to put his arms around her so she could feel the heat and strength of his body pressed against her. The smooth cotton of his shirt. The shape of the muscles beneath it.

She spoke, her voice almost a whisper.

"If you embrace me, I won't slip away."

"That's what I'm most afraid of." The spectre of her haunted him enough, the flesh and blood reality would be a devastating torment.

Juliet looked up into his face. "Could you just kiss me, once? Just to see how it feels?"

Carl knew how it would feel. He had kissed her in his dreams, in his thoughts, in his daydreams. He had amplified the memory of their brief embrace, replaying it again and again.

"I can't do that."

"But you want to."

She leant towards him, tilting her face up and closing her eyes. Carl gripped the side of the desk to steady himself. He leaned forward towards her, his face as near to her face without touching. There was barely a fraction of space between his lips and hers. He was so close, so close... he could even feel his own skin tingle. But he would not kiss her.

Feeling as though he was floating for a moment he absorbed everything he could in those few seconds: her energy, her sweet, fresh perfume, the sound of her breathing.

Then he broke away.

"You deserve better," he told her as she opened her eyes, feeling him withdraw. He saw the faint hurt and disappointment there. "You deserve better than some stolen kiss. You deserve more than I can offer you."

XIV. Airport incident

"I can't believe we have to travel in these hideous things. It's so humiliating. It's like being in a prison gang."

Cynthia was livid that the school choir were being made to wear dark blue sweatshirts when they travelled. They were printed with the school's name and logo in bright white on the front, with "St Gillian's Choir" in large lettering on the reverse.

Having looked forward to showing off her expensive clothes, the last thing Cynthia wanted was to look like everyone else.

Juliet didn't think it was such an issue. After all, who would see them on the plane? "They'll be like pyjama tops," she suggested. They were taking a night flight to Paris so it would be dark for most of the way and passengers would probably sleep.

Cynthia looked at her in disgust. "I expect you wore this kind of thing at juvie," she said. "If only it were orange. Then you'd really feel at home."

Juliet chose to ignore her. They were in the departure lounge and she was conscious of Mr Spencer hearing Cynthia's spiteful words. It was all in her file which he surely must have read by now, or one of the other teachers must have told him. No wonder he hadn't wanted to kiss her, even if he admitted being attracted to her.

However Cynthia was determined to needle her. "I'm surprised you can even accompany us. Don't you have to wear an electronic tag if you leave the country? No wonder a poor foster slut like you has no fashion sense."

"At least the sweater's baggy enough to hide your sagging ass," Margot said, losing patience with her. "Shame there isn't a hood to go over your fugly face."

"You skanky black ho!" Cynthia tried to hit Margot but Juliet managed to get in between them.

This resulted in Cynthia hitting her, and as Juliet tried to defend herself the two girls ended up in a heap on the floor, Juliet struggling to get away. "Get off me you racist bitch," Juliet said as Cynthia grabbed and twisted her hair. She was determined not to hit Cynthia, knowing her father would sue for assault if his precious daughter ended up with so much as a broken nail.

Cynthia, who had always loathed Juliet because of her poor background and the way she constantly did well in school, was only too happy to lay into her.

Within seconds they were pulled apart by a horrified Miss Mead and Mr Spencer. Juliet was dishevelled and bruised and furious, and even more furious that Cynthia had goaded her into a fight.

"Young ladies this is the most disgraceful behaviour I have ever witnessed!" Miss Mead told them. "Fighting like alley cats in a public place, while bearing the school's logo. I barely know what to think."

Juliet muttered an apology, knowing that it was useless trying to point out that Cynthia had started it. Cynthia remained silent and simply glared.

"If we were the other side of the gate I would send you both home," Miss Mead said. "Since neither of you can be trusted to behave, you will stay next to myself and Mr Spencer for the duration of the journey. Cynthia, you will sit with me," she told the outraged girl, "and you, Juliet, will remain under the eye of Mr Spencer."

Appropriate seating exchanges were made, with Juliet feeling so shocked and numb that she didn't even react when Cynthia hissed "I'll get you for this, foster slut" as Miss Mead made her take a seat next to her.

She was going to sit next to Mr Spencer for eight hours. Granted he probably thought the worst of her now and would probably insist she remained silent unit they reached Paris, but at least she got to be near him.

"Could I please visit the bathroom?" she asked. She felt a total mess and wanted to see the damage that Cynthia had done. "I promise I will just come straight back."

"That's fine. I imagine you're a little shaken up. Take your time." He smiled, his expression kind.

"Thanks."

"I saw what happened. I will have a word with Miss Mead so you aren't blamed for trying to defend yourself."

Juliet was amazed. She was so used to being painted as the troublemaker whenever there was a row: it was unheard of for a teacher to give her the benefit of the doubt. This was why she had ended up playing it so safe at school, trying to avoid ever reacting to Cynthia. It was also why Margot frequently go involved instead, because Cynthia was secretly scared of Margot even though she hated her.

The only powers Cynthia respected were money and status. Juliet had neither, Margot's family had both.

Margot snuck away to join Juliet in the bathroom. "Thanks for getting into trouble for me. It was all my fault."

"It was that bitch's fault," Juliet said, trying to fix her hair. She had scratches on her face and a bruise starting on her cheekbone. "I owe you multiple times over."

"You owe me nothing, for something that gives me such pleasure," Margot told her. She took out her camera and took a couple of snaps of Juliet. "Evidence. You should have her done for assault."

"I wish."

Margot touched up her own make-up in the mirror, pouting at her reflection. "I can't believe we don't get to sit together now. I've got to spend the whole flight next to Sister Stephanie." Stephanie, another girl in their class, was nicknamed "Sister" because she was so devout. There was even a rumour that she might be doing a novitiate after graduation.

"Whereas you," Margot turned to Juliet, "get to spend the entire flight next to holy lover boy. So I expect some progress there at least."

Juliet had a giddy feeling in her stomach just thinking about it.

"Just don't fall asleep and drool with your mouth hanging open, or he might go off you," Margot warned.

"I don't do that!"

"You might. You never know. It's not an attractive look. If Sister Stephanie mouth-breaths over me I'll drop olives in her pie-hole. That will wake her up."

Or choke her to death, Juliet thought. "Please don't you get into any trouble as well. I'm still hoping we can share a hotel room." God forbid they got separated and had to have Stephanie or someone like her as a roommate. It would ruin any ideas of sneaking out and other mischief they were planning.

Margot tipped her head on one side in mock thoughtfulness. "I wonder if I did, whether Miss Mead would make you share a room with Mr Spencer instead?"

Juliet shivered. She couldn't imagine a more lovely punishment.

XV. Flying to Paris

Juliet had the window seat. The whole group was in Economy class, Cynthia having tried and failed to get an upgrade for herself. But while most of the others were nearer the back of the plane, Juliet and Mr Spencer had seats in a small section just behind Business class. Cynthia gave her a hideous scowl as she pushed past to her own seat far to the rear.

"Let me give you a hand." Mr Spencer helped Juliet haul her carry-on into the overhead compartment, after which she squeezed into her seat - there was barely enough leg-room to fit - and figured out how to clip together her seat belt.

Then she sat there, looking out of the window. She was gripping the two arm rests out of nerves which meant that Mr Spencer's elbow bumped hers as he sat down.

"Sorry." She apologised and moved her left arm to her lap, letting him have the arm rest, though he didn't take it.

"It's fine, I have plenty of space."

The seats had their own entertainment systems though for now they were all playing some promotional video from the airline. Juliet flicked through the various magazines. It seemed an eternity before all the passengers were loaded onto the plane and she heard the crew announce "doors armed".

She watched the safety demonstration as the plane started taxiing. It did nothing to reassure her: merely putting the prospect of crashing into the ocean or needing an oxygen mask into her mind.

Juliet bit her lip when the plane started accelerating down the runway. She had planned to look out of the window but her stomach was suddenly a ball of nerves. She gripped both arm rests and closed her eyes feeling a growing sense of dread.

"Are you okay, Juliet?" Mr Spencer's voice held concern.

"I'm fine," she managed to say, not reopening her eyes.

"You don't enjoy flying?"

"It's not that, I haven't…" She was too embarrassed to tell him. She must have been the only person in the whole of St Gillian's - probably the only person on the flight except for a couple of babies and infants - who had never flown before.

"It's your first flight, isn't it?"

Juliet opened her eyes to look at him. On anyone else's face there would have been disbelief and even derision, but Mr Spencer just looked sympathetic and a little bit amused.

"Yes. I know that must sound so dumb."

"It's not dumb at all…" Before he could continue the plane's wheels left the ground with a slight weightless lurch and Juliet gave a small cry of alarm.

"It's okay." Mr Spencer put his hand on the arm rest over hers to calm her as the plane took off.

Oh God. It was like he was holding her hand again. Now she was freaking out in a totally different way. It distracted her from being thousands of feet up in the air at least.

Juliet met his gaze and he looked back at her, keeping his hand on hers for some time longer before removing it. She felt the imprint of it even after it was gone, the tingle and the warmth on her skin. "Thanks," she said.

He smiled. "I wasn't much help. You should have told me you were a first-time flyer."

"I thought people might laugh," Juliet told him. The contemptuous face of Cynthia came into her head.

"If you prefer not to tell anyone, I'll keep your secret," Mr Spencer said. He was joking but nonetheless Juliet knew she could trust him.

He fell silent and there was an awkward feeling of tension between them. Juliet was supposed to be in disgrace so perhaps he felt he couldn't keep chatting to her.

Or perhaps, like her, he couldn't stop thinking of all their previous very inappropriate conversations.

Juliet would have felt more relaxed once they were airborne were it not for his presence beside her. Every fibre of her being was conscious of him.

To distract herself she played around with the in flight entertainment system. It was frustratingly unresponsive compared to a regular touchscreen, you had to keep jabbing it to get the menu options to change. She scrolled through the choices and ended up on Classic Favourites and The Sound of Music. It was a guilty pleasure: Margot and Fhemie would have totally teased her for choosing such an old movie.

Just as she put her headphones on and panoramic scenes of mountains began playing she cast a glance at Mr Spencer's screen. Only to see the exact images on his player. They were nearly in sync.

She caught his eye and he looked at her screen and back at his, and laughed. "I guess we'll be watching a movie together," he said.

"If only there was some popcorn."

The tension was broken and the two of them sat there, both watching Julie Andrews, Christopher Plummer and assorted children sing and dance their way around Salzburg. Juliet particularly loved the nuns.

She didn't dare look at Mr Spencer when the gazebo scene came on with the romantic declaration between Captain Von Trapp and Maria. Julie Andrews was singing about how she must have done something good in her childhood to deserve such perfect love.

If that was what it took to find happiness, Juliet was going to be out of luck, considering her own past.

As often happened with this and other ridiculously schmaltzy movies Juliet found her eyes brimming with tears. She was mortified. She tried to surreptitiously brush them away but Mr Spencer saw her.

"Is something wrong?"

Juliet wanted to die of embarrassment. She could hardly blame it on onions or hay fever at ten thousand feet. "Nothing."

He frowned and then he guessed and his expression turned to amusement. He looked at her questioningly and her fiery blush gave it away. It wasn't just the romance. It was the family,

104

everything. All the things she had never had: siblings, a loving if stern father, a wonderful, kind young mother. A beautiful home.

"It's all so perfect," she told him, trying to explain. Except for the war and Liesl's heartbreak and having to flee their homeland, of course. But none of these things mattered because they were all together. Juliet would have lived in a one room hovel with a leaking roof if she could have had a family life like that.

* * *

Carl had been on edge ever since Anne Mead had put Juliet in his charge. Of all the awkward situations it was the absolute worst.

He was trying to pretend to himself that at least a part of him didn't feel secretly very glad, as conflicted as he was. He was supposed to be keeping her at arm's length, but what could he do if she was thrust upon him?

Help me, Lord, he prayed. Give me your strength to cope with this and not think in the wrong way about her.

He spent the whole of The Sound of Music trying to take his mind off the girl sitting next to him. It didn't work. The fact that Juliet was watching the exact same movie as him didn't help either since it turned it into a shared activity. A movie date on a plane.

Carl was touched to see her crying at the end of the film and trying to hide it. He was surprised that the musical's ending was her idea of "perfect", he had imagined one of the teen movies where the heroine became a model or a popstar might be more her thing.

"I'm afraid the reality wasn't quite so perfect. Hollywood changed a lot of their story," he told her.

"I know." There was no need to tell Juliet anything about the Sound of Music. She was so steeped in its trivia that she could wipe the floor with anyone if it came up as a quiz topic, even Margot with her Anne of Green Gables obsession. If you could major in Maria Von Trapp Juliet would have been a PhD.

"It's the 'something good' thing that gets to me," she confessed, trying to explain.

Carl was confused. "Why?"

"If happiness only comes as a reward like that. Because what if it's too late?"

He wasn't sure what she was getting at. "It's never too late, for anything."

But Juliet's own youth and childhood were a complete mess. There would be no handsome Austrian naval captain wrapped up in a gift box for her.

Carl remembered the spiteful student Cynthia's words to Juliet. She had mentioned "juvie", not for the first time in his earshot. He hadn't seen Juliet's file and no one had mentioned anything so he had initially assumed it was just an insult. Now he wondered but he didn't want to pry.

But she volunteered the information. "Things got kind of messed up for me after my parents died. I ended up in juvenile detention." She wanted to explain because she knew Mr Spencer had heard what Cynthia had said.

He was shocked, but sorry for her.. "That can't have been easy."

Juliet told him about it. How her parents had died when she was seven, with no near relatives and no one to look after her, and she had ended up shifted from foster family to foster family, as well as intermittent stays in children's homes.

Later on she had been caught shoplifting, more than once. It hadn't even been for clothes or anything. It was because her foster family at that time didn't provide for her properly and she had no way of getting things she needed. She was too embarrassed to say exactly what but Carl guessed that she meant items such as hygiene products. "It wasn't even twenty bucks worth but I got caught a second time, and then they don't give you a second chance. I'm the world's most useless thief," she joked, to try and lighten the mood.

Carl felt a sudden rage against these people who had been so uncaring of an orphaned girl. "Your foster family should have been prosecuted for neglect."

"No one cares about that stuff. They were what they were. They gave me a roof and that's all that CPS cared about." He looked so horrified that she tried to explain. "There are some really good foster parents out there. But you never get to stay with

106

them for long, the older you get. Little kids get priority with the better ones. Then a lot of others that take in older kids are just in it for the money. Often they didn't even let me eat what they ate," she told him.

Then there were other things that she didn't want to talk about, the dark things. She never spoke of those.

She didn't even know why she was telling him all these things, but somehow it just came pouring out.

"So it got worse and I was in a mess and I had nowhere to go. And then my Aunt Mary - she's a distant cousin of my father's - somehow tracked me down." Looking back it had been a bit of miracle, though it hadn't felt like it at the time. Leaving the relative freedom of the streets for a strict household and a strict school had felt like going back to jail.

She and Aunt Mary had fought some fierce battles in the early days, though Juliet didn't tell Carl this. Her aunt's provision of a home had been conditional on Juliet attending Catholic school, maintaining her grades and not getting into any more trouble. She had rebelled because it was all too much to cope with.

"You know I even hated her at first," Juliet confessed. "I know that's awful as I should have been so grateful to her. I am now, of course." As she had grown up she had realised what Aunt Mary had done for her, the sacrifices she had made. Her aunt wasn't a wealthy woman but she had provided properly for Juliet. The compassionate scholarship to St Gillian's only went so far. Clothes, shoes, school books: that was all thanks to her aunt.

"It's understandable," Carl told her. He was moved by what she had suffered, and the way she had confided in him.

Juliet smiled at him apologetically. "I'm sorry, you probably didn't want to hear all that. I'm not sure what came over me. I don't usually talk about it."

Against his better judgement, Carl found himself offering to be there if she ever needed to talk to someone. He should have directed her to speak with the school counsellor but he didn't want her to think he was turning her away. Not after she had put her trust in him like that.

The lights had long been dimmed on the plane and those lucky enough to be able to sleep in-flight were doing so. Juliet was one of them. Without being aware of it she had ended up leaning against Carl, her blonde head resting on his shoulder. He had to stop himself from brushing an escaped strand of hair off her forehead.

There was no way he would sleep now. The gentle pressure of her head against him was too distracting. Through the hours of the night it felt almost as though they were the only two people in the world. Carl found himself daring to wish that they actually were.

XVI. In Paris

France. Paris. People speaking in different languages as they milled through Charles de Gaulle Airport. Signs in French. Announcements over the loudspeaker that they couldn't understand a word of.

Juliet was enraptured. It distracted her from the huge awkwardness she had felt waking up to find her head on Mr Spencer's shoulder. He had looked so uncomfortable and embarrassed.

But this was like stepping into a different world. It was around the middle of the day in France and winter sun was streaming through the airport terminal. She wanted to savour every moment.

I'm actually here, Juliet thought. I'm in Paris. In Europe.

Margot had caught up with her after they exited the plane. She had also slept through most of the flight and was nearly as excited as Juliet though she had previously visited Europe with her family on a number of occasions. She had given Juliet a grilling about Mr Spencer.

"So what happened? The mile high club?"

"God no." Juliet had visited the aeroplane bathroom during the flight and struggled to imagine how anyone could misbehave in such tight space. Maybe two teeny tiny little people, but Mr Spencer was quite tall and broad.

"Cynthia was furious about it," Margot told her. "Miss Mead wouldn't even let her talk to anyone else during the flight, she had to shut up and watch movies."

Juliet would have been glad except she suspected it would make Cynthia even more vengeful. "We'll have to watch out."

There was a brief stop at a café in the terminal so people could buy food if they wanted to, before they caught the Paris Metro underground train to their hotel. Miss Mead had to deal with a couple of girls who bought wine with their baguettes, which was perfectly legal in France. They claimed they had meant to buy cokes and it was the result of poor translation skills but even Miss Mead wasn't that stupid.

"While we're over here, we'll respect the rules of St Gillian's which are those of our native country, the United States of America," she told them.

"That is so dumb," Margot remarked to Juliet. "Buying it right in front of her like that. She'll be watching them all the time now."

Juliet wanted to try something as French as possible so she ordered a brioche. She was completely confused by all the Euros and the different banknotes there.

The train journey passed in a blur - Juliet was very glad their choir teacher spoke such good French - and they finally arrived at their hotel, exhausted and aching from hauling their suitcases, and dying to freshen up. Aware how bedraggled she probably was, Juliet had been avoiding Mr Spencer since they left the plane. She feared that some of the shocked expression on his face had been at the horrible star of her when she woke.

Still, at least she hadn't drooled in her sleep.

The hotel looked much older and smaller than the photos on its website. Cynthia and her friends were bitching about it, with Cynthia claiming she had been "forcibly prevented" from staying at some five-star hotel or other.

Juliet was just thrilled to have a room looking out over the rooftops of Paris. If she leaned to one side there was even a glimpse of the Eiffel Tower. The room itself was plain rather than luxury, with twin beds and a single long window. But it was clean, there was a tiny en-suite bathroom, and best of all she was sharing with Margot.

Margot emerged from the bathroom wrapped in a large white towel, drying her hair.

"The hot water kept going cold, you have to keep adjusting it," she said.

Juliet hurried into the shower so she could get ready quickly and not waste any more time than needed in the hotel.

They had been given the afternoon to rest but Miss Mead was only allowing them to stay in the hotel or visit a café across the road. After this the schedule was tightly packed with cultural visits and singing in church, barely allowing them a moment to catch their breath.

This was intended to keep them out of mischief: the actual result was that everyone now planned to sneak out at night, after Miss Mead had gone to bed.

"Do we need to keep wearing these sweatshirts?" Juliet asked Margot.

"I'm not going to. If Miss Mead asks I'll tell her I was keeping it clean for excursions."

They had three hours before they had to assemble for dinner. Easily enough time to go somewhere interesting. Juliet wanted to go to Montmartre to see the portrait artists. They already had group excursions planned to all the main cultural icons, and Montmartre was within walking distance from their hotel.

Margot considered it. "Cute arty French guys. Sounds good to me."

They set off but to their dismay Miss Mead had taken up residence at a café table. She had a clear view of the hotel entrance so there could be no sneaking off.

"Damn. Time for Plan B," Margot said.

There was no Plan B. The hotel didn't have a back door, and a side window on the ground floor only opened into a dead-end alley from where they would have go to back to the main street.

"If this was Annie we could escape in a laundry basket," Margot suggested.

They lingered for a moment in the unattended reception, wondering what the best approach would be.

"Excusez-moi" came a rude voice and a shove from behind. It was Cynthia with a couple of her friends.

Juliet stepped out of her way.

"There's our laundry basket," she muttered to Margot as Cynthia strode across to the café. They watched as Cynthia got into a conversation with Miss Mead and used the opportunity to slip out of the hotel and around the side. It was the opposite direction that they needed to go, but no matter.

The two girls cut around through different streets until they reached the funicular railway that took people up the hill. Juliet had read about it in her guidebook. They figured out the right money and rode to the top.

Margot in particular had her eye out for cute guys but it seemed to be mainly Japanese and European tourists, most of them their parents' age.

The Place du Tertre was full of artists, their easels set up around the square as well as examples of their work. Some of them were very talented. As well as portraits there were landscape painters with endless scenes of Paris. "I don't want to buy something I haven't seen yet," Margot said, "but I might come back here for souvenirs."

After wandering around they found a café and ordered drinks. Juliet still felt dehydrated from the flight so ordered a mineral water, as did Margot. This turned out to be a much wiser choice than wine.

About five minutes after they sat down they heard their voices spoken. "Juliet, Margot."

It was Mr Spencer.

* * *

Margot brazened it out. "Bonjour, Sir. Monsieur," she corrected.

"I'm not sure you're supposed to be here," Mr Spencer said. He didn't look angry, more concerned. He didn't want them to get into trouble but he was in a difficult position, Juliet thought.

She tried to explain. "We just didn't want to waste a moment. I know this afternoon was for resting but there was no need as we slept on the plane."

Juliet then remembered where she had been sleeping, caught his eye and reddened slightly. She could sense Margot was suppressing a grin.

"I do understand, but you need to follow Miss Mead's instructions," he told them. "She's responsible for all of you, and very few of you speak fluent French. If you got lost it could be difficult."

"Do you speak French?" Margot asked him, trying to change the subject.

"Some." Mr Spencer wasn't going to be distracted. "I'll accompany you back and you can slip away to your rooms. We're visiting Sacre Coeur one night so I'll see if we can take a longer look around here beforehand. I don't think Miss Mead will mind people getting their portraits painted, if there's time."

The white-domed Basilica of the Sacré-Cœur was the main landmark of the area. Built at the highest point of Paris it could be seen from all the surrounding area. As they headed to the funicular railway its pale stones turned rose gold in the sunset. Juliet almost ached at the sight.

Carl watched her, seeing the dying sun reflected in her eyes. He hoped he had dealt with the situation adequately. He didn't want Anne Mead to think he was giving the girls a free pass but he also didn't want to ruin their Paris trip. After all, having a Coke outside a café, given they were both legal adults and not actually at school, hardly seemed the gravest of offences.

He decided to avoid mentioning it to his colleague. The choir teacher already had enough to deal with having arranged the entire tour and having to constantly check and recheck that everything was running to plan. She had some French but wasn't fluent which was one of the reasons Carl had ended up taking the French teacher's place.

"Have you been to Paris much before?" Margot asked him.

"A few times."

"What's the nightlife like? Any good bars or clubs?"

Carl knew that Margot was trying to wind him up but saw that it was making Juliet uncomfortable. When he had first started teaching at St Gillian's Juliet would probably have joined in, but he realised that there was now an understanding between them.

There shouldn't be, but there was.

"I didn't visit for the nightlife, but like any major city, it has plenty of attractions," he told her.

Margot gave him a wicked smile. "So you'll be visiting the Moulin Rouge this time? It's just down the road." Margot had been doing her homework. The red light district containing the famous cabaret was in the neighbouring suburb to their hotel, according to her guidebook.

"Tonight will be straight to bed, ahead of our very early start tomorrow," he reminded them.

Margot pouted in mock disappointment. "If you change your mind, we'd be happy to accompany you," she said.

"If Miss Mead grants permission for a cultural tour there, I'd be happy to to escort you."

Since this was about as likely as Miss Mead hitching up her skirt and joining the can-can dancers, it seemed that they were all headed for an early night.

* * *

Juliet was relieved and grateful that Mr Spencer didn't report them to Miss Mead for wandering off. That evening they were all dining at a nearby bistro and Miss Mead might have made them stay behind as a punishment.

Margot was getting itchy feet. "This is Europe. We can go out legally here. I can't see that it's any of her business what we do. It's not like I'd go clubbing wearing the choir sweater."

She had pulled on a clinging, low-cut top, arranging a scarf around her neck for Miss Mead's benefit that she would remove when the choir mistress wasn't watching. Paris was so cold that they ended up wearing jeans again. Margot had brought a sexy dress to go clubbing in but there was no way she could wear it in front of their teachers.

"We'll have to come back here after dinner anyway, so we can just change then," Margot said.

They made their way downstairs. Everyone was gathering in the hotel lobby and they were among the last to arrive.

Juliet came down the stairs trying not to look for Mr Spencer but unable to resist. He was by the door with Miss Mead. He nodded and smiled at her and she felt her insides melt. After spending the whole flight with him she longed to be with him again.

114

Unfortunately he ended up seated at a table with Miss Mead and Juliet and Margot had to share with Stephanie and a couple of other girls.

The bistro had a set menu so everyone ended up with steak frites and green salad, except for a couple of girls who were vegetarian and had omelettes. Juliet was both relieved and disappointed that they weren't presented with snails and frogs legs as she was curious what they looked like.

Stephanie insisted on saying grace which Juliet felt immensely self-conscious about. She wouldn't have minded if Stephanie had just murmured a few words under her breath, but chanting "For what we are about to receive..." in the middle of a restaurant was embarrassing.

"This steak is really undercooked," one girl complained.

"It's medium rare," Margot told her.

"I wonder if Miss Mead and Mr Spencer will have a Parisian romance," someone said.

"Hardly. She's practically old enough to be his mother," another replied.

This wasn't true: in fact Miss Mead was probably only about five or so years older than Mr Spencer, she just dressed in a dowdy way that made her look older. Juliet realised that the choir teacher was much closer to his age than she was which made her feel miserable. Mr Spencer had told Juliet before that she was too young for him.

Juliet glanced over at him and saw him deep in conversation with Miss Mead. She guessed it was only to be expected as they were dinner companions but it still made her feel flat.

She wasn't sure how she was going to drum up the energy and enthusiasm to sneak out with Margot that night as the only guy she was interested in would be back in the hotel. If Margot wanted to hook up with some French guy Juliet would doubtless end up having to talk with his friend but her heart was not in it.

Her heart was with a man who was totally off limits. Even though he confessed to wanting her as much as she wanted him, he could never be hers.

XVII. The kiss

Both Juliet and Margot had ended up falling asleep rather than sneaking out to try the Paris nightlife. The jet lag and the exertions of travel hit them both like a brick when they returned to their hotel room after dinner.

"Maybe I'll just nap for a few minutes, then we can change and sneak out after Miss Mead must have gone to bed," Margot said.

Within seconds she was out for the count. Juliet soon followed her. Her limbs felt drugged from sleep.

Daylight streaming through the gap in the curtains woke her nearly twelve hours later. They would be late for breakfast if they didn't hurry.

Juliet shook Margot awake, grabbed a shower and pulled her clothes on. The trip that morning was to the Île de la Cité, the island in the centre of the River Seine in Paris. In the afternoon they had to rehearse ahead of singing in a Parisian church that night.

Entering Notre-Dame was one of the most poignant moments of Juliet's life. She couldn't move for several moments.

She hadn't expected to be this affected by the interior of a church - or rather cathedral - but it was vast, ornate, awe-inspiring.

A guided tour had been arranged and they stood in a group at the rear, with the tour guide speaking in heavily accented English about naves and flying buttresses. His words washed over Juliet's head as she drank in the visual glory.

The school group was crowded together to hear the guide and Juliet had somehow ended up by Mr Spencer near the back, with Margot on the other side of her. They had to shift across to view something else that the guide was indicating, and Mr Spencer's arm ended up pressed against Juliet's.

By accident his hand brushed hers.

But then neither of them moved their hands.

Instead his fingers curled around hers, and hers entwined with his.

They didn't even move, or look at one another. They simply stood there, in the world's most famous cathedral, holding hands.

Juliet wasn't thinking, she was simply being. Standing there in the quiet darkness, the aroma of incense and ancient wood and stone, the stained glass like jewels high above them, holding his hand.

It both set her on edge and steadied her. Her stomach flipped and her nerves at the thought of it, that he was holding her hand secretly, no one else aware of it. At the same time she felt a wonderful stillness and safety.

She didn't dare look at him. No, it wasn't a question of daring, she didn't need to. She could see his profile in her mind, strong and as finely carved as a statue.

She didn't even ask herself why he was holding her hand. It was instinctual.

They only broke apart when the group moved outside to climb up the towers of the cathedral. He squeezed her hand before he let go.

Mr Spencer looked into her eyes briefly as she passed in front of him. His gaze was wondering but he said nothing.

From then on it seemed that wherever they could, they held hands.

Standing bathed in the cobalt and crimson light of the Sainte Chapelle, its long slender windows and vaults arching overhead, his hand again found hers. The mere touch of his fingers shot warmth and electricity through Juliet's arm and her body. She was with him. Linked. They were seeing these wondrous sights together.

His hand was strong and firm and occasionally he brushed his thumb around her palm making her feel shivery. She glanced at him when he did so but he was looking directly ahead, perfectly self-controlled.

They had to be discreet and it was entirely unspoken. A silent form of communication. And somehow, no one else ever saw.

It added to the thrill that it was secret, but also that he wanted to do it. That he felt it was worth the risk.

Lunch was at a café by the River Seine. Margot had to ask Juliet what was up as she was so quiet. "You're in a dream or something. What's up?"

Juliet just shook her head and smiled. "Just falling in love with Paris," she said. It was true: she loved everything she had seen about this city. She resolved to make more of an effort in French class in future.

"Yeah well you'd better come back down to earth. I think Paris is already taken," Margot said.

A woman with long skirts and long dark hair passed by their table. She tried speaking to them in a language which didn't sound like French and both girls were confused. The woman tried to push a postcard at them, covered in writing.

"It's a scam," Margot said. She shook her head firmly and turned away.

The woman moved on to the next table, where another unwitting girl took the postcard and tried to read it to see if she could help. She was frowning over its contents when the café proprietor suddenly came out and started shouting at the woman in French and shooing her off. The woman's face turned nasty and she spat some words back at him as she left, some of which Juliet thought she recognised.

"That poor woman," the girl who had read the postcard said. "Her mother is ill in Romania and she needed money. We should have helped her."

"How come the postcard was in English then, if they're Romanian?" Margot said.

Miss Mead and Mr Spencer had taken a table inside the café and hadn't witnessed the commotion.

Juliet wondered what was going through his mind at that moment. When they weren't able to stand together he made an effort to interact with everyone else, so it didn't look as though he was singling her out.

She longed for him.

They needed to talk but she didn't know when they would get the opportunity.

What if he never said anything? What if this was just for now, and when they went back to school, it would be all over and never to be spoken of?

Juliet found it hard to concentrate on anything when he wasn't there. Miss Mead had to bring her back down to earth a couple of times in the rehearsal that afternoon, though she was fine when the choir eventually sang in the evening service. She couldn't follow much of the service as it was in French so she let her mind wander then.

* * *

The Mona Lisa was a big disappointment. It was dimmer and smaller than Juliet had imagined, set back behind a barrier and thick glass. A large crowd of people with cameras made it impossible to get a close look.

"That's another one off the bucket list," Margot said. It was also the time to implement their plan of escape. Instead of being dragged to another museum they wanted to go shopping and have some time to themselves.

They had tossed a coin - a euro - and Margot was the one who had to feign illness. The idea was that Juliet would have to escort her back to the hotel and stay with her, and then they could get up to whatever they liked.

Margot made a good effort. She sank down in a kind of swoon on a nearby bench, trying to look nauseous. Then it was up to Juliet to alert Miss Mead.

The choir teacher was easily taken in by Margot's performance. "We may be able to call a doctor at the hotel," she said.

Juliet managed to convince Miss Mead that it wasn't that bad and that Margot simply needed to rest. Margot did a bit of swaying and clapped her hand in front of her mouth with a groan.

"I can accompany her back to the hotel and look after her," Juliet offered.

Miss Mead was thoughtful. "It would be difficult for me to come, with all the other girls here and our trip to the Pompidou. But I'm concerned about you crossing Paris alone, particularly with Margot so unwell. Mr Spencer, if you could perhaps accompany the girls. Then if Margot is put to bed and her condition seems no worse, you can both rejoin us later."

What? Margot shot Juliet a fierce glance and Juliet looked desperately back at her. They read one another's minds: how on earth could they escape if a teacher was with them the whole time?

"Sorry for you to have to leave the museum early," Juliet said to him as they exited the Louvre to find a taxi. Margot was still putting on her feeling-faint act.

No one spoke as they rode back to the hotel. Juliet was feeling stressed and guilty and she was sure Margot was furious that their plans had been foiled.

"I'll wait down here while you see to Margot," Mr Spencer told her.

Juliet took Margot up in the lift and they shot into their bedroom. Margot threw herself onto her bed groaning in genuine despair.

"What are we going to do? Maybe I can persuade him you're worse and I need to stay with you," Juliet suggested.

"He'll only want to call a doctor if you say that. Better to pretend I seem a little better and I'm sleeping. It's not so bad, I can go exploring by myself and you can enjoy a date with holy boy."

Juliet thought of Mr Spencer holding her hand and wondered whether he would do so again when they were properly alone. The taxi driver was hardly likely to notice or care.

"Are you sure you'll be okay here alone? I'm sure I could persuade him to let me stay," she said.

"If you do, I bet you any money that he stays around as well just in case I get more fake-ill," Margot said. "There's no way we can both get away now. We'll figure something else out later."

"You'd better look properly ill by the time we get back later this afternoon. And hide any shopping bags because when Miss Mead comes to check on you it will really give the game away," Juliet warned.

Rejoining Mr Spencer in the lobby and reassuring him that Margot was okay, Juliet found herself lost for words. The two of them were finally alone and she was tongue-tied.

Mr Spencer also seemed awkward around her. "I guess we'd better get back to the others. They'll still be in the museum so we can meet them outside."

They walked through the Jardin de Tuileries which stretched along the Seine in front of the Louvre. The boughs of trees were black and bare against the wintry sky. How beautiful it must be here in summer, with the fountains and flowers and people strolling in the sunshine, Juliet thought.

"It's amazing here. It's such a huge city but there's so much space and beauty," she said.

"It is. When I stayed in Paris I came here nearly every day," Mr Spencer told her.

He paused and turned. Juliet looked up at him.

His expression was unreadable, his eyes intense.

The wind had blown a lock of hair over the side of her face. Slowly he reached up and brushed it back, his fingers gently tracing over her features.

She was frozen. She wanted him so badly. At that moment there was no one else in the world, nothing else existed.

He didn't remove his hand but left it cradling her face. His other hand grasped her shoulder and then he was tilting her face up to him, his lips coming closer to her.

So close. It was like slow motion.

This time he didn't leave space between them. Didn't withdraw. She felt his lips come down upon hers, so firm and warm on hers, chilled by the winter air.

Finally.

This was what it was like to be kissed by Mr Spencer.

He drew her closer to him and gently but firmly made her own lips open so he could deepen the kiss. He enclosed her bottom lip with his and she felt the light, teasing flick of his tongue.

Her stomach lurched with desire as his tongue probed her. Wet and sensuous, it entwined with hers.

After all this time it felt like quenching a thirst. She was lost in him, dissolving in him.

Juliet reached her own arms around him, wanting the closeness of his body. His winter coat was open at the front so she could press against his chest.

Still he kissed her.

I'm kissing my teacher, she thought. We shouldn't be doing this. If anyone saw…

A part of her felt reckless and didn't even care if they were seen.

Mr Spencer was so tall and strong as he wrapped his arms around her. So good looking - he could have had any girl he wanted - but he was kissing her. Wanting her.

He broke off but still held her. "Juliet…" She could see the heat in his eyes and the conflict. He wanted her yet knew it was wrong.

She felt dizzy from his touch, from being so close to him after wanting him for so long.

Please kiss me again…

He read her mind and his mouth came down on hers once more. She loved the feel of him, the taste of him. She loved that he was kissing her despite everything compelling him not to. Despite fighting against it for so many weeks.

She closed her eyes and he was her whole world, nothing else was.

XVIII. Turmoil

He had fallen from grace. So far, so hard.

Yet he couldn't make himself feel as bad as he knew he should.

Despite going against the teachings of his church, against his professional ethics, against his own moral code, Carl knew that he would do it all again.

He stood there in the middle of Paris, looking at the girl who had upturned his entire world. What was he going to do?

Juliet smiled at him, looking strangely shy, and his heart overturned.

He had never felt like this about Rebecca or any other girl. It gave him a chill to think that he could have committed his entire life to his former fiancée when it was possible to feel like this about someone else.

"There's no point having a conversation about how I shouldn't have done that, is there?" he said.

"I guess not." Juliet found it hard to speak.

So where did they go from here?

"It's wrong on so many levels." Carl was trying to convince himself that it must never happen again.

"It didn't feel wrong. It felt anything but wrong." Juliet was looking up at him and it was hard to resist the urge just to kiss her all over again.

"I know." What had surprised Carl was that kissing her, even though she was his student, didn't really feel wrong. While he wasn't exactly expecting the heavens to crack open and punish him with a thunderbolt, he had expected to feel some kind of censure. Some Divine disapproval. Or had what he had done cut him off from God?

"I've been wanting you to do that for so long," Juliet said.

"I know. You weren't the only one," Carl admitted.

She gave him a seductive smile that shook what was left of his composure. "I wish it was just us in Paris. No one else. So we could spend all this time together."

The mention of the others brought Carl back from his thoughts with a jolt. The others - what was the time? He could only imagine the fallout if Anne Mead and the rest of the choir suddenly emerged from the museum to witness everything. He glanced at his watch and to his relief saw that they still had plenty of time before the group was due to finish their tour.

"Let's head back towards the Louvre entrance," he said.

Outside the museum they found a bench by a fountain and sat together. They could have just been any couple walking together in Paris, Juliet thought. No one around them knew that they were two people who had just crossed a massive line.

A street vendor came past with a basket of postcards and plastic trinkets in the shape of Paris monuments. He had a wire hoop strung with models of the Eiffel Tower around his neck. "You buy?" he asked Juliet. "Un tour Eiffel?" But she declined.

Carl however gave the man some Euros and handed Juliet a snow globe with the Louvre inside it. "You should have a souvenir," he said.

She shook it, watching the snowflakes fall over the pyramid, and looked him directly in the eye. "What would you like me to remember?"

He returned her gaze. "I would like to remember all of this. But it still has to stop." He saw the disappointment in her eyes.

"I don't see why. We're two free adults."

It was true. At least here in Europe, they effectively were. If they never went back, if he got a job and a place here and they both stayed… he stopped his thoughts going in such an absurd direction. "You're my student, Juliet, it's considered an abuse of power."

"It's not like you ordered me to do anything." She looked up at him again, a suggestive smile on her face. "Though I wouldn't mind if you did."

Carl wouldn't even let himself go there. "I'm a lot older than you. You might be eighteen but that's barely an adult."

"It's on the shelf by Roman standards." They had learnt in class that girls in Ancient Rome married from as young as twelve, though usually between fourteen and sixteen.

"I don't think those are the standards we want to live by today," he said.

Juliet determined to break his resolve. "You won't even be my teacher forever. It's only a few months until graduation."

"I'm well aware of that." Carl was far too conscious of it. He was letting his thoughts wander to what might happen after that time, which was totally inappropriate. "Juliet, I need some time to think about all of this. Let's talk about it when we get back."

Her heart leapt in hope. "Do you mean…?"

"I don't mean anything. I just need us to remain professional and not risk everything on an impulse," he said.

"Is that what I am to you? An impulse?"

Even as she said this Carl realised that she was so much more. "No, you're not. And that's the problem, which is why we both need some time. I promise we'll talk about this back home. For now let's just concentrate on the choir trip."

"If that's what you really want."

It wasn't what he wanted. What he wanted was to take her in his arms and shut out the rest of the world. To kiss her and hold her and be with her, ignoring the consequences.

But the consequences would be disastrous. He would lose his job, Juliet would likely be expelled and might even be thrown out of home: Carl had no idea how her aunt would react but he doubted a red carpet would be rolled out for him. There was no way he wanted to put her through that kind of ordeal. She seemed tough but he had seen the fragility in her when she had confided in him about her past.

Most of all he wanted things to be right with God, for her sake more than his. She deserved that.

* * *

"Oh. My. God." Margot fished in her purse and brought out a one hundred dollar bill. "Here you are."

"What's this for?"

"The bet. I never thought you'd wear him down."

Juliet pushed the money back at her. "I haven't. It was just a kiss. So you've won."

Just a kiss… it was so much more than that. More than if she had slept with him, in fact.

"We'll call it a draw then," Margot said. "If we'd known he was such a devout Baptist we probably wouldn't have made that bet."

Juliet wouldn't have wanted the money even if she had won. It was so much more than a game to her now.

Margot was adjusting her makeup in front of the mirror, trying to appear rested but still a little weak. She had spent the afternoon going crazy on the Champs Elysées and stashing all her purchases in her suitcase out of sight if Miss Mead visited their room. "Do I look like a recovered invalid?" she asked Juliet.

"Not wearing that jacket that you obviously just bought here," Juliet said.

Looking annoyed but knowing Juliet was right, Margot removed it. "So what's next for you?"

"As I mentioned, he wants to think about it."

Margot groaned. "The pace this guy moves at he's going to be retired and moving to Florida before he ever gets laid."

Juliet sincerely hoped not. "The thing is I really like him."

"What do you mean you like him?"

"I mean, I like him more than I thought I would," Juliet said.

Margot, who had been applying make up, paused and looked at her. "Don't tell me you've actually fallen for him. Seriously? This was just supposed to be fun."

"I know."

"He's so religious," Margot continued. "Imagine having to go to his church every night. Because if you were dating him, that's what you'd have to do."

The word "dating" gave Juliet a secret thrill. "They seemed like nice enough people."

Margot raised her eyebrows. "I can just imagine how nice they'd be if they found out you were his student and it was all completely illegal."

Time was running out for them to join the others downstairs so Juliet hurriedly fixed her own hair and she and Margot left their room. Miss Mead was relieved to see Margot looking well again and didn't show any suspicion about her supposed illness that day.

"I'm sorry you missed the Pompidou, it was quite an experience. I'm sure the others can show you their photos."

"That would be great," Margot replied. She couldn't imagine anything more dull.

True to his word Mr Spencer had arranged for them all to have dinner at Montmartre after their visit to Sacré-Cœur. This would allow them to spend some time looking at the artists and buying souvenirs.

Nuns were singing in the basilica as they entered, like a choir of angels. Juliet was entranced.

"I wish we sounded like that," she said to Margot.

Even Margot was momentarily silenced by the beauty of the voices raised in song. "Is that French or Latin?" she whispered.

Juliet wasn't sure.

Mr Spencer was standing away from her, deliberately she thought. He had greeted her but was studiously ensuring that he was always with a group of people. At least he wasn't avoiding her. But it wasn't safe to catch his eye, let alone to hope he might hold her hand.

Juliet would just have to be patient. It wasn't the virtue that came easiest to her.

* * *

On the flight back, having managed to avoid further conflict with Cynthia, Juliet and Margot were able to sit together.

"I know you'd rather be sitting by holy boy but you're stuck with me," Margot told her. "Take care not to drool over me like you did over him."

Juliet laughed. "I did not drool, I just fell asleep."

"I meant it figuratively."

They were both sad to leave Paris and determined to return one day. Margot was fantasising about studying at the Sorbonne and spending her university days hanging out at cafés with handsome French philosophy students.

Juliet joined her in imagining it, but knew that such a future would be completely impossible for her. Whatever she did after graduating high school was going to be limited by lack of money. There was no way that either she or her aunt could afford an expensive college, let alone living in Europe as a foreign student.

"Do you think your parents would let you do that?" she asked Margot. "Study in Paris"

"Probably, if I got the grades, and so long as I ended up doing international law or something my mom would consider worthwhile." Margot's mother was a corporate lawyer.

It would be good to just travel and live overseas for a year, Juliet thought. Take a round the world trip and work in bars or whatever to support herself. And figure out what she wanted to do longer term.

Margot had let Juliet take the window seat as flying was such a new experience for her, so when Mr Spencer came past them during the flight he leant on Margot's seat to talk with them.

"Having a good flight?"

"It's not so bad," Margot said. "Except for the food."

"It will be dawn US time when we land, so you should enjoy some good views," he told Juliet. For a fraction of a second there was a connection between them but then he moved on, abruptly.

After he had gone Juliet felt subdued. "You know that he's closer in age to Miss Mead than me?" she said to Margot.

"I don't think you have anything to worry about. He doesn't look like the type to go for an older woman. And he looks even less like the type to go for Miss Mead," Margot said.

This wasn't quite what Juliet meant but she said nothing further. Was the age gap between her and Mr Spencer really absurd? It was nearly ten years. If only they were both Romans, no one would blink an eye.

XIX. Back to school

Carl had thought of little else but Juliet since getting back from Paris. He couldn't deny his feelings any longer. If it was solely sexual attraction it would have been easy to deal with, or at least to make a decision about.

But it ran deeper that that. He found himself happy to be around her and looking forward to seeing her. He felt protective of her. When Cynthia or one of the other girls tried to goad Juliet, he had to restrain himself from jumping to her defence. That would really give the game away.

So what was he to do?

He couldn't confide in anyone. After all, she was his student and any relationship between them was strictly illicit.

But he knew that he had to see her again.

"How was Paris?" Dan asked him when they met at church.

"Amazing. It went very well," Carl said.

"Jenny's always wanted to go. I don't know how we'll manage it once the baby arrives, we'll probably have to wait a couple of years."

Jenny joined them at that point, trying to escape Rebecca who had cornered her. Unfortunately Rebecca came along as well. After freezing Carl out over the past month or so she was now talking to him again. It was awkward and he found himself preferring the silence.

"Carl was just telling me about his Paris trip," Dan said.

Rebecca pursed her lips. "I can't imagine giving up vacation time to take a load of schoolchildren half way around the world. You really do go above and beyond the call of duty with your job, Carl."

It was a criticism poorly disguised as a compliment.

"It's a very beautiful city. It's always worth seeing," he said, trying to keep his tone neutral. He was relieved when it was time for the service to start and he could escape Rebecca. He sincerely hoped she didn't have plans to try to rekindle their relationship. Breaking up with her had been like waking up from a suffocating dream.

It wasn't that she was unattractive but her personality left him cold.

This was another issue with Juliet. Sure, she was beautiful, but there were several other very pretty girls at St Gillian's who had tried to flirt with him in the most outrageous ways when he started teaching there. None of them did anything for him. Yet Juliet, even before she had started paying him attention, had caught his eye.

There was something about her and he couldn't get over it.

Carl managed to avoid sitting anywhere near Rebecca by going and helping a couple of older congregation members to their seats: one elderly lady needed assistance getting up and down, and had to remain mostly seated for services.

He felt a twinge of guilt when the old lady thanked him as he was mainly glad of the opportunity to sit by her and nowhere near his ex-fiancée.

Afterwards he was approached by Agnes. "What happened to those two nice young women from your school who visited our church? They seemed like very bright and well-behaved girls."

Carl suppressed a smile. There was nothing well behaved about Margot, given the slightest opportunity. He was fairly certain that her sudden illness in Paris had been a ruse. And Juliet broke plenty of rules too. Her aunt had no idea that she sang in a band.

"I don't know if they'll be back," he said.

As he said it an idea came to him. A way that he could maybe see Juliet outside school without crossing any more lines. He would have to think and pray on it, but it might just work.

* * *

Juliet felt a weird mix of excitement and flatness coming back home from Paris. She would no longer get to see Mr Spencer all day every day, but he was now taking things seriously enough to make some kind of decision.

Being in limbo was better than nothing. Certainly better than continual rejection.

She had bought Aunt Mary some religious souvenirs from Notre-Dame. Aunt Mary clucked with disapproval at the suspected cost but Juliet could see that she was secretly delighted. Her aunt gave them all pride of place around her home.

To distract her there was an email from Drew.

We've been asked to play The Green Room again, but we'll get a cut of ticket sales this time. It won't be major bucks but it will cover expenses.

He didn't specify a date so Juliet prayed it didn't clash with a school event or something of Aunt Mary's. How she had managed to conceal her participation for so long was something of a miracle.

That's awesome! See you on Tuesday.

The band had temporarily been named Dover Six after the street they rehearsed in and the number of members. The idea was to pick a better name eventually but no one ever managed to come up with anything that everyone else liked.

So Dover Six it was. Juliet was secretly happy because she felt more included, being the sixth member. Although she was effectively the lead singer now she sometimes felt a bit out of things, as she was the only female and had joined ages after everyone else.

The biggest thrill had been when Jax set some of her lyrics to music. He managed to make Juliet's verses into an actual song, it sounded far better than it had as a poem. She had been embarrassed to share them at first but Drew had persuaded her and now she was very glad that she had plucked up the courage.

They performed a couple of covers as well, as it helped to warm up a crowd. But most of the music was their own.

Juliet wondered how she would have felt if she had known that Mr Spencer was in the audience for the first gig. She might have frozen up.

Now that she felt more confident about it all she liked the idea of him being there. Maybe she should invite him to the next gig?

* * *

This the the man I want to be with.

It was all Juliet could think of when she saw Mr Spencer in their first Latin class of the new semester. He caught her eye and gave her a brief smile before turning his attention to the whole class.

She tried very hard to focus on her Latin but she was distracted, burning to speak with him. Would he kiss her again when everyone had left? Close the classroom door, put his arms around her, pin her against the whiteboard and press his lips to hers…

Juliet realised she had completely lost her place in the passage they were going through but fortunately Mr Spencer did not call on her to translate the next line. She glanced at Margot's book to try and catch up, and saw that they had long turned the page while she had been daydreaming. Vergil really deserved better attention than this.

"Line two hundred," Margot hissed at her and Juliet managed to find the right place. It was lucky she did, because she was soon called to translate something about sea serpents. Fortunately she had prepared it reasonably well.

"And they lick their hissing mouths with vibrating tongues," Juliet said.

Cynthia snickered and muttered something about "vibrators" to the girl next to her, who smirked on hearing it. Juliet knew it was targeted at her in some way and normally wouldn't have cared, except she was paranoid that Mr Spencer would hear and wonder about it. She felt her face growing scarlet.

"If we could have quiet, please. Any questions then raise your hand," Mr Spencer told them. His glance passed fleetingly over Cynthia, not giving her any extra attention but signalling that he knew that she was the source of the disruption.

Cynthia scowled and gave Juliet a hostile glare, her eyes narrowed. Juliet ignored her as best she could, hoping Margot wouldn't rise to the bait. Fortunately she didn't.

"He's got her number," Margot whispered. "And she knows it. Let her dig her own grave."

At the end of class Mr Spencer asked Juliet and two other girls to remain behind. It made his speaking to her alone more subtle. It was lunch break time so there wasn't a risk of anyone being late for the next class.

One of the girls had failed to do her homework, the other was struggling with grammar. Mr Spencer dealt with them in turn, firmly but kindly, and dismissed them.

Then it was just the two of them. Him and Juliet. She stood by his desk, waiting.

Mr Spencer seemed to be hesitating so Juliet made it easier for him by breaking the silence. "I can't stop thinking about Paris."

The tension in his face relaxed and she saw in his eyes that he felt the same. "Me too. I've been thinking a lot about everything since then. Although we can't cross any lines again while I'm your teacher, I would like to see you."

"You mean outside class?"

"Yes. What do you usually do on Sundays?" he asked.

"Mass with my aunt, and then homework, not much else really," Juliet said. Not in winter anyway, with the weather so cold and the nighttime so early.

"My church has an early evening service on Sundays," Mr Spencer said. "I was wondering if you would like to attend with me?"

Juliet was surprised. As dates went, it wasn't exactly the movies or a restaurant. "This weekend?"

"I mean every weekend. So every week we could spend some time together outside of school, in an appropriate place, and see how it goes."

This made Juliet's stomach flip. Every weekend. She could see how serious the expression in his eyes was. This clearly meant a huge amount to him, even if it was the most he could offer her right now.

Although she longed for him to hold her and kiss her again and so much more, she understood. Small steps.

"So would this be like a date? Could we hang out afterwards?" she asked him.

"We'll see. I'd like to be able to take you to dinner, but under the circumstances…"

The circumstances were other people from school ending up in the same restaurant or diner. It would be disastrous.

"We could get pizza at your place."

Juliet could see that Mr Spencer was conflicted by her suggestion. "Let's see how it goes on Sunday. I want this to be right." He meant right in the eyes of God but he didn't say it.

If she managed to persuade him to invite him back to his place… Juliet knew she shouldn't push things, but the thought of being alone with him, in private…

"I guess I'll see you Sunday then. I can meet you at your church."

"I can pick you up if you like," he offered.

"Thanks but it's really not far. I'll be fine walking." If he picked her up it would cause a world of complication with Aunt Mary. Quite apart from the fact he was her teacher, Juliet wasn't sure how happy Aunt Mary would be for Juliet to regularly attend a non Catholic church.

"If you're sure." Mr Spencer hesitated. "I'd really like to see you there." His voice was softer.

Juliet was moved. "I'd really like to be there." She remembered the band invitation. "I was also wondering, the band I'm in is playing again in a couple of weeks, would you like to come along?" She bit her lip, anticipating that he might make some excuse.

To her relief he smiled. "I'd love to."

"There are tickets but you don't have to pay, I'll get you one, or put you on the list." She wasn't exactly sure how it would work.

"That's fine. I'm happy to get my own ticket, either way."

They were both silent for a moment. Juliet wished they could just go somewhere and spent time together without all this caution and the fear of discovery. This patience thing was not easy.

"Great, I'll let you know the exact details when I have them," she told him. Now she was going to have to make sure she looked her absolute best. She would have sung her best anyway, for the sake of the band and because she loved performing with them, but she needed to wear something that would get Mr Spencer even more worked up than before. Fhemie was good with clothes and sewing, maybe she could help.

XX. Going to church

Aunt Mary seemed surprisingly unconcerned when Juliet mentioned she was attending a friend's church service on Sunday evening. Her conservative choice of dress probably helped. She certainly didn't look as though she was really about to sneak out to a party.

She had even been honest enough to tell her aunt that it was a Baptist church. By lucky chance it turned out that a woman in Aunt Mary's knitting group, whom she particularly liked, was a Baptist.

"It doesn't seem to have done Doris any harm," Aunt Mary said. "I dare say the Lord doesn't disapprove of us visiting His other houses."

The Lord might well disapprove if he had an idea of Juliet's true motive for going there. "I won't be late back," Juliet promised. She was relieved she hadn't had to lie. "There may be coffee afterwards." This wasn't exactly a lie either, as there might well be. Although she hoped that any coffee would be at Mr Spencer's place, just him and her.

She walked briskly through the cold night air. The streets through the suburb were well lit but even with her winter coat she didn't want to linger. She also didn't want to arrive at the church with bright red shiny cheeks but there wasn't a lot she could do about that.

Juliet felt increasingly nervous as she approached. The church was lit up at the front and looked really bright and shining. It had been the same when she visited with Margot and by herself, but this was different. She was invited.

Inside Mr Spencer was already there and her heart leapt to see him. He was talking to a couple of other people including the man she recognised from the Green Room, but he stopped speaking with them and came over to Juliet.

"Juliet. I really am very glad to see you." Mr Spencer's eyes held even more that he didn't dare say. "Come and meet some people."

It was another fifteen minutes until the service started and not everyone was taking their seat yet. Mr Spencer introduced her to the man she had seen before, who was Dan, as well as to a very pregnant woman who turned out to be Dan's wife, Jenny. She seemed very nice but Juliet felt awkward as they were all around the same age and she was younger. Did they know who and what she was?

And what about Rebecca, was she here? Juliet sincerely hoped not.

Her dilemma at how to introduce herself was solved by Mr Spencer. "This is Juliet, one of my students from St Gillian's."

Dan gave her a slightly curious look. It wasn't unfriendly but he was appraising her. "You're the one we saw singing in the bar that time, aren't you?"

"Yes, that was our first ever time performing together," Juliet said.

"What kind of music is it?" Jenny asked.

"It's sort of a mix. Kind of trip-pop. I just sing, I'm not really the musical one. Jax, our keyboardist, writes most of the music." Juliet didn't want to take the credit as Jax really was the mastermind of it all.

"You sing very well, from what I heard," Dan told her.

"You'll have to let us know when you're next performing, we'll come and listen," Jenny said. She had a gleam in her eye and she cast a brief look at Mr Spencer. "Only it had better be soon, because time's running out for my days of fun and freedom." She indicated her belly.

Juliet thought how friendly Jenny and Dan were. "I'd be happy to get you tickets. We'll be at the Green Room again in a couple of weeks."

A few people stopped to chat, including Agnes who recognised Juliet and was very glad to see her. Juliet was feeling overwhelmed with niceness. It was almost surreal.

Then finally the organ started and those that weren't already seated hurried to their chairs. Juliet sat beside Mr Spencer, relieved to be have something else to focus on.

* * *

Dan had obviously said something to Jenny. Carl dreaded to think what, but the look that Jenny had given him after the Green Room was mentioned said it all. Carl knew he could trust them, but Jenny had a dangerously lively imagination. She had probably already put two and two together and made a very incriminating number.

Though she wouldn't be far off the mark, of course. Because there he was, sitting next to Juliet, barely able to concentrate on anything Pastor Brown was saying as he was completely distracted by her presence beside him.

He realised that he really wanted to be alone with her. Wise or unwise, it was going to have to happen. After all, how risky could pizza at his place really be? They both knew what was at stake, Juliet was hardly going to broadcast it around school.

He would hold out for this week, he thought. Take it slowly. Next week he would see about asking her back for a meal. She would need to clear it with her aunt anyway.

Juliet's voice sounded clear and beautiful as she sang the hymns even though she wasn't very familiar with them. He felt a sense of pride at being next to her. She wore a small silver cross that glinted in the hollow of her neck and even the brief glimpse of skin was giving him very unholy thoughts.

Prayers came as a relief because he could make his own imprecations to the Lord. Most of which were about resisting the girl kneeling next to him.

"Is your friend staying for tea and coffee?" Agnes asked after the service, cornering Carl and Juliet as they filed out of the congregation.

Carl looked at Juliet questioningly. "I'd love to," she said.

"What would you like, dear?" Agnes asked.

"Let me fetch them, Agnes." He didn't want to leave Juliet stranded but he didn't want to trouble Agnes. Dan and Jenny had come up again so Juliet wasn't left by herself.

As Carl returned with the mugs he couldn't help scanning the room for Rebecca. He hadn't seen her before the service and she didn't usually attend on Sunday evenings because of preparing for the week ahead.

Jenny missed nothing. "She's not here," she told Carl. "Though I wouldn't be surprised if she shows up next week," she said, flicking her gaze to Juliet, who didn't notice as she had been asked something by Agnes and was absorbed in conversation with her.

"Really?" Carl asked.

"If word gets out," Jenny said. Then she added quickly: "Not that I'm suggesting there's anything to gossip about, but you know how things are."

Carl felt tired just thinking about it. He had really hoped that Rebecca wasn't minded to rekindle things between them, but from what Jenny was suggesting he might face another confrontation with his ex-fiancée yet again. She had been so unpleasant after they broke up that it had made him feel very comfortable with his choice. He understood that she was hurting, her pride more than anything, but it didn't incline him to change his mind. Quite the opposite.

The group chatted for a while longer on church affairs, Juliet mainly listening, and then things started to break up as people drifted home.

"Let me drive you home," Carl offered to Juliet, thankfully out of earshot of the all-knowing Jenny.

"Are you sure?"

"Absolutely. It's dark and cold and it makes no sense for you to walk all that way. I'm sure your aunt would be happier for you to get home quickly."

* * *

Juliet followed Mr Spencer to his car. It wasn't the first time she had been in it, of course, but she felt unaccountably nervous this time.

The cold night air made her shiver even as she wrapped her coat around herself, stepping out of the brightness and warmth of the church.

"Cold? I'll put the car heating on as soon as we're inside," he offered.

Juliet could think of far more effective ways that Mr Spencer could warm her up but she didn't dare to suggest any of them. It was kind of ironic that she felt so on edge around him. She'd seen plenty of other guys and got up to far more heavy stuff than had ever happened with Mr Spencer. But with him it felt different. More significant.

They walked across the street to where his car was parked. Mr Spencer went around to the passenger side, opened the door for her and closed it after she had got into the seat. Guys her own age never did that. It added to her nerves, the sense of being weirdly out of her depth.

Everyone at church had seemed older than her as well, there were no other teenagers there, maybe a couple of people who looked like college students but that was it. Younger families presumably went to the morning service.

Juliet chewed her lip as Mr Spencer drove through the darkness. He didn't say anything to her, though she noticed that he had remembered the way. She flicked her eyes to his profile a couple of times, but his gaze was fixed on the road. She wondered what he might do if she put her hand on his thigh.

Mr Spencer finally pulled up on the road just down from her aunt's house. The neighbours were entertaining and their guests had parked in the space right outside Juliet's home. So by fortunate chance Mr Spencer had to park out of view from where Aunt Mary might see through the curtains.

He unbuckled his seatbelt, obviously planning to open her door for her, but she turned to stop him. "Mr Spencer…"

He moved his hand back from the door and looked at her. The angles of his face were flawless in the semi-darkness, lit only by a nearby streetlight. "I think you had better call me Carl, outside school."

"Carl…" She said the name, testing it. Somehow it shifted everything, to call him by his Christian name.

"Juliet." He waited for her question.

"Would you kiss me?"

He was silent for several seconds after she asked this and she didn't dare breathe. She hoped he wasn't angry.

"You know that I really shouldn't." He sounded conflicted.

"Please?"

Their eyes connected. They both wanted the same.

Without speaking he reached out one hand to cradle her face. He looked at her for several seconds as though still trying to decide.

Then he tilted her head towards him and brought his lips down on hers, tender and warm and firm all at once. She felt a throb throughout her body, melting as it intensified, as he moved her lips apart and deepened the kiss.

Juliet hadn't imagined anything could be as good as Paris but in the intimacy of the darkness it was even more sensual. Just the two of them with no one else watching.

He broke off. "I could do this all night. But I don't want your aunt to send out a search party."

"She won't be worried just yet." This time Juliet kissed him, winding her hands in his hair. She heard him suppress a groan as she kissed the corner of his mouth, then across to the centre, drawing his top lip in between hers, her tongue lightly flicking inside his mouth.

Then he gripped her more firmly, taking control of the embrace. She was drowning in him. His breathing was growing ragged as she ran her fingers up his neck, making him tighten his grip on her.

But just as she thought he might push her down onto the car seat and get really heavy, he pulled back again.

"I think we'd better call it a night."

Juliet felt bereft. She was thrilled at the effect she had on him, and bewildered by the effect he had on her. How could simply kissing be this earthmoving?

"It's not late," she pointed out.

"I know. But I shouldn't even be doing this."

"We," Juliet corrected.

Carl looked confused. "We?"

"We are doing this. It's not just you, you don't have to take all the blame."

"I'm the one in the position of authority. The one who should know better," he said.

Juliet gave him a sexy half-smile. "I don't think the world will end if you kiss me."

He was silent for a while. "I didn't exactly plan this. I figured we would just go to church, and manage not to cross the line again."

It was the exact opposite of Juliet had planned, but the concern in Carl's voice worried her. "Do you want me to not come again?"

He looked at her and his eyes softened. "Of course not. It's great seeing you there. I just need to remember that I'm your teacher, not…"

Juliet hoped he was going to say "your boyfriend" but he left the line unfinished. As soon as she thought it she realised that it was what she wanted more than anything else in the world: to date Mr Spencer. Carl. To officially be his girlfriend, exclusively.

It gave her a sudden sharp pang of envy that Rebecca had been able to enjoy this privilege, while she, Juliet, couldn't.

She felt in a daze as he opened the door for her and waited until she had entered her aunt's home before returning to his car. Now she had to snap out of it and look normal so her aunt woudn't guess anything was up.

She took a couple of deep breaths, hung her coat up and smoothed her hair. She was living two lives: band-and-Carl Juliet, and good - or at least reformed - niece Juliet. At some point it would all collide and collapse.

XXI. Suspicious ex

The memory of the kiss had to last her all week. Juliet had secretly hoped that Mr Spencer might ask her to stay after class and repeat it but he remained perfectly professional.

It just made her burn up inside even more.

She couldn't wait until the following weekend so she could get to see him outside school again. Carl. She had to keep reminding herself she could call him that now.

But it was hard, because he had to be Mr Spencer in the classroom.

"I can't believe you're this excited to go to church," Margot said. "It's like you're living in some kind of weird parallel dimension."

Since Paris, Juliet had been living in another reality. Her entire world was upturned. She was dizzily crazy about a guy who was holding her at arm's length. He seemed to have so much more control than she did which only intensified her own desire for him.

Band practice was the best escape from the chaos in her mind. Singing gave Juliet focus. Her bandmates were completely disconnected from school, there was nothing to remind her of Mr Spencer when she was with them.

Their sound was really starting to come together. Juliet had thought they sounded okay a couple of months back when they first performed, but it was only now that she realised how much better they could have been. Before, everyone was consciously trying to fit together. Now it was seamless.

Jax and Drew were managing other things behind the scenes too. Juliet had initially thought of it as a hobby, just fun, but Jax in particular was deadly serious. This was his life. He had a day job, as did the drummer and the bassist. Drew and the other guitarist were both college students.

Juliet hadn't paid a lot of attention to what was going on with the management of the band but there was starting to be talk of demos and even a video. Drew had a friend who was a videographer, Jax knew someone who worked in a recording studio. The drummer knew someone who had recording equipment in their basement which might be even cheaper.

It was all favours and freebies and grabbing what they could get, but there was the increasing sense that something was happening. Juliet simply tried to focus on her singing. There was too much other stuff going on in her life to think about more complications. If they started getting more bookings it would only be trickier to hide it from Aunt Mary.

And she had something far bigger to hide from her aunt: that she was becoming involved with her teacher.

* * *

Rebecca. Of all the people Juliet had hoped never to be confronted by, there she was at church. Not actually touching Carl, but all over him in every other sense of the word.

Juliet couldn't help herself analysing Carl's ex-fiancée, trying to figure out what he might have seen in her. She had to admit that Rebecca wasn't unattractive, just kind of severe and serious looking. Her hair was neatly plaited into a braid and she wore a navy cardigan over a long navy skirt.

But Rebecca's face lost any pleasantness when Carl extricated himself and came to meet Juliet at the door. Any smiles were replaced with suspicion and hostility. Of course she put on her fake charm when Juliet was introduced to her but Juliet could clearly see through it.

"I do remember you, you're Carl's student. How interesting that you should start attending the same church," Rebecca said.

Juliet was going to mumble something about exploring her spirituality again but Carl cut in. "Juliet's actually here as my guest," he told his ex-fiancée.

144

Juliet was shocked that he would admit this. So was Rebecca.

"Really? I shouldn't imagine a Catholic school would approve of you inviting students to another church."

Before Carl could reply Juliet was relieved to see Dan and Jenny arriving. Jenny greeted Juliet warmly and Rebecca raised her eyebrows and looked even more displeased.

Members of the congregation started to move towards their seats. "I guess we should go and take our places," Rebecca said, addressing Carl directly to cut Juliet out. She clearly meant "we" as him and her.

But Carl took his own lead, turning to Juliet. "Let's go and sit down," he said to her, ignoring Rebecca.

Rebecca's eyes narrowed but before she could react, Jenny jumped into to save the situation. "You'll sit with us, won't you Rebecca?" Somehow Jenny managed to usher the furious woman off with her and Dan. Carl cast her a grateful look.

Juliet couldn't bring herself to look at the other woman so kept her eyes down and followed Carl to a row.

"I'm sorry," Carl said. "I should have anticipated that it might be awkward if she came."

"It's not your fault," Juliet told him. She felt bad that her own presence was causing so much disharmony, in a place of faith.

* * *

Carl wanted to avoid Rebecca and he also wanted to invite Juliet back. He had been postponing the invitation, still conflicted on how appropriate it would be.

He also wasn't entirely sure how long his self-control would last. It would be a battle.

But the prospect of enduring tea and stilted conversation with Rebecca was worse. She was clearly suspicious about his friendship with his student, as Jenny had warned him would be the case.

So as they started to file out of their seats, he whispered to Juliet: "would you like to get pizza?"

Surprise and delight showed on her face. "I'd love to."

Carl guided her straight to the door, he didn't even want to stop for a drink and chat with friends.

"Leaving already?" It was Rebecca, trying to corner him by the door.

"Yes, I have to drive Juliet," Carl said. He omitted the word "home" so it wasn't technically a lie.

Rebecca gave Juliet a patronising smile. "I expect you have to get back early, what with school tomorrow," she said.

"Something like that," Juliet said. She tried to be polite but she wanted to kick Rebecca.

Carl wished Rebecca goodnight and he and Juliet left. As before he opened the car door for her. They set off, turning towards his place rather than Aunt Mary's house this time. It was a drive into the unknown for both of them.

* * *

Juliet liked Carl's house. It was tidy without being overly neat and he had shelves full of books. Juliet hated immaculate homes with polished glass all over the place, where you never felt you could relax.

Though she didn't feel very relaxed yet. They were alone in his home, somewhere she had longed to be, and now she was boiling over with nerves.

She looked around. Many of his books appeared to be in Latin and some were beautifully bound in leather with gold lettering on them. He clearly read them - they weren't just decorative shelf-filler - as several were on a coffee table and had bookmarks sticking out from them, and pieces of folded paper with notes. Juliet wondered if he was studying for something or just read them for leisure.

Next to the books, a pile of marking reminded her that he was her teacher.

Carl stacked the books into a pile. "I should have cleared this up before, I had to do some research earlier."

"Research?" Juliet looked at him questioningly.

"For a possible doctorate."

She was intrigued. "You're going back to college?"

146

"I don't know yet. It would probably be part time while I worked, but I haven't decided."

Juliet looked at one of them. "*Magna Vita Sancti Hugonis* - the great life of holy Hugonis?" she attempted to translate.

"Close. The great life of St Hugh," Carl told her. "So what about you, have you decided on college yet? What you'll study?"

Juliet hadn't. It was something she had been giving some thought to recently. "Everyone expects us all to go to college. But without knowing what I really want to do, it seems like a lot of debt to get into."

"You could start general, pick a major later on," Carl suggested. "And there are scholarships. You're easily talented enough to try for one."

"I know. It's just that I'm not even sure of going at all, at least not immediately." It was hard to explain. The one thing she was sure she did want, something that she had always wanted, was something she couldn't admit even to her friends.

But there were other reasons too. Juliet had spent her whole life at someone else's direction, under someone else's rules. Living with Aunt Mary and going to St Gillian's had been very safe and structured. She wanted to be free of all that. "If I go now, not knowing what I want to do, it will just be an extension of school. But if I wait and then there's something I really want to do, it will be worth all the money and everything."

"I guess most of your friends at St Gillian's have college funds?" he said.

"Yes." Juliet didn't resent it, it was just the way it was. "Above everything, I'd like to travel some more. So I might work and save up for that. Maybe even work overseas."

"That sounds wise. I've never regretted studying and working overseas, though it can make you restless when you come home," Carl said.

"Do you get restless?"

"At times. Which is partly why I'm thinking of doing the doctorate," he hold her. He changed the subject. "You must be hungry. Does pizza still sound good?" It did. "Great. I'm out of soda so we can order some with the pizzas."

Juliet looked through a pile of DVDs by the television while he ordered. There were a couple of movies, a British TV series on the Ancient Romans, and then a DVD on Christian marriage. The woman on the front of it looked like Aunt Mary.

Carl noticed her looking at it. "It's Rebecca's," he told her.

Juliet was relieved it wasn't his, but refrained from saying so. She hoped he wasn't holding onto it out of any desire to reconcile with his ex. She was pretty sure that Rebecca wanted to get back with him.

"Anything you'd like to watch?" Carl asked.

What she wanted to do was sit on the couch with him and break down his defences. None of the movies looked the right kind of thing for that, and the marriage video least of all. "What's this Rome series like?"

"It's pretty good. We can watch it if you like." He went over and put it in the player.

Perhaps deliberately, Carl had chosen an arm-chair while Juliet sat on the couch. So no physical contact was possible between them. He really knew how to torture a girl, Juliet thought.

They watched the start of the first episode without speaking, and then the pizza arrived - something of a relief, as it broke the tension. It also meant that Carl sat on the couch beside her as it was easiest to share that way. But neither of them ate much of it. Juliet was too conscious of him sitting so close to her.

She deliberately leant back and towards him, just a little. It didn't take long for her to be leaning against him, his arm around her. There was something very natural about the way it just happened.

Juliet was trying to concentrate on the history series but it was impossible. She turned her head to look at Carl, who looked back in response.

All she had to do this time was close her eyes to feel his lips come softly down on hers. Against the comfort and space of the cushions as he leant towards her, he was almost lying on top of her. He was only kissing her, but his body was pressed down against hers and Juliet had never felt more turned on. His strength and superior size made her feel both at his mercy and protected.

As though he could do what he wanted with her, but also keep her safe.

She could feel the force of his own desire, pressing rock hard against her through the fabric of his clothing. He realised too and shifted, embarrassed, sitting up again.

"I'm sorry. I really lack self-control around you."

"I'm glad." Juliet wound herself around him this time, moving her leg across him so she was sitting on his lap, facing him.

"Juliet…"

He was trying to tell her no but he couldn't manage it.

She took the lead and kissed his lips, across he angle of his jawbone, onto his neck. She heard his breath catch in his throat. He had moved his hands off her but now he was clasping her again onto him, his hands caressing her back.

"Lord help me, I want you so badly," he said. "Being so close to you is like playing with fire."

Juliet moved her head back to face him. "I want you even more."

"I don't think that's possible," Carl told her, bringing his lips on hers yet again. He managed to regain control. "We really have to stop. This isn't right."

Juliet slid off him and sat back against him, resting against his shoulder, her faced tilted towards his. Her entire body ached for him to touch her.

"I wish I could sleep with you. I don't mean that," she added hurriedly, seeing the consternation on his face. "I just mean be with you the whole night and wake up with you."

Carl felt his heart turn over and other parts of his body grow even more heated despite his willing them not to.

"Until now it hasn't been that hard following God's teachings, even when I was engaged," he told her. "I thought it seemed hard at times, but compared to this it was nothing. If I took you into my bed I couldn't trust myself to do the right thing."

Juliet's idea of the right thing was very different from Carl's, at least at that moment.

"Didn't your fiancée stay over?" she asked. She couldn't bring herself to mention Rebecca's name.

"We were waiting until marriage," Carl said.

"But weren't you ever tempted?"

Carl didn't want to be disloyal to Rebecca, not that she had shown him much loyalty spreading rumours, but he also didn't want to lie. "Truthfully? No. It wasn't until I met you that I started feeling this way."

Juliet was happy and weirdly nervous at hearing this. At the same she found herself disturbed by the reference to Carl's marriage. It seemed like such a distant, grown-up thing to have been planning. Yet he had been on that path, in a separate, adult world that she didn't yet feel a part of.

Before she had felt thrilled at the gap between them: that he was so much older and had more life experience than her. Now she felt at a disadvantage.

Carl picked up on her mood change. "I am here for you, Juliet. I realise it must seem like I'm always holding back but it's the only appropriate way right now. I genuinely love spending time with you."

XXII. Ready to rock

"You know, you should try pushing some of his buttons," Margot suggested as she and Juliet hung out one lunch break.

"What do you mean?"

"Wind him up. Get some more action happening," Margot said.

Juliet was taken aback. "Why would I want to do that?"

"Because you're turning into the Virgin Mary. Seriously. I can't believe how slow he's taking things."

It was true that things were going at a much steadier pace than Juliet was used to, but there were reasons for that. Valid if frustrating reasons.

Juliet bit into an apple. "I'm okay with how it's going."

"I wouldn't be." Margot was still seeing Terrance on and off and they certainly hadn't taken things slowly. "Doesn't it get dull, just kissing?"

Weirdly it didn't. Juliet would have been happy with more but she had to amid that even just kissing Mr Spencer - Carl - was more intense than stuff she had got up to with other guys.

"I don't know. There's so much going on this term, what with study, and then the band. Maybe it's better this way."

"Whatever." Margot wasn't convinced. She'd been Juliet's partner in crime for too long to believe that her best friend was satisfied with a chaste romance.

As she walked to band practice that night, Juliet found herself thinking about Margot's words. Maybe it would be fun to step up the pressure with Carl. After all she wanted him badly.

She could hardly start acting like a vamp at school or in church, so that left the band. She hadn't really thought about what to wear, other than imagining she would wear a similar outfit to last time. But maybe she should try and improve it.

Juliet was hopeless at sewing but Fhemie had a flair for it, mainly from fixing up dance costumes over the years. It might be worth asking her.

* * *

"You can pay me in muffins, but not those healthy ones. Just chocolate, no zucchini or chia or shit or whatever you put in them usually," Fhemie said.

"You like them usually. You always eat them," Juliet pointed out.

"Yeah. But I'd like them more if they were just chocolate without the health food." They were at Fhemie's house, having gone there after school. Juliet had brought her outfit with her for Fhemie to take a look at.

Fhemie gave it a critical eye. "It needs a bit of work but we'll get there." She took out some scissors and started savagely hacking at the plaid of the skirt. "You rolled it over for that other time, didn't you? I can make it look better than that."

She shortened it, cut slits in it, and tacked it up. "I'll machine it later. The blouse is going to be more work."

Juliet never knew exactly what Fhemie did or how, but an hour or so later she was trying on something that seemed to be about a tenth of the size of what she had worn before. Fhemie had combined parts of the blouse with a cut up lycra vest, so it was skin tight but with the collar and a couple of other elements to retain its look of being a school blouse. Many lifetimes ago, anyway.

Juliet wasn't really sure what to say. There was no way she could wear it. "It's a bit revealing, isn't it?" she asked Fhemie.

"Have you seen what I dance in?" Fhemie said. Most of her costumes would have given her grandmother a stroke.

"I know, but I'm singing not dancing."

"Trust me on this. You have to start thinking of it as a costume, not clothes. It will move better and look better on stage this way. Just tying the shirt up like you did before make it all lumpy and bunched. This will have a good line," Fhemie promised.

Juliet had nothing else remotely suitable to wear so she guessed she would have to take Fhemie's word for it.

"And you'll need stockings. Hold ups not suspenders," Fhemie said.

"You really don't think this is going to be too much?" Juliet asked.

Fhemie shook her head. "It's not so bad. You can see a bit of your midriff above the waist as you move, but the neckline is high at the front, you can't even see any cleavage really. It's really just your legs that will be on show, and what's the big deal about legs?"

She was probably right, Juliet thought. Still, she was going to have to summon up some courage to wear it.

"Look at these." Fhemie picked up a music magazine and flicked through a few photos of female singers in concert. "You see it's really no different. You need to look the part."

* * *

Her door firmly locked, Juliet tried the costume on again in front of her bedroom mirror. She applied make-up, much more heavily than usual. Like stage make-up, Fhemie had advised.

She looked like a different person. Like a performer. She had a weird feeling all of a sudden, as though she were becoming someone else, or that there was someone else she needed to become.

Juliet had to look at herself in the mirror for a while, trying to get to know this new image.

What would my parents think of me now? she thought. They would barely recognise her dressed and painted like this. Would they even recognise her at all, aged eighteen, not having seen her since she was a small child?

Thinking about it, and knowing that she could never know one way or the other, made her tear up. Why did you leave me? she asked the mirror, wishing she could see her mother's face in her own. She only really knew it from photos, her own memories were blurred and faded.

Would they be proud of her? Even though they would probably freak out over this outfit, they might be proud of her singing. She tried not to think about all the lost years. The grief and the loneliness and the neglect and the abuse. And the other thing, the thing she couldn't tell anyone.

Her eyeliner was smudged and streaked down her face from the silent, aching tears.

Whatever she did, she must not cry on stage or ever get too damp with perspiration. It turned her from a vamp into a deranged panda.

* * *

Fhemie was right about the costume. Wearing it made Juliet feel like she was putting on a new persona, playing a role. Inside she was still a wreck but outside she looked… convincing.

The reaction of the band further confirmed Fhemie's skills.

"That is awesome," Drew said. "So hot. The crowd will love it."

Drew had come close to flirting with Juliet a couple of times earlier on but she had managed to convey she wasn't quite single.

Originally it was because she had wanted to avoid complications, nothing would be worse than dating someone and it all going wrong and messing the band up. She preferred the platonic dynamic of it all anyway.

And now, was she single? She wasn't exactly dating Mr Spencer. But they went to church together and kissed in his car and at his place, and if he had asked her out properly she wouldn't have hesitated to say yes. He was the one holding out on her, taking it all so cautiously.

Juliet's head went into a different place when the music started. It was a switch-off from normal reality, and switching-on to a kind of bubble of just her and the band on stage.

The Green Room was packed out that Thursday night. There was another, longer established band playing after them so Juliet couldn't flatter herself that all these people had bought tickets just to see Dover Six. Still, it was exciting.

Margot and Fhemie were out there, pretending to have been dragged along reluctantly, but Juliet knew her friends were secretly pleased for her.

"Do you have band t-shirts?" Fhemie had asked.

"No, nothing like that. It's only our second performance, we don't exactly have fans lining up to buy merchandise," Juliet said.

"Don't expect me to wear one when you do," Fhemie said. "But I will buy one, if I can get to meet that cute guy you have."

Cute guy? Juliet wasn't sure whom Fhemie meant. "Drew?"

"No, idiot. The cute guy on keyboards."

Juliet nearly burst out laughing. She guessed Jax wasn't bad looking, but compared to Drew or even a couple of the others she wouldn't have picked him out as the hot one.

"He's single, so I can try," she promised Fhemie.

"Single or not, it makes no difference to me," Fhemie said. "Just get me introduced."

Hiding a smile, Juliet said she would do what she could. Fhemie never admitted this kind of stuff, so she must really have a thing for Jax. Jax had never indicated any interest in girls or guys to Juliet, so she didn't even know if he was straight. She could probably find out from Drew.

* * *

Carl caught his breath when he saw Juliet appear on stage. She was lit up like a flame, and her outfit was... he told himself firmly that it was what singers wore, and tried to resist the urge to blindfold every other man in the place.

Including Dan, who was grinning in Juliet's direction then back at Carl.

"Your face," Dan said.

Jenny was also suppressing a smile.

"What's wrong with my face?"

"Like you can't decide whether to get a shotgun or a hotel room," Jenny said.

Before Carl could protest she continued: "I'm claiming pregnancy privilege. With my hormones and this ever more enormous belly, I get to speak my mind or I'll burst."

Carl should have guessed he couldn't hide anything from his best friends. "I should never have brought you here."

"It wouldn't have made any difference whether you had or not," Dan told him. "It was written all over your face and hers when we saw her here the last time. Let alone when you brought her to church."

"It really isn't like that," Carl said. "She's my student."

Jenny gave him a wicked smile. "Not for much longer. Just a few months until graduation, right?"

"Seriously though, do her parents know about all this?" Dan asked.

"Her parents are dead, several years ago. She lives with an aunt. I believe the aunt gave her approval to Juliet coming to church, but probably doesn't know about the singing," Carl said.

Jenny was moved. "The poor little thing." She rested her hand on her stomach. "Imagine this one losing us, Dan, it's unbearable. No wonder she's not like the average high schooler."

"What do you mean?" Carl was curious.

"It's hard to say. How would you put it, Dan?"

Her husband shrugged. "More self-possessed, maybe? She's obviously crazy about you, Carl, but she didn't act like some dumb teen might."

"She looked at you like Rebecca should have looked at you, but never did," Jenny told Carl. "And you're the same, when you look at her." She saw Dan's frown. "Alright! I'll button my lip and bite my tongue. But you ask Agnes."

Carl had a fair idea of what asking Agnes about Juliet would do, and had no intention of stoking that fire. He was startled by what Dan and Jenny had said, he had hoped to have appeared far more professionally detached. It was a good thing he didn't play poker if he was that bad at masking his emotions.

It was true though. He was crazy about her. He watched her now, singing, and felt a surge of pride. She was easily the most beautiful girl in the room, every eye was upon her.

At the same time she seemed different. The whole band did. Before they were a talented group of musicians, performing together. Now, they were - he searched for the right word - slick, professional. They had got their act together in the literal sense of the phrase.

* * *

Juliet was on a complete high after they finished the set. Everything was perfect: they had performed flawlessly, the crowd had loved it, and they had all enjoyed every moment of it. Her friends were out there, and best of all, so was Carl.

She went straight to him afterwards. He was with Dan and Jenny, and although Juliet had felt super confident on stage, she felt oddly shy on seeing him. He was wearing a dark blue shirt and looked taller and more mature than most of the other guys, except for Dan.

"What did you think? Were we okay?" She found she ardently wanted his approval.

"You were more than okay," Carl said.

"You were absolutely awesome," Dan told her, with Jenny agreeing.

"Seriously, all of you were amazing. I'm so glad you got us tickets," Jenny said. Tactfully she steered Dan off to the bar to get more drinks, leaving Juliet alone with Carl.

Juliet didn't dare touch him although given the crush of people she was nearly pushed against him. "So you really liked it?"

"Absolutely." Her face lit up with happiness as said this, and he was surprised and touched that his approval meant so much to her. He couldn't help flicking his eyes up and down her body. "And you look incredible."

Juliet felt herself blush though she hoped he wouldn't see it in the lighting. She had totally forgotten what she was wearing, and reminded of it now, she felt half naked. "Fhemie helped make it."

"It's very distracting."

"Would you like me to wear it in class?"

Carl felt his body respond just thinking of this image. "I don't think we'd get much Latin done."

"I don't think I would mind that." She was looking up at him, her eyes darkening with desire. It took all of Carl's self control not to put his hands on her body. The close fitting design of her costume revealed the exact shape of her body, he could imagine how it would feel to run his hands over the curve of her waist.

He wanted her so badly.

Thou hast ravished my heart with one of thine eyes, with one chain of thy neck…

Her lips parted slightly as she looked at him, willing him to embrace her.

Every fibre of his body was tested, strained. The crowds of people no longer existed.

Fair as the moon, clear as the sun.

"Juliet…"

If Fhemie and Margot hadn't arrived at that moment to break the spell, Carl wasn't sure that he could have resisted kissing his student in public. The two of them were a welcome interruption.

* * *

"Hi Mr Spencer. What did you think of Juliet?" Margot's expression held a sly grin.

"Very talented. All of them," Carl said, managing to recover himself.

"The costume was my creation," Fhemie told him, though he already knew this. "Did you like it?"

They could see that their teacher was disconcerted and were trying to wind him up. It reminded Carl that he was the authority figure and had to face them in class tomorrow. Juliet and Margot anyway, since Fhemie didn't do Latin. He avoided rising to their bait.

"It looked very professional," he said to Fhemie, whose eyes glinted even more evilly than Margot's.

Carl wondered exactly what Juliet had told her friends about the situation. Fortunately there wasn't too much to tell: he had obviously compromised both of them by inviting her back to his place, but at least things hadn't progressed past kissing.

"I'm so glad you like it," Fhemie said. Carl was relieved he didn't have her in his Latin class. Margot was bad enough, but the two of them together would be torment with all their innuendo.

"You guys thought it was okay then?" Juliet asked them.

Fhemie grimaced. "Well, you know, it was bearable. I've suffered worse."

Juliet interpreted this as the high praise that it actually was and hugged her friend.

"You know you did good, girl. You managed not to embarrass us." This was Margot's approval.

"Anyway. So that cute guy on keyboards, are you going to introduce me?" Fhemie asked.

Juliet looked around to see were Jax was. He and Drew were over by the side of the stage talking to some man while the others were packing up equipment. "Come over with me now," she told Fhemie. "I need to go and help anyway, we're not famous enough yet to have roadies."

As they left Dan and Jenny arrived back with drinks and Margot slipped back to her boyfriend, casting Carl another knowing grin as she did so.

"More of your students?" Jenny asked.

"Yes. Juliet's friends."

Dan handed him a drink. "This will have to be the last one for us, it's getting late. Do you still want a lift back?"

"If you can, thanks," Carl said.

"What about Juliet?"

"She's staying with her friends."

Carl secretly wished she were staying at his place. He remembered what Juliet had said about wanting to wake up with him. The vision of having her in his arms all night had haunted him ever since.

He couldn't imagine how it could ever be a reality. There were some things he didn't dare pray for.

XXIII. The agent

Juliet couldn't believe what Drew was saying. He had called her up on Saturday morning for a band meeting at a nearby café.

"I feel bad that we kept it from you, but I didn't want to stress you out. After all it was only our second gig," he said.

It turned out that Jax and Drew had managed to get some music industry contact to come and watch them play at the Green Room.

"He was really impressed, and he wants to manage us."

Juliet warmed her fingers on her coffee. She could feel how excited they all were, though everyone tried to appear casual about it. She felt just the same.

"We need to sort out a few things," Drew continued. "He wants to see some kind of demo video and we need some preliminary publicity photos. Those are easy to sort out but the video will be more work. We also have to decide which track to perform."

Everyone had their own ideas about this but there was a tacit understanding that Jax, since he wrote nearly all the music, should get the casting vote. Fortunately he picked one of Juliet's favourites and Drew agreed with his choice too.

"It's the most anthemic," he said. "It's memorable. Musically it may not be the best we've got but it will stick in people's minds."

There was some discussion of what the video should look like. There wasn't the budget for anything fancy, they were calling in freebies and favours as it was. "It could just be us playing, from a few different angles," the bassist suggested.

Juliet had an idea. "My friend's a dancer," she said. "I bet she'd be happy to help out."

"Was that the girl you introduced me to last night? We couldn't pay her," Drew said.

"That's her, the little one. She's really talented, truly."

Drew stirred his drink. "She certainly looked hot."

Juliet cast a glance at Jax to see if he was reacting. He had appeared completely oblivious to Fhemie's attempts to get him to notice her in the Green Room. Whether it was deliberate or not, she wasn't sure, but it had infuriated Fhemie and only made her even more determined to get his attention.

"I can get her to meet with you properly. She could maybe do some kind of audition," Juliet suggested.

"Sure. She probably knows way more about choreography than any of us do, so that could be helpful," Drew said.

Fhemie would be thrilled, Juliet thought. She would pretend to be all dismissive and non-committal, but Juliet always saw through it. Dancing and Jax: there was no way Fhemie would turn it down.

* * *

Fhemie, the world's skinniest glutton, was stuffing her face with Juliet's triple-chocolate muffins. They were gathered at Margot's place on Saturday afternoon, having planned to go to the mall but ended up staying in Margot's room watching DVDs.

"Food is what you should try," Fhemie advised her. "The way to a man's heart is through his stomach. You should cook for him."

Juliet laughed. "Cook what?"

"Anything. You're great at it, it's your talent. Lasagne maybe. Everyone likes lasagne." Fhemie liked lasagne.

"Guys like meat," Margot said. "Steak. Ribs. Something like that."

"How about chicken? You could do a pot roast," Fhemie suggested.

Margot shook her head. "No, that's too mom and family dinner. It has to be date food."

Juliet figured that steak would be easiest. "What do I do, take it round there?"

"No!" Fhemie was derisive. "You invite yourself to his place and you cook it there. Make sure it all takes ages so it's really late by the time you finish. Then Mr Spencer will have to ask you to stay the night."

"It's a good plan," Margot said. "Does he have a spare bedroom? If not then you'll have to share his bed."

"There's definitely a second bedroom, but I don't know if it's set up with a bed," Juliet said. If there wasn't, she imagined he would insist on being a gentleman and taking the sofa. If he even invited her to stay back at all, of course. They were probably getting way ahead of themselves.

Margot looked disappointed. "That's a shame. Maybe you could accidentally sleepwalk into his room in the middle of the night."

"A guy once told me he only had one blanket so I'd have to share his bed," Fhemie said.

"You surely didn't fall for that?" Margot was incredulous.

Fhemie grinned. "Of course not. But still, I decided to share it with him anyway."

"I don't think Jax will be that kind of guy," Juliet warned her. "I think he'd be really slow and wary. His main thing is his music, he never seems to have mentioned any girls since I've known him."

Fhemie shrugged. "Wait until he sees me dance. We'll see who's slow about making a move then." To Juliet's relief she had agreed to be in the video. "Anyway, he's no more serious about his music than I am about dancing."

"What will you do when you're too old to dance?" Margot asked Fhemie.

"First I plan to get on one of those celebrity dancing shows as an expert dancer. Then I plan to become well known enough to get an agent and get offered acting roles. Then I want to be the glamorous bitch on some long-running TV soap. The bitches always have more fans and more fun," Fhemie said. "Then I'll be rich and famous and do less and less work while I earn more and more money."

Coming from anyone else this would be absurd. Coming from Fhemie it would probably happen, Juliet thought. Fhemie could be

162

absolutely driven when she wanted to be. Her grandmother's desire to send her to a convent only fuelled her ambition to dance.

"Yeah, like any of that will even happen," Margot said.

Fhemie shrugged. "If it doesn't, something else will. I'm going to dance and I'm going to be rich, regardless."

* * *

Juliet arrived home later that evening. It was dark but not late.

She opened the front door with her key, slipped off her coat and hung it up. The house was strangely still. Usually she would hear the television or the radio, but tonight both must have been switched off.

She walked through to the living room, startled to see Aunt Mary sitting very upright at the table. Her face was set rigid, her mouth fixed in a tight line.

"And where have you been?" Her aunt's voice was accusatory.

Juliet was alarmed by her manner. "Just at Margot's. Did I forget something?" She couldn't remember her aunt asking to be back especially early.

"Are you sure that's where you've been? Not out with some boy, at some bar?"

What on earth was going on? "No, I..."

Aunt Mary slammed her fist on the table making Juliet jump.

"I am very disappointed in you, young lady. I thought we were long past all this. The lying, the sneaking around with boys." Her face was white with fury, two red spots of colour in her cheeks.

"But I haven't been..."

"Don't lie! I know exactly what you've been up to. Out disgracing yourself with such shameful behaviour. I was a fool to ever put any trust in you."

Juliet's heart dropped like a stone. Aunt Mary must have found out about Carl.

But how?

* * *

Juliet was momentarily bewildered when Aunt Mary pushed a newspaper across the table towards her.

"There!" she declared.

Wondering how on earth she and Carl had ended up in the local paper, Juliet glanced down.

There, covering most of the top of the page, was a photograph of her singing with the band and the headline: "Hot new band Dover Six thrills crowd". Her skirt looked obscenely short but fortunately the colour of the lighting disguised it as being St Gillian's school plaid.

Her mind was racing. Was this what Aunt Mary meant? She felt a conflicting mix of relief and panic. So her aunt didn't know about Carl. Yet, anyway. The band seemed like such a small thing in comparison to practically dating her teacher.

"This what you're angry about?" Juliet asked.

"What else?" her aunt snapped. "How long has this been going on for?"

There was no point lying now. "Some months. I did mean to tell you," she said quickly, looking at the shock flare on Aunt Mary's face. "But I wasn't really sure if it was going anywhere."

"This is your idea of music appreciation and poetry, is it?"

"Well it is music, and I have written lyrics for some of our songs," Juliet said.

Her aunt was only further enraged. "This is not what I expected of you, young lady, as well you know. Appearing in a nightclub, dressed up like a…" she didn't complete the phrase and Juliet wondered what word Aunt Mary couldn't bring herself to say. Harlot? Prostitute? Out of context it was probably far worse than either.

"It's just a costume. I don't wear it at other times," she said.

"It's a disgrace. The whole thing is disgraceful," Aunt Mary said. "Lying and sneaking around for the purpose of this - " she tapped the newspaper " - it's shameful."

"Maybe it's more shameful that I didn't feel able to tell you," Juliet said.

"I beg your pardon?"

There was no salvaging this, so Juliet decided to be honest. "I'm eighteen, Aunt Mary, I'm a legal adult and if I want to sing a certain type of music, that's my choice."

"Not under my roof," Aunt Mary said. She looked furious.

"It's not under your roof, is it? You never have to hear it. I don't even sing it in the shower," Juliet pointed out.

"I mean that while you live under my roof, under my rules, you will not comport yourself like this. Heaven only knows what the neighbours must think, what your school must think. For they will all find out, now you have been splashed across the newspaper in this appalling way."

Juliet felt cold. "Are you saying that I have to quit the band if I am to continue living here? Even though everything else is fine and my grades are good and there are no other problems?"

Aunt Mary's mouth was pursed tighter than ever before. "That is exactly what I am saying. You are to give this up immediately. Or as you have mentioned, being as you are a legal adult, you can find somewhere else to live."

* * *

Juliet couldn't stay in the house with Aunt Mary in such a mood, after such a terrible row. But she had no idea where to go. She felt uncomfortable about rocking up at Fhemie's or Margot's house again, though of course they wouldn't have minded.

As she walked out again into the dark and the cold, there was only one direction that her feet took her. The only person she wanted and needed right now.

It was a long walk, and she was shattered and past crying by the time she saw the warm glow from his windows and suddenly fighting nerves, made her way up his driveway.

"Juliet, what is it? Come inside out of the cold." Carl ushered her through, closing the door behind her. He could instantly see that something was very wrong. He led her into the living room and got her to sit down on the couch. He sat next to her. "Tell me what's wrong."

She told him and it all came out in a rush.

"Aunt Mary found out about the band and she's furious. She's thrown me out - or she's threatening to throw me out - if I don't quit. But I don't want to, it feels like letting everyone down. I mean I guess they could find another singer..." she trailed off, miserable.

"What's happened? How did she find out?" Carl asked.

"There was a photo in the newspaper. So she saw what I was wearing and everything. That didn't help."

Carl raised his eyebrows. "Of course, I saw that. It was a great review. But no, your outfit probably wouldn't have helped."

"Did you think it looked awful?" Juliet asked, suddenly insecure.

Carl looked directly into her eyes making her stomach flip. "It was the hottest thing I've ever seen. But I'm not your aunt."

"So what do I do?" She was honestly out of ideas.

"I can talk to her if you would like."

Juliet looked at Carl. He might be her teacher but he was also a young and very good looking man. She could only imagine where Aunt Mary's suspicions would head if he came over and started advocating for her. The situation was bad enough as it was.

"I think that might make things a thousand times worse," she said.

"I understand. But if you need me to, I will. Now, has she actually sent you out of the house tonight and if so, do you need somewhere to stay?" Carl asked. "I can drive you to a friend's house or you're welcome to stay here. Unfortunately there's no bed in the second bedroom as it's filled with storage boxes, but I can take the couch."

Juliet suppressed a smile which Carl saw. "What is it?" he asked.

"It's nothing. It's just something that Fhemie said. But my aunt hasn't yet officially thrown me out, just threatened to, so I'll be fine to go back there for now."

"If you're sure." She could see that he was very concerned for her. "You can always come here if you need to. Your safety is more important than any other considerations. Have you eaten?"

Juliet hadn't. She had walked a long way in the cold and she found that she was actually hungry. She shook her head and Carl went to fetch them both food. While he did she looked at his copy of the paper. She hadn't even read the article herself except the headline. Her own name leapt out at her.

"Singer Juliet Martin has attitude and flair, and ethereal vocals that elevate Dover Six to a league apart."

The review, which wasn't long, continued by briefly mentioning a couple of tracks, and then Juliet was glad to see a reference to Jax as the main songwriter. She assumed the others would have seen it, but in case they had missed it she asked Carl if she could have his copy. She suspected Aunt Mary would have burnt hers.

Carl was happy for Juliet to take the newspaper. He had brought soup and bread which was just what she needed, it warmed her up from the inside. Which reminded her of what Fhemie had suggested.

"Could I cook for you sometime?"

Carl looked up from his bowl. "Is that a subtle way of telling me that this soup is inedible?"

Juliet was mortified. "No, it's great. Truly. I just like cooking and I get restricted at Aunt Mary's as she tends to like plainer dishes."

"What did you have in mind? Roast peacocks and lobster?" He was teasing her.

"Nothing so exotic. Just a change from chicken," Juliet said. "Do you have any allergies?"

"None that I know of."

It was getting late, and Juliet knew if she was out all night without warning there would be more than hell to pay with Aunt Mary. Carl also noticed the time. "I should drive you home," he said.

Both relieved and disappointed because she didn't want to leave him, Juliet put her coat back on. She turned towards the door as Carl put his on, but then he said: "Come here."

She turned back to him and he took her in his arms and kissed her. "I really am sorry for everything you're going through. I'm sure your aunt will come around. Your grades are outstanding and you have no disciplinary issues at school. Wait until she's over the shock, and promise her that you'll wear something less revealing when you next perform. Jeans, maybe."

Juliet met his gaze. "Would you prefer me to wear jeans?"

There was heat in his eyes. "When I think about you in front of all those guys, yes. But when I see you there performing, absolutely not. It's the right costume for what you do." He dropped his voice. "Besides, you look amazing in it."

Feeling happy for the first time since the row with her aunt, Juliet flung her arms around him and kissed him again. It took all of Carl's willpower to actually get them both in the car and drive her home.

* * *

When Carl arrived back home there was a phone message.

"It's Dan. I'm at the hospital. Jenny's in labour, but so far everything's fine. We'll have to take a raincheck on lunch tomorrow."

Carl frowned. Surely it was two weeks early? He hoped Jenny was okay.

Even more so, he hoped that Juliet was alright. He couldn't imagine her aunt would actually throw her out, it wasn't as though Juliet was taking drugs and playing truant from school. But if she did end up homeless it was going to be tough for her.

Hopefully one of her friends would be able to give her a home until graduation. Carl knew that many girls at St Gillian's came from wealthy families: both Cynthia's and Margot's parents had been mentioned as benefactors of the school. So they must have huge houses and the means to be charitable.

And if not… ultimately he cared more about Juliet than his job. He would give her a place to stay if no one else would.

If he was fired over it, he would take the consequences. Her wellbeing was paramount.

XXIV. Getting hotter

On Monday night Dan dropped round to Carl's.

"Just on my way home from the hospital, it's all good. Jenny should be coming home tomorrow around lunchtime."

"How are they?" Carl asked.

"Both doing beautifully. Jenny says she's got my ears and chin but I can't tell with these things."

"Poor baby," Carl joked. "She's alright then? I was concerned, given the early arrival."

Dan, cracking open a can of Coke, looked somewhat shamefaced. "About that."

"About what?"

"The premie thing. She's not premature at all, bang on time in fact. Even a couple of days late."

Carl was confused. "But how?" There had been a big deal made at church of the baby being a "honeymoon baby", along with some kindly meant jokes, but it was only eight months since Dan's and Jenny's wedding.

"Let's just say there were more than two of us walking up that aisle. In fairness we didn't know at that point, so it wasn't a shotgun wedding or anything."

Knowing Dan and Jenny, Carl wasn't as shocked as he might have been. Dan had dropped hints previously that he and Jenny hadn't maintained perfect celibacy until their wedding day. But this was the first proof that Carl had of this, let alone that they had conceived their first child before marriage.

The most important thing was that mother and child were healthy and well. Privately, Carl thought that Dan was going to have a job concealing the true dates from Agnes and some of the other old ladies and church. He'd heard snatches of their conversation before: they'd seen enough babies over the years to know what was what.

But they were generally kind women, and Jenny was well liked, so Carl hoped tact would prevail.

He changed the subject. "You're off work for a while then?"

"Two weeks. Jenny's mother flies over then, and she'll help out. What about you? How's your little blonde temptress?"

Carl wasn't certain he liked Juliet being referred to in those terms, for a host of reasons. "She's hardly little." The term carried implications he didn't like. After all Juliet wasn't a child, and she was reasonably tall. Taller than Jenny, and Dan would never refer to his wife as "little".

"You know what I mean. You're absolutely hooked on her, aren't you?" Dan said with a grin.

"She's my student."

"Yes, of course." Dan made a pretence of being serious. "Until June, and then she's not."

"That's beside the point. She'll be going off to college, starting her life. The timing is all wrong, regardless."

Dan scrutinised his friend. "And if the timing wasn't wrong?"

"What do you want me to say? What do you think?"

"That if I was in your shoes, I'd have far fewer inhibitions," Dan said.

Carl hadn't wanted an answer, his question had been rhetorical, but now he had one.

"Jenny likes her too," Dan added. "Of course she has the advantage of being ABR."

"ABR?"

"Anyone But Rebecca. Jenny's term, not mine, and I shouldn't have repeated it. But at least you know where we stand on it all."

* * *

There was an uneasy ceasefire between Juliet and Aunt Mary. Nothing more had been mentioned about the band, though Juliet knew her aunt expected her to give it up.

170

The newspaper review had gone around St Gillian's like wildfire, impressing some people and causing others like Cynthia to be more spiteful than ever.

Juliet could tell that Cynthia was jealous and it wouldn't have bothered her, but Cynthia was relentlessly in her face about it.

"It's the singing foster slut. Which of the band members are you banging? All of them, I shouldn't wonder."

Margot and Fhemie did what they could to defend Juliet but it was an uphill task. Cynthia was very clever at getting other people into trouble for retaliating when she bullied them.

None of the teachers made mention of Juliet's band except Miss Mead. She made a remark about it being "rather disappointing to use God's gifts for such an unholy purpose" and didn't give Juliet any more solos. This would have been okay but instead the verses went to Cynthia, which stung.

Cynthia unwisely tried to ridicule Juliet in Latin. Her own crush on Mr Spencer still hadn't entirely abated, and from time to time she would make last gasp attempts to win his approval of her and his condemnation of Juliet. Little did she know that she only made herself look a thousand times worse in his eyes.

In the end the Latin teacher lost his patience. When Cynthia muttered yet another snide remark to her friend, looking sidelong at Juliet, he ordered her out of the room.

"Get out. When you can finally stop talking in class given all the occasions I've asked you to do so, you can return."

Cynthia's mouth fell open and several girls gasped in shock. Cynthia never got taken to task by any of the teachers, no matter how malevolent she was.

"You can't send me out. I need to be in this class," she protested.

"If you needed to be here, you would have been paying attention," he told her. "Now leave."

Furious, Cynthia gathered up her things. As she left she shot a vicious glance at Juliet and Margot and hissed at them. "You'll pay for this."

The mood in the classroom was very much on edge after Cynthia departed. Everyone was shocked by Mr Spencer refusing to overlook her behaviour. People were dying to discuss it.

It was hard for anyone to concentrate on Latin verse. Mr Spencer had won a new level of admiration for standing up to Cynthia but there was also concern for him.

He nodded and smiled to Juliet as she filed out with Margot. His eyes told what he couldn't say. That he was worried about her and that he was sorry for what Cynthia was putting her through.

"Get a room," Margot muttered, seeing their gaze, and Juliet shoved her in the back to hurry her out of the room before Mr Spencer could react.

"He nearly heard!" Juliet said.

"He must know I know. Anyway, that's the least of his worries. I shouldn't be surprised if Cynthia tries to get him fired," Margot said.

Juliet was worried. "What do you mean?"

"Get her daddy to threaten to withdraw his donation towards the new sports hall."

"Surely she wouldn't try something like that?"

Margot shrugged. "She's enough of a spoilt little bitch to try anything. She now knows unequivocally that Mr Spencer can't stand her, which is humiliating because she was crushing on him before. God forbid she ever finds out about you and him, because your life won't be worth living."

A cold fear crept up Juliet's spine. "But she wouldn't, would she? I mean there's nothing actually happening. Officially we're just friends."

"Yeah right, girl. You'd just better hope she doesn't get an urge to convert to Baptism."

* * *

Shooting the video was far more exhausting than Juliet had imagined. She had thought it would be a relatively simple affair, but it took hours with endless takes.

Drew's videographer friend was very meticulous and insisted on the light and angle being perfect in each shot. Some of the guys started grumbling but he wouldn't relent.

"You're not going to use every shot, are you? Surely you've got enough of us miming?"

Juliet tried to be as cooperative as possible and not complain. She was also on edge because of the issue with Aunt Mary. Doing this video was in direct defiance of her.

The one who impressed everyone was Fhemie. She danced and danced and danced, never seemingly getting tired. Juliet couldn't tell if it was fitness, stamina or sheer determination.

She was glad they had decided to use Fhemie. It took a lot of the pressure off her and also enabled her to wear more regular clothes: jeans and a tight top. Which was freezing since it was a cold day, but she wore her warmest jacket between takes and Drew regularly fetched coffee for her.

"Can you dance in double time?" the videographer asked Fhemie. "I can use a technique to slow it back to normal speed, then it will look like the world around you is all smooth and slow."

Fhemie looked him directly in the eye. "There's nothing I can't do," she said.

The band might have snickered at her supreme confidence at the start of the day, but as time wore on they could see that it wasn't a boast. It was simply Fhemie.

Juliet saw that Jax's eyes were lingering on her friend more than he probably intended them to be. Or at least more than he intended anyone to notice.

The song they were filming was called "Write you out". It was about someone writing their ex out of their life after he falls for someone else. Juliet, as the singer, was obviously the rejected party, Drew was playing her ex boyfriend, and Fhemie was the girl who had lured him away.

"I don't get this song," Fhemie said when they took a break. "Why doesn't she just move on? All this stuff about writing him out of her history. If a guy cheated on me, I would have forgotten him already. I wouldn't sing about it." She cast a glance at Jax. "I like the music though."

Juliet, who had written most of the lyrics with Drew, tried to explain. "It's from this thing we learnt about in Latin. *Damnatio memoriae*. If someone was a traitor, they wrote them out of history and destroyed their statues."

"I should have guessed Mr Spencer would come into it somewhere," Fhemie said.

Drew was curious. "Mr Spencer?"

"Our school Latin teacher. Juliet's boyfriend."

None of the band knew about Juliet's complicated private life and it raised a lot of eyebrows. "You're dating your teacher?" Drew asked.

"We're just friends." Juliet hoped the redness she felt in her face wouldn't give her away. Thank goodness for thick make up. She kicked Fhemie who grinned evilly.

The videographer called them back for another take. Juliet had to mask a wave of fatigue that overtook her. It wasn't just the exertions of the shoot. The ongoing stress with Aunt Mary was wearing her out. She just wished it could be resolved.

* * *

Juliet nearly dozed off during the service at Carl's church the following evening. She had slept badly, tired from the video and worried about further conflict with her aunt.

He was anxious about her. "Should I drive you straight home? You look like you could do with some sleep."

"I told Aunt Mary I would be out for dinner, so she's not expecting me," Juliet said.

"We won't hang around here then, we'll go straight back to mine."

There was another motive for this and that was avoiding Rebecca. She seemed to make a beeline for Carl every time now. She would try to cut Juliet out of the conversation or slight her in a way that was just too subtle for someone to actually pull her up on it. It was worse now Jenny was away with the baby because she had acted like a kind of shield before.

Despite wanting to leave immediately they got waylaid by Pastor Brown who wanted to talk to Carl about some youth event the church was holding.

Dan, who wasn't involved, chatted to Juliet. He had started coming back to the evening service as his mother-in-law was now helping with the baby.

"You should pay Jen a visit, she'd love to see you," he told Juliet. "The baby's fine for visitors."

174

Juliet was surprised by the invitation as Dan and Jenny were Carl's friends, not hers. She didn't feel that she knew them very well though she liked them both.

"I'd be happy to visit," she said to Dan.

"Great. Carl can give you our address. Only if you have time, I imagine your schedule's pretty tight with all your band stuff. You'll also have to let me know when your next gig is."

Juliet promised to do so, and as Carl was finally finished with his discussions with the pastor, the two of them farewelled Dan and left for Carl's place.

* * *

Juliet told Carl about the invitation as they drove to his home. "Do you think he meant us both to come?" she asked.

Carl, knowing Jenny, doubted this. "I think she's interested in getting to know you better," he said. He imagined his ears would probably be burning if Juliet did go round there, but Jenny at least meant well.

Juliet felt happy to be at Carl's. She felt increasingly relaxed there despite the unresolved tension between them. How he managed to be so self-disciplined she had no idea.

"What would you like to eat?" he asked her.

"I'm actually not that hungry." She had other plans.

They stood there, gazing at one another, an invisible thread between them, drawing them together.

"I've missed you," he told her.

"You see me at school everyday."

"It's not the same. You know what I mean." He cupped her face in hands and tilted it so he could kiss her.

Her stomach flipped and she was dizzy, drowning in him.

Juliet broke off and looked up at Carl. His eyes were hazy with desire. "There's nothing stopping us, if you want to," she said.

She knew full well he wanted to.

She reached up and kissed him again, drawing him down to her. Feeling his tongue push with more force into her mouth. Then he was pushing her onto the couch, shifting her underneath him so he could lie above her and keep kissing her, moving from her lips down to the sensitive hollows at the base of her neck.

His hands were on her shoulders, staying there. Juliet took his right hand and moved it down over her breast. Above her clothes, but it was still the most intimately he had touched her.

Carl froze for a moment and she panicked she had gone too far. Then his fingers moulded around the curve, his thumb gently pressing and squeezing the soft roundness into his hand. His thumb brushed across and she let out a small cry, pressing her hips up against him. Even through the layers of clothing her nipple peaked and tightened at the feel of him.

Carl could barely think straight, he was so turned on. To have his hand on her breast, her warm body beneath him: no matter how he shifted he couldn't prevent his hardness from pressing into her thigh. He was too distracted to even try praying.

Juliet squirmed, to try and centre him against her. She wrapped her legs around him, trying to get the pressure of him where she needed it. She started rocking against him and he ended up matching her rhythm. She moved her hands down his back, revelling in the feel of his lean muscles, and put her hands on his butt, trying to draw him against her more tightly.

She could only imagine how much better it would be to be naked with him, skin on skin, with him deep inside her instead of this through-clothing frustration. If only he would move his hand lower, slip it below her waistband, let his fingers curl around...

"I need you," she whispered.

Carl groaned. "I can't do this, I'll lose it," he warned her.

"Couldn't we just lie naked together? Not actually do it, but be closer to each other?" she begged.

They both knew that removing the barrier of clothing would result in only one thing. Neither of them had the physical capacity to hold back, despite Carl's earnest intentions to keep things under control.

He screwed his hips into her, as hard as he could. "I have never wanted anyone as badly as I want you right now," he told her. His breathing was ragged and his brow was damp. "But you know we can't go further."

Juliet slid her hand between them, trying to feel for him. That brought him up with a sharp movement. "Don't! I will literally explode if you do that," he said.

Somehow Carl managed to gather enough resolve to get a grip of himself, and he slowed down and moved away from her. He saw the disappointment and unsated desire in her face: it was no less than his.

"I'm sorry." He really was. He felt like he was leading her on through his poor self-control. After all, he was the adult. She was his student and it was his responsibility to prevent them from going too far.

And he felt bad because he had failed to pray to stop things, and even now, he didn't feel like he even wanted to pray. He almost envied Dan and Jenny their more relaxed approach. Though in fairness they had at least been officially betrothed.

That wasn't even a possibility with Juliet. She was nearly a decade younger than him, still not out of school. In a few months time she would doubtless move on to college and it would be worse and harder for both of them if their relationship became too intense.

He was ready for the next step: she surely wasn't. And nothing could be done about it.

XXV. Seeking advice

"Would you like to hold her?"

Carefully, Jenny handed the precious swaddled bundle over to Juliet, who held the baby girl as though she were fragile china.

"Don't worry, she won't break," Jenny told her. "She's a tough little thing."

Juliet studied Sara Grace's sleeping face. She was so perfect. It was hard to imagine how just a couple of weeks before she hadn't even been outside the warmth of a human body.

Jenny was tired but was otherwise doing very well. "It's hard to know with a first, but I think she's pretty easy," she told Juliet. "She's feeding well and gaining the right amount of weight. My mom is staying with us so I don't even have to worry about housework. Or baking," she added, taking another one of the homemade cookies that Juliet had brought her. Her mother had gone shopping that afternoon and Dan was still at work so it was just Juliet and Jenny there.

"She's adorable. You're so lucky." Looking at the tiny being, long eyelashes resting on a plump pink cheek, Juliet thought of what it might have been like when her own mother held her for the first time, and felt a pang.

She'd never have the same kind of support that Jenny enjoyed if and when she had a child. She wondered how her mother had felt the first time she had held Juliet as a newborn. They weren't things she would ever be able to ask. "You know I'd give anything to have what you have," she confessed.

Jenny gave a chuckle. "There are plenty of days when I'd quite happily gift wrap Dan and send him to you."

"I didn't mean Dan," Juliet said, then quickly added, "not that he isn't really great. I just mean having your own family." Not being alone, she thought, but didn't say it. "Having children, being with all the people you love. It's something I want more than anything."

Jenny raised her eyebrows. "At your age all I wanted to do was party. The thought of getting stuck and home with kids was the last thing on my mind."

"Really?" Juliet was surprised.

"I haven't always been the good little housewife. Not that I'm even that now, as Dan will tell you any time you like. At your age I was the wildest member of Phi Beta Kappa, partying every night and making my parents and professors despair. Goodness only knows how I didn't get thrown out," Jenny said.

"I never imagined you like that."

Smiling, Jenny recalled the past. "I nearly burnt the sorority house down once. The singe marks are still there as a memorial to my wild ways. And now - " she looked at her daughter, her face softening, " - here I am with a husband, a home, a job and a baby, living in the suburbs. So much for my plans to be a hotshot Carrie Bradshaw type in New York. No 'Sex and the City' for me."

It didn't look as though this bothered Jenny. "But you're happy with the way it all turned out?" Juliet asked.

"Ecstatic. I mean what you want at twenty changes a lot when you're nearly thirty. Imagine spending every night at a frat party now, with drunken college boys throwing up on my shoes." She shuddered. "I'd be the oldest person there. That's not to say it wasn't fun at the time, but I've got it out of my system. But you should do all that stuff, live wildly while you can."

Juliet was silent, looking at the baby. Then she spoke. "I've sort of been there, done that. Much of it, anyway."

Jenny looked intrigued. "What do you mean?"

"I don't know if you know, if Carl said anything, but I was in and out of foster care when I was younger. I went a bit wild: drinking, boys, sneaking out all the time. When the only thing waiting for you at home is someone who spends most of their time shouting at you or hitting you, you tend to avoid being there as much as possible." Juliet closed her eyes, remembering the painful times.

"There were a few of us who hung out together, on the street, at older guys' houses. There were cigarettes, alcohol, other stuff. I was a total mess when my aunt finally tracked me down. Then it was really hard to follow her rules, though the last couple of years have been easier. We got used to one another," she said.

Jenny's eyed held sympathy. "I can see why you wouldn't be into the idea of drunken college parties. With me it was different, I'd led a very sheltered, small town life so I wanted to rebel."

Juliet was looking anxious. She toyed with the fringe of the shawl that Sara was wrapped in. "Carl knows some of it." She had managed to tell him about juvenile detention, though he'd heard it from Cynthia first of course. "I told him about some things. But he doesn't know about all the drinking and everything. And we did some other stuff." Her eyes held anguish as she looked at Jenny. "Do you think he would think very badly of me?"

Jenny felt her heart well up for the girl holding her baby. "Of course not, you were only a kid! And even if it had happened later on, he wouldn't judge you." Seeing that Juliet wasn't convinced, she tried to explain. "If Jesus were here today, as a young person, whom do you think he'd be hanging out with? Me and my hometown friends, living in our comfortable homes and going to school each day and attending church youth group?"

Juliet could see this childhood in her mind, like a movie. It was all pink and pastel and sunny.

Jenny continued. "Or would he hang out on the streets, with homeless kids, troubled kids, kids doing drugs? Kids who didn't have any of what I was lucky enough to have, what I took for granted. Because I think I know what he'd do. And Carl - not that I'm trying to say that Carl's Jesus, though there are times even I find myself wondering - he would be just the same. There's no way he would ever reject someone for having a difficult past. None of us would. Even if you were going through all this now and worse, we'd be there for you, Juliet."

Juliet had tears running down her face. One fell onto the sleeping Sara, which made Juliet cry even more. "I'm so sorry, I've got your baby wet."

Jenny laughed and smiled kindly. "I don't think a few tears will hurt her." She put her arm around Juliet. "Carl really likes you, you know. I know you're younger than him but you've been really good for him. He's held back because he's your teacher and because of all the other issues he has with doing things correctly. But don't give up. And never think for a moment that anything in your past would count against you in his eyes."

* * *

Carl brought takeout around to Dan and Jenny later that week. Jenny's mother had gone to the movies with another neighbour.

"You'll be godparent to this little one then?" Dan asked him. They'd discussed it previously and Carl had readily agreed, touched to have been asked.

Now, actually looking at the small human whose spiritual wellbeing he would be committing to, it seemed a more solemn task than he had previously contemplated.

"Of course she'll need a godmother too," Jenny said, casting a sidelong glance at Carl as she fed Sara Grace.

"You've asked my sister, haven't you?" Dan said.

"I have. But she lives far away, and it's nice to have more than one," Jenny told him.

Carl wasn't sure how he could help. Presumably if he had still been engaged to Rebecca they would have asked her. There was a knowing look in Jenny's eye that unsettled him.

The baby finished feeding and Jenny patted her gently on the back before handing her to Dan. "Your turn. She always needs changing right afterwards," she told Carl.

"I'll bathe her too then, given it's time for her bedtime," Dan offered.

This left Jenny and Carl alone in the sitting room.

"Your friend Juliet brought some delicious cookies around the other day," she said. "She's a very nice girl."

Jenny had orchestrated this conversation, Carl realised. She had something to say to him. He wasn't sure if he was going to like it. He suspected he was going to get a lecture about Juliet's age and his responsibilities as her teacher.

"She is, yes," he said.

"You two clearly adore one another," Jenny continued.

Carl tried to pre-empt her. "I know it's inappropriate, I've been wrestling with it. I agree she's far too young and she'll be off to college soon. I thought that church would help us both keep it platonic."

Jenny grinned, her eyes glinting. "You have no idea what I was going to say, do you?"

"I couldn't blame you for disapproving. It's completely unprofessional for me to have seen a student outside school." Let alone to have invited her back to his place, to have kissed her, to have been on the verge of going so much further, he thought.

"Carl, Juliet is eighteen. She's a young woman not a child. Legally an adult. Except for the school thing which will be over in a matter of months, there's no issue with you two seeing one another."

Carl was shocked, having expected Jenny to give him a stern telling off.

"It wouldn't be fair to hold her back. She'll be off to college, you know what that's like." You of all people, he thought, having heard more than a few anecdotes about Jenny's wild college days. "She has enough restrictions in her life now. She'll want to be free, not tied down."

"Have you actually asked her what she wants?"

"We've talked, yes. More or less," he said.

"If you had a proper conversation with her, you might get a more accurate idea. She told me about some of her past, which was truly awful, poor girl. It sounded to me like the last thing she wants to do after high school is to go crazy and date half of Harvard," Jenny told him. "The complete opposite of my plans at her age, but then my upbringing - just like yours - was pretty much the opposite of hers as well."

Carl was silent, digesting this.

"After all, there are loads of people who end up marrying their high school sweethearts. I can't see that it makes a huge difference if one of them was the football captain or the sports coach, can you?" Jenny continued.

Carl could see an enormous difference, particularly thinking of the sports coach at his own school. A paunchy, middle aged married man who had creeped on female students. He sincerely hoped he was nothing like that. He had spent enough time fending off the flirtations and crushes of the St Gillian's girls.

Except for Juliet, of course.

But marriage? It was the furthest thing from his mind, particularly after the near-disaster with Rebecca. Now Jenny had put it in his mind he had a flash vision of Juliet standing next to him in church, in bridal white. He tried to push it from his mind but it was stuck there now.

As if the image of her performing in the scanty schoolgirl outfit wasn't enough to haunt his dreams, he was starting to imagine her in bridal lingerie, lying on a bed, wanting him.

"Think about what I've said, anyway," Jenny told him. "I'd like to see you happy. Both of you."

* * *

Carl was determined not to be selfish. Juliet was his student, she was vulnerable, she'd suffered years of neglect and abuse. Whatever he wanted for himself had to take second place to what was best for her.

He had assumed that they would be saying goodbye at the end of the school year, and even if it wasn't for his faith, this was a reason to hold off from getting too serious.

But the fact was he felt seriously about her. It was going to be incredibly hard to let her go: to walk away when she went to college.

Now Jenny had stirred up ideas in his head that he wasn't sure were helpful. He wasn't even sure how to pray about it, because it felt wrong to pray for something that he wasn't sure was right.

But how could he pray to give her up?

Once again stricken with doubt and confusion, he found himself inside a Catholic church. The incense and dust and dark wood took him back to the previous occasions. It might not be the same priest this time, but it was the same God.

"I came here some months ago, Father."

"I remember you, my son." It was the same man as before. Carl wondered how on earth he could remember him from that one time. "What is it you seek?"

Answers. Guidance. Someone to judge whether what he wanted to do was right or wrong. Fair or selfish.

"How do you know if something is right? If you pray and no answer comes?" Carl wondered why he was able to ask a near stranger this, and not his own pastor.

He could hear a warm amusement in the priest's voice. "Have you been listening for one?"

Had he? Somehow he had expected there to be a voice in his head. Or some text that resonated with him from his bible.

The priest continued. "You ask me for guidance, but have you asked others? The Lord does not only speak through one voice."

"You mean I should ask my own pastor?"

"Your pastor, your friends and family. The answer to what is right rarely impacts just one person. Just as those around you are affected by your choice, they may also have answers for you."

Jenny. He had been trying to reject what she said to him, feeling it was wrong to even think alone the lines she had led him. Now he wondered. Dan too, the conversation that Carl had dismissed some days previously. He also thought of Agnes and her knowing glances.

Were these his answers?

Carl felt a faint flicker of hope in his heart but quickly suppressed it.

Carl, Jenny, Agnes, Pastor Brown, the Priest, Rebecca. Every one of them had given him some kind of response even if he hadn't sought it. But there was a glaring gap in this list.

Perhaps the problem was not the question, but the fact he hadn't yet asked it of the right person.

XXVI. In the bedroom

It had to be perfect. She had to prove she could do this.

Normally Juliet wasn't nervous about her cooking skills. But making a meal for Carl for the first time seemed like a huge deal. He had cooked for her several times and she wanted to reciprocate, though it had to be at his place as she could hardly bring him back to Aunt Mary's.

On Margot's advice Juliet had decided to cook steak. Carl offered to get the ingredients for her but Juliet insisted on providing everything and managing it all.

Steak. Café de Paris butter. Baked sweet potato fries. Salad. Chocolate mousse.

Juliet was trying to include as many French elements as she could as a reminder of the Paris trip. Their first proper kiss.

Despite her nerves and the unfamiliarity of Carl's kitchen, she managed not to burn or overcook anything. She had always had a knack for cooking. It was the reverse of her knitting ability, to Aunt Mary's great disappointment.

"You may as be knitting with your feet," she had remarked in the early days of Juliet coming to live with her. Two straggly, unravelling, mismatched squares for a scarf later and they were both relieved when Aunt Mary gave up the lessons.

But cooking, that was different.

Carl watched Juliet as he passed the kitchen on his way to the living room. It felt like his house was full of light and warmth having her there, even though it was a dark and rainy evening.

Not once had Rebecca ever done this, he thought. He had always been the one cooking for them both at his house.

They'd eaten at her place, of course, many times. But he'd more often than not been the one fixing the food while she caught up with overdue work. On the occasions Rebecca cooked it tended to be takeout or something frozen and heated up.

Carl wasn't looking for a domestic goddess in a wife. He simply wanted a partnership. He figured that if they both worked, they could always afford domestic help if they needed to.

"Do you need any help?" he asked her.

"It's all fine, but thank you."

Carl insisted on setting the table as he didn't want Juliet having to do everything. It was a good strategy having something to do. When they just sat and tried to watch TV they could never keep their hands off one another. An activity gave the evening structure and kept them both too busy to fall into temptation.

Finally the meal was ready and they sat down. Carl was hungry by that point and the food smelt delicious.

Juliet was watching him anxiously as he ate his first mouthful. "Is it okay?" she asked, before he had even finished chewing.

He reassured her. "It's amazing. From now on you're cooking all the steaks, as I always burn them."

From now on… Juliet knew it was just a thing to say, just politeness, but she so wished it could be true. That she would always be able to do this, indefinitely.

"I haven't made this sauce before," Juliet said. "Aunt Mary sticks mainly to chicken with fish on Fridays. She doesn't really like much more than salt and pepper as flavourings."

"She's missing out," Carl said.

"I know it's not as good as if we went out to a restaurant," Juliet said. "They have different abilities with a commercial kitchen. And years of training."

Carl finished another bite of perfectly medium rare sirloin, exactly how he liked it. "This is as good as any restaurant. Besides, a Middle Eastern friend once told me that they consider home cooked food to be better, because it's *mubarak*. Blessed," he translated.

Juliet hadn't prayed over the ingredients so she wasn't sure if that was the case with her cooking.

"Did you work things out with your aunt over the band?" Carl asked her.

Juliet shook her head. "I'm still not sure what to do. I love being part of it, but she's serious about kicking me out. I hoped she would eventually come around or forget about it but she's not going to. And I can't hide it forever."

"I guess not." He was concerned for her and wished there was an obvious solution.

"Even if I could keep hiding it the problem is more than that. I don't expect her to approve, but I wish she didn't disapprove so much. She's actually upset and I feel bad about that. At the same time I can't - " Juliet struggled for the right words " - respect her upset because it's not rational. I don't think it harms my mortal soul to sing in a band, or whatever she fears, nor does it disgrace me in anyway. At least that's how I feel."

Carl remembered Juliet on stage: the passion with which she sang, her beautiful voice, the talent of the other musicians. The response of the audience who clearly viewed the band with respect.

"It doesn't disgrace you at all," he said. "Quite the opposite. Remember that your aunt has never actually seen you perform, she's only read the newspaper article. If she saw you she might have a different opinion."

The article. The rest of Dover Six had been so hyped by it, even Jax though he tried not to show it. It had been perfect timing with the music industry guy coming to see them. It might only be a local publication but at least it showed they could get good press.

Juliet hadn't dared tell them what trouble it had got her into.

As for Aunt Mary ever seeing her perform, Juliet couldn't imagine how that could ever happen. "I'll just have to risk it for now. If the worst happens Margot has offered me a place to stay. And it's only a few more months until graduation."

At the mention of graduation Juliet looked at Carl intently. After graduation he could surely have no more excuse for keeping her at arms' length. Though she didn't think she could wait that long.

Afterwards he tried to prevent her from washing up but Juliet insisted on doing it. "You don't want to wake up to a sinkful of dishes." As it turned out he had a dishwasher and they stacked it together. Somehow it seemed right to have her there, with him, sharing this task. Carl felt glad to simply be with her.

Then it was done and they were standing there in the kitchen. In his house. No one to disturb them.

Juliet reached up and put her arms around his neck. Carl found his hands automatically went to her waist: touching her rather than pushing her away was starting to become instinctive.

He could breathe in the warmth of her body and the faint trace of perfume she wore. It gave his body and instant and powerful reaction and he held her away from him.

But she pressed herself against him, gazing at him questioningly. "Could we go to your bedroom? Just for a while?"

There was nothing Carl wanted more. Just for a while… to lie with her and be with her. He was sure he could control himself. Even though a huge part of him no longer really wanted to.

"It's this way."

* * *

It felt almost surreal. After all the months of trying so hard for this, Juliet was now lying down with Carl on his bed, face to face. She had no idea where this was going and for the first time she felt unaccountably nervous.

He slipped his hand underneath her top and cupped it over her bra, his gaze never leaving hers. She found herself wondering whether he had even done this before, or certainly not routinely, the way he did it was so like exploring. As though he were testing himself.

Then his lips were on hers and it was an amazing feeling. Warm, sensuous, but with a firmness that suggested he was in charge of the situation. Juliet felt her stomach flip.

His other hand stroked down her back, over the curve of her waist and around her rear, and as he was drawing himself closer to her, body to body, she suddenly froze.

He broke away instantly. "What's wrong?"

How could she tell him? "You know about me not being a virgin…"

188

He interrupted her. "Juliet, it's fine. Your past is your past. I like you for who you are, it makes no difference."

"No, it's not that." This was so difficult. Not even her best friends knew about this. She was really struggling to find the words. Would he be disgusted? Freak out? Reject her?

She plucked up her courage. Tried not to get the usual flashbacks that distressed her whenever she thought of it.

"It's that when I lost it... it wasn't by choice."

"What do you mean?" Carl looked puzzled.

"The last foster home I was in." She couldn't even speak it fully. "Before they sent me back to the children's home. The foster father..."

Juliet didn't need to continue, the truth was written in the pain in her eyes.

She saw shock and anger in Carl's eyes. But it was anger for her, on her behalf, not at her.

"I take it he's in jail now."

"No." She buried her face in his chest and couldn't stop the tears. "I told the foster mother - his wife - what happened, and she didn't believe me. She said I was a whore, and whores like me deserved everything they got. Then they sent me away, and told the social workers that I was a promiscuous liar who was putting their own kids at risk. No one believed me."

He was holding her, stroking her hair.

"So I'm ruined," she said. "And if you think I'm a slut, then I guess she was right."

He raised her head to his, and now he looked really angry. But his voice was kind.

"You're not a slut, Juliet, or a whore. And you are still a virgin, regardless."

"How can I be?"

"You've never willingly chosen to have sex. That's what being a virgin is."

If it wasn't for the trauma, for the nightmares she still occasionally had, she might well have voluntarily had sex. After all, Margot and Fhemie frequently slept with the guys they dated.

"I nearly did, a few times. But when it came close, I couldn't go through with it. I kept seeing him..."

"It's alright." Carl had his arms around her, tightly. She was safe.

Then somehow although Juliet had been crying just moments ago they were kissing. Passionately. He was the one person in the world who seemed to blot it all out. She needed him like a thirst. His kindness. His warmth. The way being with him made everything feel better.

His lips were on hers, hers on his, they were tasting each other, drinking one another in. Hot and wet and soft and sensual. She was opening for him, his tongue entwining with hers.

Now she broke off. "I want you." She looked at him directly in the eyes and he knew what she meant. "I want you, to make a new memory."

He looked back at her, his eyes serious. She could tell that under any other circumstances he would have refused. But he saw that she needed him, that she had a need that went deeper than rules or morals or commandments, beyond the teachings of his religion.

"If you're sure?"

She was.

He lifted off her top so she was just in her bra. Traced her stomach just at the waist of her jeans, making her shiver.

"This should feel like sin," he said. "But it feels like love." He was looking at her body almost in wonderment.

Juliet was startled by what he said. Her eyes held the question she couldn't speak.

"Yes, I love you," he said. "I didn't expect to, or even want to. It certainly wasn't in my plan for my life to fall in love with someone so much younger than me, someone in my care as a student. But sometimes there are other plans for us."

He didn't mention God, but Juliet knew that was what he meant.

"Do you want me?"

He gave a laugh that was half sad. "Yes, I want you. I've wanted you for ages, but we're taught to fight temptation. This, though, is something different. It feels right."

"Even after what I told you?" she asked.

"Because of that. Because I want you to understand that you can be loved, and whatever happened to you wasn't your fault and doesn't define you," Carl said.

He loosened the front of her jeans and his hand slipped down. She bit her lip at the feeling of his fingers slipping between her wetness.

"I haven't done this before either," he said. "So we're both going to learn together."

He was still in command of the situation. Still her teacher.

"Are you sure? You won't regret this?" Juliet asked. He was moving his fingers around her, exploring, and practically making her whimper.

"Afterwards I'm probably going to want to marry you - " he paused, seeing the shock flare up in her eyes and feeling her body tense, "- but there's no rush. I know how young you are. If things happen later on then they happen, I'm just telling you honestly how I feel. And doing this with you is only going to cement that."

Slipping off her clothes he allowed his hands to move over her body. As he traced the curves that seemed almost sculpted to fit his grasp, he found himself wondering about the first union of man and woman. Carl didn't take all Bible stories as fundamentally literally as some others of his faith did.

But as he ran his hands over her stomach, her thighs, past the hollow of her waist, over her breasts, marvelling in the beauty of her and the way it felt so natural to touch her, her wondered. His hands seem to know where to move and how to caress her even though this was new to him.

Bone of my bones, and flesh of my flesh: she shall be called Woman, because she was taken out of Man.

Was this how Adam felt, with the help meet created from his own rib?

Juliet's responsiveness also amazed him. Rebecca had rejected any advances throughout their courtship, and the women of his church generally seemed to find it easy to guard their virtue. So it was a surprise to Carl to find that Juliet seemed to want him as much as he wanted her.

The flush of her skin, her shallow breathing, and as he slipped his hand in the most forbidden places the softness and the warm wetness of her.

Juliet looked up at him. Despite her supposed experience he could see a trace of apprehension in her face, but also trust. She was entrusting herself to him, putting her self in his hands.

How could something this elevating be a sin? It was far more than raw lust, which Carl had always been taught was the root of extra-marital activity.

Rather it was a sense of reverence, of wanting to honour her body. To worship her.

Carl felt a pang of guilt at what must surely be a blasphemous emotion. But after all, wasn't that one of the vows that man made to woman? *With my body I thee worship.*

For the first time he understood it: how the sacrament of marriage mirrored the love of Christ for his bride, the Church.

There were other thoughts he had, questions he had that he didn't want to dwell on right now.

Instead he let Juliet's beauty, her warmth, her sensuality block them out. If he had to atone for his later then he would do so. But for now, in this moment, nothing had ever felt quite so sacred.

He knew what lust was, he was a man of flesh and blood after all, not made of stone, but this was so much more than that. His whole being was infused by wanting to explore her, discover her, taste her, know her.

Even as he felt himself ready for her, to take the next step, he held back.

He wanted more.

He wanted to take her for the first time in his marriage bed.

It wasn't even about religion or righteousness, but simply wanting it to be the very ultimate that it could be.

XXVII. Holding out

"What's wrong?" Juliet sensed him withdraw.

"I want us to wait."

"Really?" She was incredulous. Her whole body was on fire with wanting him, her nerves stimulated and inflamed by his caresses, and now he was stopping?

Carl moved back from above her, lying down alongside her.

Juliet became insecure. "Is it me? Is there something wrong?" Had she repulsed him in some way?

"No, of course not. It's the opposite," he said, his arms around her. He was willing his nearly painful hardness to subside. "It's because you're so perfect that I want us to be perfect."

"What do you mean?"

He was face to face with her. "I want us to be married."

Juliet had thought he was kidding before. But his gaze was completely sincere. It made her stomach do strange things.

"You want to marry me? Seriously? Why?"

"Because I love you, like I have never loved anyone. Because this is it for me. Because I want to spend the rest of my life with you."

She was silent. "Really?"

He saw that she didn't believe hm. But he sensed that she wanted to. "Wait a second." He left the bed and opened a drawer. Brought out a small box. It was vintage looking, covered in gold embossed leather.

Carl knelt down on the floor next to the bed. "Juliet Martin, will you do me the honour of one day becoming my wife?"

"One day?" Juliet was so taken aback by everything that she could hardly speak the words.

"If and when you're ready." He handed her the box and she opened it. Inside, its gemstones dazzling like white fire, was a beautiful antique ring.

Juliet drew in her breath. Now she couldn't speak as she was so overcome.

Carl was anxious, thinking she didn't like it. "It was my grandmother's. We can choose something new for you, this can be just for now. No one has ever worn it before. Rebecca made it clear she wanted her own ring, and when I showed it to her she wasn't really interested."

He remembered with some pain now the faint distaste on Rebecca's face at the suggestion of what she called a "second hand" ring. He should have realised then that it was never going to work with her. Their values, despite following the same religion and attending the same church, had been too different.

Carl saw that Juliet was actually crying and was horrified. "What's wrong? I didn't mean to…"

He broke off as she looked up at him through her tears, and she realised she was crying with happiness. Seeing his confusion she tried to explain.

"Being offered this, it's like being asked to be part of someone's family," she told him.

He sat by her on the bed and brushed a lock of hair away from her eyes. "You are part of my family, Juliet. Or I want you to be. I would love us to be a family one day."

She was kissing him now and crying, overwhelmed with everything. Then she gathered herself together and moved apart from him, pushing the box back towards him.

Carl felt a sudden alarm. His eyes met hers, questioningly.

Juliet looked shy. "You're supposed to be the one who puts it on." She held out her left hand.

"Does this mean…?"

"Yes. It's a yes." Totally, absolutely. She smiled at him, radiant now, and he felt both relief and joy. He took the ring from the dark velvet it rested in and slipped it on Juliet's finger. He had assumed it would need resizing but it was a perfect fit.

"It feels a bit of a leap," Juliet confessed to him, playing with the ring on her finger.

194

"A leap?"

"From not being anything to being engaged. It's a lot to get used to."

He was confused. "Not anything?"

"Because we weren't ever officially dating. I wasn't ever your girlfriend, exactly."

Carl put his hands on her shoulders and turned her to face him. "In my heart you've been far more than that for a long time. I love you. I've loved you for ages."

"I love you too." It was the first time Juliet had said it. The first time she had said it to anyone, ever.

His lips met hers in a kiss which, as usual, intensified and headed out of control.

"Now we're engaged, couldn't we…?" Juliet wanted him so badly.

"We could, but wouldn't you rather wait?"

She could see from his eyes that being celibate until after they spoke their wedding vows meant a lot to him. "I can manage to, but it's probably going to have to be you who stops us from crossing the line," she told him.

Carl smiled. "I can take the lead with that. Not that it's gong to be easy, but we've got this far. Even if you want to wait a few years."

Juliet was shocked. "Wait a few years. Why?"

"This isn't something to rush, you haven't even graduated high school yet. I know what I want, but I want you to be really sure. Then there's college and everything."

"You mean you wouldn't want a wife who was still in college?" Juliet asked.

Carl took her hand. "Not at all. But you might prefer to go to college without ties. Spend a couple of years enjoying your freedom, experiencing dorm life. I don't want to limit you. If you decide afterwards that this is still what you want, I'll be here."

The thought of sharing a dorm filled Juliet with horror. She'd been forced to share rooms many times in her life: in foster homes, group homes, juvie. She'd had her belongings trashed and stolen. People waking her up at all hours. And worse… The thing she treasured most about being at Aunt Mary's was the safety and privacy of having her own bedroom.

"I've already decided this is what I want. I can be married and still attend college, can't I? Unless you'd rather wait?"

"If you weren't my student I'd be tempted to call up Pastor Brown now, but I imagine you'd like a proper wedding. Speaking of which, I'm totally happy for us to get married in your church, in a Catholic ceremony. I realise that's probably important to you," he said.

Juliet was silent for a few moments. "Actually I wouldn't."

"You wouldn't?" Carl was surprised, but he didn't press her for a reason. He was even more surprised when she gave him one.

"The thing is, I don't think I'm really Catholic." She could see that she was going to have to try to explain it. "When my aunt first fostered me, she assumed for some reason I would be. And also that I would have been confirmed. So when I found out that if I wasn't, I'd have to go to all these Sunday school classes and learn the catechism, I just let her think that I was. It's probably a mortal sin for me to be taking Communion. I can't let her know now because she'll be furious. And devastated."

From Aunt Mary's perspective Juliet's fake Catholicism would be a worse deception than the band, or even dating her teacher. Being engaged to her teacher, in fact. She found she had to pinch herself to believe it was real.

This strong, handsome, intelligent man was going to be her husband. A man she had already grown to love and adore, and who amazingly loved her back.

Juliet was worried Carl would be shocked about the Catholic thing but instead he was fine with it. "There's no time limit with religion. If you want to take catechism classes it's not too late. You needn't even let your aunt know."

"I don't really want to take them. Also I'm not sure I could even do that because I'm not sure I was even baptised." Her parents, from the little she remembered, hadn't been churchgoers. There had been no godparents coming out of the woodwork to help her when they died. So even if they did exist they may as well not have. She explained all this to Carl.

It was a relief being able to tell someone after all these years. In the early days at St Gillian's she had always had a sense of terror that someone might find her out. Over time she had got to learn the rituals as well as anyone else so no one guessed there was anything wrong.

"You can get baptised in my church if you like. Either way, we can easily get married there," Carl said.

Juliet was silent again. "It's not that I don't want to be part of your church," she said eventually, "but I still haven't figured a lot of this out. It's not that I don't believe but I feel like I need to find my own way through this."

She had been worried her response might disappoint him but there was only love in his eyes. "I understand completely. Leave it with me, I have an idea."

He kissed her and stood up, bringing up her with him. "Let's get you home because I don't want your aunt worrying, and it's already late. If you stay here I'm only going to be lying awake all night on the couch thinking of you in my bed, and I think we could both use a decent night's sleep."

XXVIII. Engaged

Fhemie's face showed bewilderment and a kind of disgust. "You cooked for him, got half naked on his bed, and you ended up with no sex but a ring on your finger? What is this, The Sound of Music?"

Juliet had been nervous about telling her friends about Carl's proposal but hadn't expected this reaction.

"Anyway," Fhemie continued, "we'll be choosing our own bridesmaid dresses. I don't trust you to select something that isn't awful. All brides do."

Juliet hadn't even started thinking about bridesmaids and said so.

"But obviously we will be. I mean who else would you pick? Cynthia? Sister Stephanie tripping up the aisle behind you in a wimple? Anyway, my gift to you will be to coach you for your wedding dance."

"Thank you for the offer, but I have no idea if we'll even be doing that. And I'm sure we'll be just fine."

"You won't. I've seen you dance," Fhemie said. "This husband of yours will seek an annulment before you even consummate. Besides, anyone who doesn't dance as well as me, which is everyone, is painful for me to watch."

She grabbed her bag and stood up. "I have to get to class. You think about what I said."

Juliet laughed and bid her farewell.

Margot had been largely silent since Juliet revealed her news, but when Fhemie had rushed off she turned on Juliet.

"It wasn't supposed to be like this. You were supposed to be the Anne, not the Diana."

Juliet was confused. "Who?"

"You were supposed to be the one going places. The orphan with an amazing future ahead of her. Not the small town girl marrying the small town boy and giving up all her dreams."

There were actually tears in Margot's eyes, which moved Juliet.

"I'm not giving up my dreams. I'll still be going to college and everything. I was never going to be able to go to some Ivy League place, you know that. I don't have the money."

"There are scholarships," Margot pointed out.

"I know, but there are no guarantees I would get one. And what I really want is what you've always had. Not money, but your parents. Your brother. Your sister. A family of my own."

Margot sniffled. "You're welcome to them. They'd adopt you anyway, my mom considers you like a daughter."

Juliet was touched. "You'll always be the nearest I have to a sister. Both you and Fhemie. But even since my parents died, long before I even met you guys, there's this ache. It doesn't go away. But with Carl…"

She found it hard to put what she felt into words. He was the first person who would be truly hers. On her side, part of her team. She would never have to worry again about being on her own, alone, lonely.

"Well, so long as you're happy," Margot said grudgingly.

Juliet was ecstatic. Walking on air. "I am, truly. And if you remember, Anne pretty much gave up her career to marry Gilbert and have a load of children with him. Whereas I totally plan to have a career, I'll just be married as well."

* * *

Carl's grandmother's beautiful stone sparkled on Juliet's finger. She loved that it symbolised other happy marriages and had been worn on the hand of other happy brides.

She couldn't wear it at St Gillian's of course, so she was dying to wear it to Carl's church. It was also the easiest way to let people know they were engaged without making some huge announcement.

Carl had already told Dan and Jenny. Jenny wasn't currently attending the evening service due to the baby. This wouldn't have been a problem except that Rebecca saw it as an opportunity to muscle her way back in.

By some horrible coincidence, Carl saw that Rebecca had decided to wear the engagement ring he had given her. He hadn't asked for it back, considering that it had been a gift to her, and she had never offered to return it.

She had moved the ring to another finger but the implication was clear. She was angling for Carl again. Otherwise why wear it to church?

When Carl and Juliet arrived at church - they travelled there together now, with him picking her up from the end of her road - they met an uncomfortable Dan trying to extricate himself from a conversation with Rebecca.

Rebecca flashed them both a smile that Juliet found very fake. She also made a point of flashing her ring which Juliet guessed instantly was the engagement ring that Carl must have bought her. It was a nice ring, not what Juliet would have chosen as it was very modern and angular, but Carl had clearly been generous.

"How nice to see you, Carl. And you Juliet." Rebecca avoided saying "you both".

Juliet greeted her politely and felt mortified about her own ring. As awful as Rebecca was she didn't want to totally humiliate her or cause a scene in church. Perhaps she could discreetly slip her ring off her finger, and reveal it on a future occasion?

While she wavered over this dilemma, Agnes came up and clasped her hands in greeting. Of course she instantly detected the heirloom ring, large as it was, and brought Juliet's hands up to see.

Agnes opened her mouth and then gave a wide smile. "I think I can guess what that is. It's quite beautiful on you. A wonderful symbol. Congratulations, my dears. I'll confess I'm not surprised, but I am very happy for you both."

She kissed them both and then of course the secret was out.

Juliet never forgot the expression on Rebecca's face.

No one else saw, but Juliet did. Rebecca was stricken: hate and contempt burned in her eyes as she looked briefly at Juliet, then turned her gaze away. From that point on she avoided both Carl and Juliet.

But Juliet knew she had made an enemy. An enemy potentially even more dangerous than Cynthia, as Rebecca had a very personal reason to hate her. She shivered. It seemed as though a shadow had fallen over her world.

* * *

It never rains but it pours. Just as Juliet thought she couldn't be more blessed with good fortune, Drew had news that simultaneously thrilled and devastated her.

"The record company wants to sign us, and they want us to tour this summer in Europe. Mainly festivals."

They wouldn't be a headline act and it would be on the most basic budget ever - no five-star hotels or buckets of champagne - but the exposure would be huge.

Most importantly it was the right kind of exposure, and the right audience, according to Drew. The trip-hop that Jax was influenced by had started early that decade in the UK and was bigger in Europe than the US.

"There's more interest there, so we can cut our teeth - as Rich puts it - before a more receptive crowd." Richard Lloyd was the guy from the record company. Juliet had only met him briefly as Drew and Jax had been dealing with that side of things.

"It's not until the end of June then?" Juliet asked.

"Yes, well into summer break," Drew said, then frowned. "There'll be a lot of work to do before then, though. Way more than now. Will you be okay with that and school?"

It wasn't school that Juliet was thinking about. June was when Carl had been talking about setting a date. Neither of them wanted to wait any longer than they had to.

"School will be fine," she said to Drew who smiled in relief. "So how long will we be over there?"

"Just the summer. If it goes well, we'll be touring back over here from September and recording an album," he told her.

As if the summer wasn't problematic enough, September as well? How was she going to manage that?

Juliet already had her future mapped out. Marrying Carl, moving in with him, getting a job and starting community college in the fall. She tried to conceal her dismay. It was the most incredible, awesome opportunity she could have imagined. It was like a whole new path was opening up: just not one that she could take.

If only this had happened a year ago, before she had met Carl. To travel throughout Europe and be paid for it - and as a singer as well - it was beyond a dream.

"That's amazing news. It's hard to take in," she said.

Drew grinned. He was clearly over the moon and Juliet could only imagine how excited the other band members must be. Her heart felt like a heavy stone.

"We all have a meeting with the record company and the tour manager next week," he said. "Contracts, lawyers, everything.

Dover Six was going places. But was Juliet?

* * *

"So now I have to cancel my summer plans and drag myself around Europe to watch your band play?" Margot asked. They were at Margot's house, supposedly studying. Dover Six's news was a far more interesting topic.

Juliet's mouth fell open. "You'd actually come over?"

"What do you think? Someone needs to make sure your awful singing doesn't start a third world war."

Even Margot couldn't pretend to be dismissive for long, and a smile flashed on her face.

Suddenly both she and Juliet were yelling and screaming and hugging, dancing all over Margot's bedroom in the crazy way they used to years back, over something exciting like a cute guy asking for their number.

"I can't believe it! You're actually going to be a rockstar!" Margot said.

"Not quite yet but yeah, one day maybe!" Right now it seemed okay to dream. Except then reality came flooding back. "I don't know if I can do it, though."

"What do you mean you don't know? You just get up there and sing and rock it," Margot told her.

That wasn't what Juliet meant. "How can I do all that if I'm marrying Carl?"

Margot put down the hairbrush she had been using as a fake microphone. She frowned. "Yeah, that's awkward. He'd understand though. Couldn't you postpone the wedding?"

It was more than that. It was the engagement too. Juliet was terrified of losing him but equally troubled about letting down the band. "He's not going to want to hang around waiting, is he? It's not like being in the army or something." Something worthwhile, Juliet thought. Something that people respected. Like being a missionary or going to the International Space Station for six months.

"You really love him, don't you?"

"More than anything."

It might have started off as a game or a crush, an infatuation, but Carl was now her world. She had grown to know him, trust him, to like him and love him. It wasn't something that could be thrown away.

How could she possibly tell him about the tour? How could she possibly tell her bandmates about the wedding?

* * *

There really was no more perfect revenge than Cynthia finding out about the tour. But Juliet took little pleasure in her fury and jealousy. Cynthia simply couldn't get to her any more.

"You're going on a European tour? Like for real?"

"What about college? Can you study over there?"

"You are so lucky, that would be my absolute dream!"

Cynthia tried not to show any reaction but her resentment was obvious. Juliet had moved on and up. She was now beyond Cynthia and her high school mean girls clique. Cynthia realised this and was all the more furious.

When she saw how other girls reacted to Juliet's news - which Margot and Fhemie took care to hype up and spread around as widely as possible - Cynthia knew she was beaten. Juliet was now accepted as beyond cool. If there had been an election for Queen of St Gillian's, Juliet would have walked it without trying.

As a result Cynthia gave up on goading Juliet and calling her "foster slut" and simply ignored her.

For her part, Juliet was relieved. She even found herself feeling sorry for Cynthia at getting rejected from the colleges she had applied to. Happily, Margot had been accepted by Harvard which her parents were even more thrilled about than she was.

Fhemie had several offers to study dance performance including Juilliard, but hadn't yet made up her mind.

"You'll need dancers on tour," she said to Juliet as they sat outside in the sunshine, eating lunch. The winter was so long ago now and it was Juliet's favourite time of year: late spring. All the promise and excitement of summer lay ahead.

"I wish. It's all totally low-end, playing on the smaller stages at festivals, but if we ever do get successful we'll totally hire you."

Tossing her head, Fhemie was dismissive. "I'll be far too famous and expensive by then."

"You'll be on the pole by then, girl," Margot said. "Stripping for your supper."

Fhemie glared at her. "Like hell. You wait until you're standing in the rain and my limo sweeps past you and sprays you with dirt." She turned to Juliet. "So how does this all work with the marriage thing? Is your holy husband happy with it?"

Juliet's face fell.

"She hasn't told him," Margot said.

"What?" Fhemie started laughing. "Your fiancée doesn't know that you're heading off to Europe right after the wedding. What's he going to think, that you're spending an overly long time in the bathroom?"

"I don't know," Juliet said, feeling miserable. "I can't lose him and I can't let the guys down either. I kind of wish I could split myself in two."

"Sliding Doors," Margot said.

"What?"

"That movie where she lives two parallel lives. Figure out which one is best, kill off the other one."

Juliet vaguely remembered the movie. "What if you liked both equally though?"

"You can't have everything you want in life," Margot told her.

* * *

Carl was careful to treat Juliet normally at school. He was still her teacher and wanted to behave as professionally as possible. It was important that she graduated well so she could have her pick of colleges. He was concerned that marriage shouldn't hold her back or limit her options in any way.

But he couldn't stop his eyes softening when he saw her nor the feeling of joy and pride that she had agreed to become his wife. It was impossible not to catch her eye and silently communicate how he felt about her.

Her friends clearly knew. "Ave, Magister Spencer," Margot greeted him in correct if badly pronounced Latin, a glint in her eye.

"Margot, Fhemie, Juliet," he nodded to them, catching sight of Fhemie nudging Juliet and grinning just as he passed them.

He entered the staffroom with its aroma of stale coffee where he was approached by Anne Mead. The choir mistress wanted to discuss some Latin anthems that the choir would be performing.

"I am conscious of the *Sacrosanctum Concilium*," she was saying. "The exhortation that others should still be able to share and understand the worship. That's why I thought we might include translations in the programme. Your help would of course be most valuable with that."

Carl looked over the songs selected. "These are great choices, Anne. I'd be very happy to assist in any way I can with translation."

Anne Mead smiled gratefully. As colleagues they had become friendly since the Paris trip, though Carl sometimes felt a sense of misgiving. He doubted he would retain her good opinion if she ever found out he had fallen for one of his students. Let alone that he had first crossed the line in Paris.

But his sense of misgivings were about to intensify beyond all imagining.

Miss Villiers, the deputy head, stood there. Her expression was grave. "Carl, the principal and I require your presence immediately. I'm afraid there has been a very serious allegation that we need to investigate."

XXIX. Reported

"We've had a report that you are involved in an inappropriate relationship with one of your students."

The headmistress of St Gillian's had summoned Carl to her office. Her tone was formal and serious. Sitting next to her was Miss Villers, with an accusatory look in her eye.

"An inappropriate relationship?" Carl, stunned, played for time.

"With Juliet Martin, in your senior Latin class. You have been seen outside school together."

Together? Unless someone had been peeping through the windows, the only place they had been out together was at his church.

Carl's mind was racing. "Juliet comes to my church and I have given her a lift home a few times."

Miss Villiers raised her eyebrows in clear disbelief. She had never liked Juliet.

The headmistress's expression remained more neutral. "And how far would you say this relationship has developed? Have you crossed professional boundaries?"

He had, of course. But while lying was completely against his faith, the desire to protect Juliet was stronger. He tried to find something credible to say that wouldn't also be compromising. "Through church I have got to know Juliet more…" he began, but the headmistress cut him short.

"Are you involved in a sexual relationship with Juliet Martin?"

Little did the headmistress realise what a relief this black-and-white question was. Carl could truthfully answer: "No, I'm not."

He saw Miss Villiers purse her lips. She clearly thought the worst even if the headmistress appeared to believe him.

"And is there any reason why someone might think you might be in such a relationship? Has your conduct around her been unprofessional?"

Carl avoided answering this for the time being. "Can you tell me who has been making these claims?" he asked.

The headmistress looked apologetic but firm. "I'm afraid I can't disclose that."

"I'm trying to understand why someone might have developed such an impression," Carl said. He was also wondering about their motive for ringing up. After all, Juliet was eighteen. To ring up the school suggested another motive than genuine concern.

Meddling, perhaps. Or vindictiveness? Even as he wondered this he felt his heart sink. He was pretty certain who the call was, after all, who else could it be?

"Is it possible that Juliet Martin has developed a crush on you? Such a thing is not unusual with teenage girls and male members of staff," the headmistress asked him.

"Not that I'm aware of." It wasn't exactly a lie. Carl wouldn't have ever described Juliet's feelings as a crush. It had been a mutual physical and emotional attraction.

"If that's the case, while I can hardly suggest you avoid your church, I do recommend that you limit your interactions with her outside class as far as possible. Continue to follow the school guidelines: don't be over familiar with students, always leave your classroom door open if you need to speak privately with them. This is for your protection as much as theirs," the headmistress said.

Carl thanked her, avoided the mistrustful gaze of Miss Villiers, and left. He realised they would probably grill Juliet as well. There was no way to safely get a message to her so he just had to pray that her story corroborated his.

If not - well, he would have to take whatever came. There were only a few more weeks until graduation. Compared to the years and decades he hoped they would spend together this was a minor issue.

* * *

"Sit down please, Juliet. I'm afraid I need to ask you some sensitive questions."

Bewildered, Juliet took a seat before the headmistress and Miss Villiers. Being asked to sit down was a good sign, she supposed. If you were being disciplined you were made to stand.

"I need to ask you about your relationship with your Latin teacher, Mr Spencer," the headmistress began. "I understand you have formed a friendship with him outside of school?"

Don't panic. Don't go red. Don't go pale. Play for time. Juliet felt her heart thudding as the world seemed to go into slow motion.

"Do you mean at his church? I go to his church," she said.

"Church is no issue. But has your friendship with him crossed a line? Has Mr Spencer made any inappropriate or unwelcome advances?"

Juliet had to bite her lip not to giggle at this. Amid the shock and panic of this interview she had a sudden desire to laugh. She fought it down.

"Not at all." It was true: he hadn't. She had pretty much made all the moves. They certainly wouldn't have been unwelcome if he had made them though. And by Juliet's own moral code, given she was eighteen and a free consenting adult, she didn't consider any such moves would have been inappropriate either.

"Don't be frightened to admit if he has," he headmistress said. "You won't be in trouble. He's the one in a position of responsibility."

Juliet's head whirled. Had they already spoken to Carl? What had he said?

She was guessing he must have denied it or played it down, as the headmistress was still digging. "He's… just my teacher," she said, trying to appear surprised and confused by the question.

"The reason I have to ask is because we've had a report that your friendship may have crossed a line."

How did they know? What did they know? Who had said something?

Juliet played dumb. She frowned. "I asked him for a lift a couple of times, when it was raining. Was that wrong?"

"A lift is fine, Juliet. It's whether anything else happened. Did he try to touch you or kiss you, when he drove you home?"

"No." She was the one that had done that. The headmistress would be the worst ever police interrogator, Juliet thought. She had no idea how to get to the truth. Juliet could have passed a polygraph with these questions.

"If you're sure, then we'll leave it at that. People sometimes do get the wrong impression and I'm sure they were only trying to look out for your wellbeing," the headmistress said. "Remember though that you can always come here if anything does happen to make you feel uncomfortable."

"Thank you, I will, but truly everything is fine," Juliet told her.

* * *

Juliet didn't see Carl for the rest of the day and later that evening she was too wired and too freaked out to dare to go around to his place. She imagined spies lurking behind every bush.

Aunt Mary was out, but it seemed too risky to even use the home phone. So Juliet slipped out to a payphone down the road.

"Hello, it's me."

"Juliet." The warmth in his voice relieved her. "Are you okay? I wanted to speak with you earlier, but…"

"But it's too risky, right? Somebody knows."

Even being in the phone booth was freaking her out. She kept imagining someone peeping through the window or tapping her conversation.

They swapped notes about their respective interviews. Fortunately they had corroborated one another nicely.

"I'm sorry you had to go through this," Carl said. "I would have liked to have been honest but figured it made more sense for you graduate high school without a huge row."

A huge criminal investigation, possibly. Juliet wasn't exactly sure what the law was. Could they try to prosecute Carl, even though she was over the age of consent?

For the first time she was almost glad he had refused to consummate their relationship yet, even if it was due to entirely different motives.

"Who do you think said something?" she asked. "Someone from church?" Pastor Brown, maybe. After all he was Carl's spiritual leader. Maybe he thought he was saving Carl's soul. Though she didn't like to suggest a name without proof.

"I'm not sure." This was true - Carl wasn't sure - but he had an idea. He hoped very much that he was wrong.

"I guess we may never know," Juliet said. "But in a couple more months - if this hasn't changed your mind - we don't need to worry any more."

His voice was huskier when he replied. "Nothing would make me change my mind about you, Juliet."

The seriousness of his tone made her shiver a little, and even though he wasn't there she felt her body throb for him.

"I wish I could be with you now." Safe. In his arms. In his bed. Making the most inappropriate moves ever...

"Likewise." His voice held the same desire. "What are you doing Saturday?"

Juliet dragged her thoughts out of Carl's bedroom. "Saturday? Nothing much."

"Want to come for a drive? There's something I'd like to show you," Carl said.

Hadn't they better be more careful now? "Would it be safe?" she asked.

"It will be perfectly fine. You'll see why," he told.

He arranged to pick her up mid-morning when Aunt Mary would be out shopping.

Juliet wondered what he wanted her to see but Carl wouldn't tell her. "It's a surprise."

XXX. In the forest

Carl picked Juliet up on Saturday morning.

Amid everything at school she still hadn't told him about the band touring, but now it started to weigh more heavily on her mind. She pushed it away.

"So where are we going?" she asked. It was a beautiful spring day, warm and sunny. She had deliberately worn a lower cut top than usual, making the excuse to herself that it was to stay cool.

In reality it was because she wanted to tempt her sexy fiancé as far as she could.

Juliet leant back in her car seat, managing to deliberately undo a button so she revealed even more, and ensured her skirt was rucked up a little. She saw Carl flick his eyes to her then back to the road. She could tell he was trying to concentrate on not being distracted by her.

She wriggled so her skirt was even higher up her legs.

"Juliet."

"Yes?" She feigned innocence.

"Are you trying to make me crash?"

"Maybe."

Carl tried to focus on driving. "I can't pull over, we're meeting someone there."

Juliet gave a sly smile. "Are we?" She loosened her neckline even further, arching her back, leaning her head back and closing her eyes.

Five seconds later Carl had parked off the side of the road.

"It's hard enough seeing you at school all week without seeing you like this now." His gaze was thick with desire. He kissed her, pressing her into the car seat.

Juliet took his hand and put it over her breast. She felt him groan as his fingers moulded around her flesh while he continued to embrace her. His thumb brushed over the sensitive peak, making her gasp at the sensation even through the thin cotton of her clothing.

She longed for Carl to touch her bare flesh but he was teasing her through the material. Gently squeezing and tugging between his fingers.

His mouth moved from her lips, kissing down her neck, on the sensitive skin below her ear. "I want you but we're still going to wait," he murmured and Juliet moaned in frustration from wanting him.

"Seriously?"

"The more you try and wind me up, the more I'm going to make it as hard for you as it is for me," he threatened her. He was only half joking.

"Is it really that hard for you?" she asked, deliberately pretending to misinterpret as she slipped her hand to the front of his jeans. It was the first time she had managed to put her hand on him there without him stopped her, and she froze momentarily feeling his size and the rock hardness of it.

"That's how much I want you," he told her. "And if you can't behave then it's going to be torture for both of us."

Sexy torture though… Juliet wasn't sure if she minded…

Until he suddenly pulled off her and she was left with her entire body longing for him, abandoned.

"Some practising can't hurt," she pleaded.

"We'll definitely get some practice in but we're not going all the way. The first time I make love to will be after you become my wife."

Juliet shivered at the determinedness in his tone and the possessiveness of "my wife". Graduation couldn't come too soon.

He drove off again and it wasn't long before he turned down a track. They were in the hills outside the town, an area of woods and fields. Carl parked at the end of the track and they got out. He led her down a path through some trees.

As they came out on the other side Juliet was overawed at the view. It was on the top of a hill and you could see for miles across the valley to other rolling hills beyond, misty from this distance.

Around them were what looked like benches laid out, seats roughly hewn from tree trunks. There were birch trees at intervals, forming airy walls with the sky open above them.

"This is beautiful," Juliet said. "What is it?"

"It's called the Forest Cathedral. It's used by a Unitarian Universalist church led by an old friend of mine, Mike Talbot." Carl looked back. "Who's just arrived. I wanted you to meet him."

A man of about the same age as Carl approached and greeted them warmly. "This is Juliet?" he asked. "Welcome to our church, or nature's church, I should say."

Juliet was confused. "It's very beautiful."

Carl saw her bewilderment. "Let me explain. Or rather, maybe Mike can tell you about his church."

Juliet, who hadn't really heard anything about Unitarian Univeralism beyond the name, was curious.

Mike told her the basics. How it was a non-denominational tradition that welcomed all people seeking for spiritual truths. "We have other religions here, not even just Christians. Even agnostics and non-believers who are open to searching," he said.

"I thought you might like us to get married here," Carl said. "It means you can choose how you would like the service to be, whatever you're comfortable with, and of course it's a great location."

"You wouldn't mind?" Juliet asked Carl. She was anxious that he might prefer his own church.

"It truly doesn't matter to me," he told her. "To me, God is everywhere. Whether I get married here, or back at my church, or even in a Catholic church, He's still there. I don't think the specific ritual matters so much as what's in our hearts when we commit to one another."

Juliet loved the idea. She was holding his hand and she squeezed it to let him know. "What it if rains?"

Mike laughed. "Everyone asks that. We have many large umbrellas, and there's a kind of wooden structure further in the forest that we can use instead if we need to. The view isn't as spectacular but it's still pretty cool."

"I absolutely love it. It's perfect."

Carl saw how happy she was and he knew it was exactly the right thing for her. For them both.

As they walked back to the car, Juliet felt the cold anxious feeling in her stomach. She wanted this so badly, it felt right. But so did being in the band.

It was time to make a decision. How was she going to choose?

* * *

Carl knew from the moment that she couldn't meet his eyes in church that he had been right.

Rebecca.

Who else?

Juliet hadn't come that evening, having had an overload of assignments ahead of upcoming exams. At least that was what she had told him. Half of the reason was that she was still suffering an agony of doubt over how to let Drew and Jax and the rest of the guys down.

Dan and Jenny were also at church, with all the old ladies cooing over Sara Grace who looked angelically quiet before the service. It would have been the most normal thing for Rebecca to try and hang out with them but she kept her distance.

"Is your young lady not with you tonight?" Agnes asked him.

"Too much homework."

"That would be your fault then, for setting too much," Agnes said. She chuckled. "Latin verbs instead of church indeed!"

Juliet was actually buried in a history assignment but Carl didn't correct Agnes. His mind was elsewhere. He wasn't sure what to do about Rebecca. He didn't want to cause a scene and he couldn't prove it, but he never wanted to interact with her again.

He also had no intention of telling Dan or Jenny, though he knew they would be horrified if he did so and Jenny would likely refuse to ever speak with Rebecca again.

"Rebecca's acting weird this evening," Jenny said to Carl after Rebecca studiously avoided them. "Perhaps she's finally got the message that there's no going back."

"Maybe." Despite everything Carl felt sorry for her. Or perhaps because of everything. Because Rebecca was the architect of her own unhappiness, and her latest spite had isolated her even further.

He wasn't going to mention anything to Jenny or Dan though. For one, he had no proof, and the two of them had enough on their plate anyway what with the baby.

There were better things to think of, Juliet for one. She had told him that she was going to tell her aunt soon about their engagement. Carl had offered to be there with her but Juliet had thought it was best for her to do it alone. "Once she's done freaking out, I'll introduce you. I think she'll be okay once she's met you."

"If you're sure?"

"It's best this way. I might not tell her quite everything though." She had looked at him anxiously when saying this, worrying he would disapprove of anything but the full and absolute truth.

But he smiled. "I think that very wise." It would be kinder and more sensible not to shock Juliet's relation more than necessary, at least to start with.

Thinking about this, he caught Rebecca's eye in church. Pastor Brown was droning on in a sermon that wasn't managing to inspire Carl for some reason. His eyes wandered, and he saw the guilty and accusatory glance his ex-fiancée gave him.

Carl wished for her sake more than his that she hadn't done it. Despite everything he still didn't want to believe she was so truly awful as she had seemed these past few months. Partly because it made him feel bad for her, and partly because it made him feel like an idiot.

He hoped she would find someone else quickly and move on. He was so happy himself that he wanted everyone else in the world to know the same joy.

XXXI. Future talk

Despite his own happiness, Carl guessed something was up. He knew Juliet well enough by now to know that when she was worried about something she often bottled it up.

"Is everything okay?" He thought that she might be feeling overwhelmed by the idea of the wedding, now they had seen the venue. They had both been busy at school the past week but he had hardly seen her. He couldn't phone her either.

In Latin that day she had seemed stressed and unhappy so he called her back at the end of class. As risky as it was, it was the only time he could really talk with her.

"It's fine." Juliet felt so guilty as she looked at him. She still hadn't managed to find a way to tell the band and she felt like she was betraying Carl by not doing so.

He wasn't satisfied. "Juliet, we're a team now. You're not on your own and you no longer have to carry your burdens alone. Whatever it is, you can tell me. Even if it's about us."

Juliet looked at the board behind him, the desks. The Latin posters on the walls. It was a hard enough subject to bring up, but here he was the authority figure. She still felt kind of in awe of him, in his teacher role.

Carl saw her hesitation. "Would you like to come around to mine tonight? For dinner?"

She would love that. Even if she couldn't bring herself to say anything it would be an opportunity to be with him.

"Great. Want me to pick you up?"

"I'll walk." She could use the time to clear her head.

Wishing he could kiss her, and wishing she could kiss him without the enormous risk it would represent, Juliet left and went to find Margot and Fhemie for lunch.

* * *

"It's pizza. I had so much marking that I ran out of time to cook."

Juliet grinned. "So long as mine doesn't have pineapple on it. You know I hate pineapple."

"I'm doing my best to learn everything you like and don't like. When you move in here, you can go through the entire place and throw out anything you don't like."

Move in with him? Juliet got a sudden jolt realising she would be doing exactly that once she was his wife. It was an exciting and scary thought.

"That's if you want to live here," he continued. "We can start in a new home together if you prefer."

"I love this place," Juliet said. "Besides it costs loads to move." She was already worried that she wouldn't be contributing equally to their marriage as she had no assets and no real earning potential yet.

Carl sat her down on the couch beside him. He took her hands. "Money really isn't going to be an issue," he said.

"But I don't have any," Juliet said.

"It doesn't matter who brings what to this marriage. I'm not about to make you sign a pre-nup. When we become husband and wife, everything I have is yours."

"I know, but…"

"Besides." Carl hadn't really wanted to raise this, as it was something he still felt conflicted about himself. But he needed to be completely transparent with her. "I had an inheritance from a great uncle a few years ago. It's not something I live off as I prefer to make my own way. But it means that so long as we're careful, we'll basically never have to worry about money. So you can go to any college you want to. Then if you do decide you're going to be a rich and successful executive and want me to be a house husband, that's fine too."

Juliet felt strange.

Carl was confused. "What's wrong?"

"I just always imagined I would be doing everything alone," she told him. "I don't need you to provide for me."

"I will provide for you, because you will be my wife and one day I hope the mother of my children," Carl told her.

Juliet's stomach flipped at the thought of this and at the firmness of his tone. "Want to get started on that?" she offered, teasing.

"You know the answer to that." She could see from his eyes that it was both yes and no. Yes, he wanted her very much. No, he still wasn't going to yield to temptation until she was legally his. "So was that what you were worrying about, the financial side of things?"

Juliet became serious again. "Not exactly."

"What is it, then?"

How to tell him? Straight out, she supposed. "It's just how to tell Drew and Jax and all of them."

Carl frowned. "Tell them what?"

"About getting married. Pulling out of the tour and everything."

Now he was really lost. "What tour?"

Juliet fiddled with the hem of her blouse. "They got this offer to tour in Europe this summer."

Carl's face lit up. "That's amazing! Congratulations."

"I know, but obviously they'll have to find another singer."

"Why on earth would they have to find another singer?" he asked.

"Because of me getting married. I can't get married and then go all around Europe for months, can I?"

Carl was quiet for a moment. "Is this what's been worrying you?"

"Kind of."

"Did you honestly think I would want to stand in the way of you taking an opportunity like this?" he said.

Fear gripped Juliet. She looked up at him, her eyes pleading. "Most of all I want us to get married. I truly want that, more than the tour. Honestly." Please don't end it, she prayed.

Now Carl was laughing. "Did you not even consider you could do both? I'll happily wait for you, married or not. And if having a husband over there wouldn't get in the way, I could easily use some research time in Europe for my thesis. I was going to have to go back to Oxford and a couple of places in Germany anyway."

"You mean you would come with me?"

"If you'd like me to. I don't want to stand guard over you, but if you would like me to travel with you for some of it and it fits with the band's plans, I'd be happy to."

Juliet was enraptured. "I want you there for all of it. At least one of the guys is taking his girlfriend for the whole time." The bass player's girlfriend was on the payroll to help with logistics and wardrobe and other tasks. Juliet was very glad there was going to be another female coming along with them.

"Then let me know the dates and I'll book my flights."

She threw her arms around him. "I can't believe this. Having everything, I mean. I've been so stressed about how to let them all down and now I don't have to."

"I'm more amazed that you would consider giving something like this up for me," Carl said.

"Because I want you even more. You're more important to me than anything," Juliet told him.

This time he kissed her, deeply, tenderly, passionately. "I will never know how I got so lucky to be with you."

* * *

"I've got two things I need to tell you, Aunt Mary."

Her aunt lowered the spectacles that she used for knitting. She could knit blindfolded but there were some intricate details that needed close attention.

"From your tone I imagine you don't expect me to be pleased with either," she said.

Juliet swallowed. She summoned her courage. She tried to remember that she was a responsible, legal adult and someone's fiancée. Not a child.

"The first is that the band I was singing with has been offered a recording contract and asked to tour in Europe this summer."

She waited for a reaction. There was none forthcoming. Aunty Mary's mouth remained set in a firm, hard line. She had expected something like this, Juliet thought.

"The second is that I'm getting married."

At this her aunt's mouth fell open and her knitting dropped from her hands into her lap. "Married?" An expression suddenly crossed her face. "You're not..?"

"No, I'm not." Juliet interrupted her. She refrained from saying: "but thank you for thinking the worst." She supposed it was likely a lot of people would think that, given she was marrying at a relatively young age, and if they knew of her background. Give a dog a bad name and hang him. It would hardly be the first time people had made assumptions about her.

"Who is he then?"

Juliet took a deep breath. "His name is Carl. He's a member of the Baptist church I've been attending. I think - I hope - you'll like him. I'd like to invite him around for dinner next week so you can meet him."

Aunt Mary didn't yet consent to or refuse this request. "What does he do, this young man?"

Juliet had deliberately decided not to tell her aunt that Carl taught at her school. Most likely she wouldn't connect "Carl" with "Mr Spencer", if she even remembered the name of Juliet's Latin teacher. There would be time enough to tell her in future, after such time that it would all seem very long ago and no longer a reason for outrage.

"He's an academic." After all, he sort of was. He was quitting his job to return to study. "He's doing a doctorate in medieval studies." Once again she avoided the word "Latin" just in case.

Surprisingly, her aunt's expression softened. "You don't have to do this, Juliet. I know I said what I said, but you'll always have a home here. You don't need to rush into marriage if that's what this is about."

It gave Juliet a lump in her throat. She saw for the first time sadness and regret in Aunt Mary's eyes. "It's not, truly. I know it's early but it's the right thing for me, and we don't want to wait."

"Can he provide for you, this man? If he's still a student?"

"He teaches as well." Let Aunt Mary think she meant at university. "Besides, he won't need to, because I fully intend to have a career."

The disapproval was back. Her aunt sniffed. "I hardly see how that's possible, if you're gallivanting overseas with a musical band. What does your future husband think of all that?" A thought came to her. "He's not one of its members, is he?"

Juliet laughed. "No. But he doesn't disapprove. We'll be touring in over the summer, when he's on vacation anyway. So we'll travel together."

"I suppose it may help keep you out of trouble. All the drugs and drinking that I read about with young people today."

"As you know, I've been there, done that." Juliet saw her aunt flinch as she said this but kept going. "So I'm long over that. I simply want to travel, sing, see the world. Be married to a good man whom I love, and see what the future has in store."

The hands had picked up the knitting again and were working along the rows. "It all sounds very ideal."

Compared to her childhood, anything would be ideal. "I hope it will be. And I hope you'll come to my wedding and give me away." She looked Aunt Mary directly in the eye. "Because you're all I have. There isn't anyone else, and I'd like you to do that if you will."

"I'll meet him first, and then we'll see," Aunt Mary said.

Juliet had an impulse to hug her aunt but didn't dare. Maybe becoming a great aunt one day would soften Aunt Mary. She liked children after all, she frequently seemed to be knitting for other people's babies or grandchildren.

Other than Carl, Aunt Mary really was all she had. And she suspected that her aunt, though she wouldn't have admitted it in a million years, had come to think the same.

XXXII. Honeymoon night

"So now I'm your wife I get to submit to you, however you would like?" Juliet said.

She was lying down on the bed of their hotel room, wearing a filmy ivory slip that left little to the imagination. Against the white sheets and pillows, her blonde hair spreading out over the pillow, she seemed like an angel to Carl.

An angel with flushed cheeks and a very un-angelic look in her eyes who was waiting and willing for him.

Carl looked down at her, surprised and also even more turned on. "You know I'd never ask you to do anything you didn't want to."

There was a gleam in her eyes. "I might not mind if you did."

Carl unbuttoned his own shirt and cast it aside. By some instinct he moved on the bed over her, took her wrists in his hands and pinned them against the pillows. Juliet gasped in desire and her body writhed in the silken fabric, unable to escape his grip and not wanting to.

Carl was powerfully hard. This beautiful girl was his to take, always. He would never hurt her, he adored her, but if she wanted him to pretend to assert some archaic marital right, he was only too happy to oblige.

"You're going to submit to me and do your wifely duty, then?" he said, only half joking.

Her lips parted, craving him, and his mouth went down on hers. He crushed her a little with the weight of his body and she squirmed and let out a whimper.

To his surprise he found her submission an extra turn on. They were only playing around, but it awoke some deep, physical and emotional instinct in him.

She was his. This was his woman, his mate.

He grasped both of her wrists in one hand momentarily as he manoeuvred out of the rest of his clothes, lying naked on top of her. He was tempted to rip the silk right off her body.

Instead, he tugged it over her head and then let himself sink against the contours of her body, flesh to flesh, hard muscle above soft curves. He brought his mouth down on one of the rose tipped breasts that were now his to tease and tantalise. He loved her instant reaction as his tongue swirled around the sensitive point.

He slipped his hand between her thighs, feeling her there for the first time. So warm, wet, slick.

He was more than ready for her and he could tell from the way she was straining towards him that she wanted him too. She was ready for him.

Carl moved up over her, his knees naturally moving her thighs apart. Their bodies were made to fit one another. His length was against her, he was so rock hard he didn't even have to position himself. He simply moved up and slowly, with the most agonisingly amazing sensation - heat and wetness and tightness - he was inside her. His wife. They were one.

Juliet gasped as he entered her. She had been nervous about something not working or not fitting, but happened as though it was always meant to.

She had to get used to his size. It was larger than she had anticipated from feeling through his clothes, almost uncomfortable. But he was gentle and she loved the sensation of fullness.

He was possessing her. Her husband, making her body his.

Carl rocked into her gently. He wanted to last as long as possible but with all the build up and this final, perfect feeling it was going to be hard to stop himself going over the edge. Each time Juliet writhed against him he nearly lost it.

"I love you," he said, looking down at her. She was gazing back up at him, all his.

"I love you too."

He switched back to gripping her wrists with one hand - it wasn't really a hold, she could easily have got free - but Carl liked the way it raised and exposed her breasts and the darkening of desire in her eyes when he tightened his grasp.

He slipped his other hand lower, between them, the flat of his thumb going between her legs and pressing against her nub. He moved it around in a circle, gently at first, testing her.

Juliet's nerves were already on edge but when he touched her there it was like electricity. She cried out and pushed up harder towards his fingers so Carl intensified the movement.

This is my husband, she thought. Even this first time he already seemed to know her body and exactly what she needed. They were perfect together, a perfect fit.

Focusing on pleasuring her had briefly helped hold Carl back, but as Juliet suddenly moaned, twisted, pressed and spasmed against him he was totally lost. He could feel her climaxing around him and it brought his own release.

Exactly together. The same second.

Carl felt himself filling her, pumping into her. She had said it was too late in the month for anything to happen, but the possibility that it could gave it an extra edge. Juliet had said she didn't want any barrier between them for the first time, but to be as close as they possibly could.

He ran his fingers over her belly, imagining her one day swollen with his child. He wanted at least a couple of years of married life with her first, before they started a family, but if it happened earlier they would cope.

"Are you glad we waited?" Juliet asked as she lay in his arms afterwards.

"Yes. It's a good thing I hadn't anticipated how amazing it would be, or there's no way I would have been able to hold out."

Juliet smiled, feeling warm, happy and sated. "I did my best to let you know."

"I know you did. You drove me nearly crazy for months." It had become a game for her to tempt him and for him to hold out. A battle which he had only barely won.

There were so many things they hadn't done together. Juliet shivered just thinking about it. How she now had unrestricted access to his body, and he to hers.

Being with him had laid all the ghosts of the past. They had had the most beautiful wedding, with Aunt Mary eventually agreeing to break with tradition and give Juliet away in her father's place.

Margot and Fhemie had been bridesmaids, in completely different colours and styles because Juliet had let them both choose what they wanted to wear.

It had caused something of a scandal at St Gillian's. But since the term had ended, Juliet had graduated and Carl had resigned, there wasn't much anyone could do. Some people had thought she was crazy to get married so young but Juliet knew that it was the right time and the right decision for her.

She had never been more certain about her decision than now, as she lay with her new husband, enjoying his strength and his warmth and his love.

She was truly blessed. Next week, following months of intensive rehearsals, she would be flying to Europe as a potentially rising star. And she would have this amazing man at her side, to share in all the excitement that the future held in store.

XXXIII. Epilogue

Three years later

Carl had thought Juliet looked radiant when he married her. When they first made love. When she won her first Grammy.

But nothing could compare to the way she looked lying in the hospital bed, her hair damp and tousled, her eyes shining despite her exhaustion.

A tiny pink face nestled in the crook of each arm. Carl looked from one to the other.

"I can't tell which is is which," he said. The nurses had wrapped them both in white.

Juliet smiled. She had never looked more beautiful to Carl.

"We have Elizabeth Carla Spencer on my right, and Gabriel Julian Spencer on my left. Your daughter has your nose, so it should be obvious," she told him.

It wasn't at all obvious to Carl how this tiny delicate flower in any way had his nose, but he took her mother's word for it. Lily and Gabe, his children. They were named after Juliet's parents, a tribute he had been delighted to make.

The room was filled with flowers, cards and gifts from well-wishers. Juliet had distributed as much as she could to the hospital staff but it still looked like a florist's.

"So how are you all today?" he asked. Juliet had had to stay in hospital for a few days, getting the twins' feeding established, and Carl was looking forward to taking them home.

He had thought Juliet might say "tired" but instead she said: "Happy. Very, very happy." His heart swelled with love for her.

Most days Carl couldn't believe how lucky he was. They had enjoyed an idyllic three years of marriage so far. His decision to return to Europe to work and study had worked perfectly as her band toured and built up its reputation and fanbase. Moving into academia had made it even easier, as he could work from wherever he needed to.

He had thought their initial desire for one another would ease over time, but he felt as passionate about her now as on their honeymoon night, if not even more so. Making love to one another, nearly every night since they had been wed, had been a revelation to both of them.

Carl wanted her right now though he suspected it would be some time before they could resume the physical side. It would be more than worth the wait, regardless.

"The woman from the magazine rang," he said. "I put her off for a couple more days, they understood." A celebrity magazine was donating a huge sum to a children's charity in return for the first baby pictures when Juliet was out of hospital.

"Did you tell them it was twins?" Juliet. "Have people found out?"

"No and no. I figured you could reveal that surprise in your own time."

Juliet's pregnancy had come at a good time: Dover Six were burned out from touring and Jax wanted to take a few months to write more material. He was determined that their second album should eclipse the first. Which, given their debut album had gone triple platinum, was no small task. Juliet had been deluged with offers ranging from adverts to movie roles, so even when they weren't performing she was still constantly working.

The break from touring had given Juliet some privacy, though news of her pregnancy still made the celebrity press. So far no one knew it was twins. It was the one little thing that she and Carl had been able to keep private - their secret alone - and she treasured it.

She looked at Carl, her face momentarily anxious. "Do you want me to give all this up?" she asked him.

"These two?" He stroked Lily's tiny cheek with his finger.

"You know what I mean. The band. Touring. The next album and all the promotion." Once it all happened it was going to be

228

long hours, seven day weeks, endless different time zones. Juliet wasn't sure if she could manage that and a family.

"Not unless you want to. I'll be with you, and we can always get a nanny. You're earning such crazy money and I know you love it. It's an investment in their future too," he said, indicating the twins.

Juliet loved that Carl didn't mind being the one who moved around with her. He was secure enough in himself that he didn't need to be the main breadwinner: though if she wanted that, and to stay at home with the twins, he would have done so immediately. She still might, she thought. She really wasn't sure how she was going to feel.

"I'm so lucky," she said. "Having you. I couldn't do any of this without your support." All the times she was exhausted from jet lag, the times she was terrified ahead of a major show, when she had been sick, when she had just wanted to get away and shut the world out for a while. He was always there for her.

Carl leant over and kissed her. "I think it's the other way around. I have a beautiful, famous wife whose work enables me to travel, who has just given me the two most amazing children."

Juliet was quiet for a while. "Do you ever mind how it all happened?" she asked.

"Do I mind how what happened?"

"All the torment I put you through. I didn't exactly make it easy on you, did I?" She still blushed when she remembered that Hallowe'en years ago, turning up at his practically flinging herself at him. She occasionally still had a moment of insecurity that she had pushed him into it all.

"Sometimes I wonder if it was all part of a plan for us. If you hadn't acted how you did, we might never have reached where we are now. When I look at you, and at these two, I know that it was meant to be," Carl said.

Juliet thought of everything that had happened over the past three years. She thought of her friends: Margot doing amazingly well at Harvard and dating a hot new guy every six months. Fhemie, who had joined them as a dancer on their last tour, one of the biggest upcoming stars at Juilliard.

Aunt Mary was well, Jenny and Dan - god parents to the twins - had had a second child of their own, a little boy.

It hadn't been such plain sailing for everyone. Pastor Brown had been forced to resign and Rebecca had also left the Baptist church after it was discovered they were having an illicit affair. It made little difference to Juliet and Carl as they now attended the Unitarian Universalist church together.

Carl had wanted to support Juliet in prosecuting her former foster father. But it turned out he was dead, with his wife serving twenty years in jail for his murder. Justice had caught up with them both: Juliet could finally close the book on that sad and traumatic part of her past.

There had been some surprises at St Gillian's. Ann Mead and Miss Villiers had caused an even bigger scandal by falling in love and moving to teach at a non-religious school elsewhere in the state. Sister Stephanie - the most pious girl at St Gillian's - had ditched her planned novitiate and stripped to fund her way through college.

Perhaps the biggest shock of all was Cynthia. She had discovered a vocation and was now a novice at a convent in Massachusetts. Margot had made a couple of sarcastic remarks about witches but so far Cynthia was proving them all wrong.

Juliet bore no enmity or ill-will towards her former tormentor. She recognised that Cynthia must have been deeply unhappy and insecure at school to be such a spiteful bully, and if becoming a bride of Christ brought her the inner peace she sought, so be it.

But the happiest of all and the most blessed was Juliet. Somewhere in her youth or childhood, perhaps she had done something good.

For she had the perfect career and the perfect family. The perfect man who, even if he was no longer officially her teacher, still taught her every day about life and what it was to be loved: completely and eternally.

* * *

About Noël Cades

Noël Cades is a British writer who currently lives in Sydney, Australia. A fan of romance from historic to erotic, some of Noël's favourite authors include Jilly Cooper, Jackie Collins, Elizabeth Rolls and Victoria Holt.

Noël is always delighted to hear from other fans, readers and writers of romance.

You can contact Noël at noelcades@gmail.com

Noël's website is at **http://www.noelcades.com**

Visit Noël's blog to sign up for exclusive news and the chance to receive new free book giveaways.

Excerpts from *French Kissing* by Noël Cades

They passed other walkers and a couple of people jogging, taking advantage of the shade in the hot day. Marcy always loved the pale golden-green light underneath the trees here. It was like being a leafy castle.

After a little while Gray stopped and turned her to face him. "Tell me if this is too soon," he said.

"If what is?"

"This." He tilted her head up to his and brought his lips down on hers. They were simultaneously soft and firm, and warm. Her stomach gave a flip.

Her lips parted in response and he deepened the kiss, tasting her. It felt so right, so perfect, like quenching a thirst.

I really like him, Marcy thought. Even though it probably was too soon she had no doubt about her feelings. She was just surprised it could happen this quickly.

Again reading her mind, he broke off. "I wasn't expecting this."

"This?"

"You. Meeting someone practically the first day I arrive in town."

The way he said "meeting someone" gave Marcy a shiver. It made it sound significant, somehow.

"I had to make it up to you for the crash somehow. To give you a better welcome," she joked.

He raised his eyebrows. "Is that the only reason you kissed me?"

He was joking as well, but she played along. "Of course. Just being hospitable."

Gray narrowed his eyes. Without a word he took her in his arms again, more forceful this time, his lips plundering hers. She melted against him as his hands gripped her sides, his thumbs brushing near her breasts.

She was out of breath when he finally let her go. Shell-shocked, while he was grinning. "How would you like to extend me some more of that hospitality tomorrow night?"

Marcy was momentarily startled but he broke in again. "I mean have dinner with me. Nothing more," he told her.

Nothing more? She found herself half-wishing he did mean something more. But still the kisses… both of them… this wasn't "just friends".

"I'd love that."

Maybe this year wasn't going to be such a disaster after all. Maybe it was for the best that Josh had dumped her.

Thinking about how Gray's lips felt on hers, she was sure it must be.

* * *

Mr Grayson studiously avoided looking directly at her during class or addressing any questions to her. Marcy wanted to roll her eyes when she saw how some of the other girls simpered at the merest word from him. They were practically all over him, playing with their hair and trying to seem cute and dumb. Well they were dumb, most of them.

If Addy had been there she would have been rolling her eyes and making secret vomiting gestures to Marcy. Marcy missed her so much.

At least Mr Grayson didn't seem to be responding to them. He treated everyone in the same friendly but businesslike way.

Looking at him, she couldn't really blame others for drooling all over him. He was TV star hot. In fact given that he'd mentioned he liked acting she found herself wondering why he hadn't gone that career route. It had to be better paid than teaching.

"Anyone? Marcy… Winters, isn't it?" he said, looking down at his register and feigning that he didn't know. "What would your interpretation be?"

Oh God. Her face flushed bright red. One moment's daydreaming and she had lost track of what he had been saying.

Keep calm, she thought. "Could you please repeat the question?"

There was a snicker behind her from one of the guys near Brittanny.

Mr Grayson raised his eyebrows. "What is Monsieur Martin asking the hotel concierge for?"

She hadn't even read it. Fortunately Marcy found French relatively easy. She glanced down at the book. "Whether he has a non-smoking room."

He was silent for a brief moment. "Good." Then he looked away and addressed another question to someone else.

The lesson continued, an endless ordeal for Marcy. She had one eye on the clock, willing the hands to go round faster.

Finally they ticked over to noon. The lunch bell sounded. Marcy practically slumped with relief. Grabbing her things together quickly, she got up to make a rush for the door.

Only to be stopped by a command.

"Marcy Winters, would you stay behind please?"

* * *

"I'd also like to know why you lied to me?" Gray said. His eyes were a hard, dark green.

She wanted to sink through the floor. "I didn't exactly lie."

"You led me to believe you were at college. An adult. God, Marcy, do you realise the position you've put me in?"

Marcy wished she could cover her face and make it all go away. But her arms were hugging her bag.

"I didn't think it mattered. It wasn't like it was illegal or anything. I had no idea you were going to be teaching at Springdale."

They hadn't ever really discussed his job, which was odd when you thought about it. Or maybe not. Marcy had shifted out of the subject of college and careers as much as possible, to avoid revealing her own situation.

"Going into a bar was illegal. Buying alcohol for you was illegal. Taking you back to my place…"

"…was not illegal." She finished for him.

"That hardly matters now, does it? I could lose my job at the very least."

"I'm sorry." She really was. "I just liked being with you so much." I liked you, she thought. I still do.

Something softened in Gray's eyes when she said this.

His voice was husky. "I liked being with you too." Then he became stern again. "But that's it, Marcy, I'm your teacher now. Nothing more can happen. And no one can ever find out what did."

* * *

Marcy didn't know what instinct made her look around, back towards the bar, but when she did her stomach nearly fell through the floor. Gray - Mr Grayson - was there, looking directly at her. She froze. Maybe he would ignore her.

But no, he made his way over to her.

"You shouldn't be here." He did not look pleased.

She could smell alcohol on him and his hair was ruffled at the front. It was sexy, it reminded her of the other night with him.

"I'm only watching my friend sing. It's Coke, look," she said, holding out her glass towards him after his eyes went to it accusingly.

"You need to be twenty-one to get in here."

"I'm on the guest list," Marcy told him.

He was still glaring at her. "It's still illegal."

"Well, I was invited so it's not an issue." She didn't actually know whether it would be an issue or not if there was a police bust, but it was hardly a rowdy bar.

"That's your friend?" Gray asked, looking at Revel. "How old is she?"

"She's a senior at Springdale as well."

Gray swore. "I can't even drown my sorrows in peace without being surrounded by students."

Marcy realised he had had quite a bit to drink. "Drown your sorrows?"

He obviously hadn't meant to say it. "Forget it."

They were in front of one another, closer than he probably intended because of the crush of people. She was nearer his eye level due to being on the stool.

She could smell his cologne, his skin. Practically feel the warmth from his body, he was so near her.

She looked at his lips, firmly set in anger yet still soft. She knew how they would feel on hers.

He swayed even closer towards her. For a moment she thought he was going to kiss her, and every fibre in her body longed for him to do so.

But then he straightened up and got a hold of himself. "When the band is over, you need to go home, Marcy."

Her disappointment was almost like a lead weight, dragging her down, as he walked away. He moved out of sight and she thought he had probably decided to leave altogether.

Wound up about it all, Marcy tried to concentrate on the rest of Revel's singing. She eventually finished her set with a modernised version of "When I fall in love" which Marcy found almost physically painful to hear. Music occasionally got to her, but never this strongly. It was as though every lyric somehow spoke about how she had been starting to feel for Gray, or would have done if the whole teacher-student thing hadn't strangled it.

Afterwards Revel came over to their table, and Marcy wasn't able to leave as Revel had asked someone to get them more drinks. Someone else had left, so Revel slid up onto the seat next to Marcy.

Marcy knew by now that Revel wasn't the kind of person to directly ask what someone else thought about her, or care. But Marcy had enjoyed her singing, so she said so.

Revel smiled. "It's fun. I'll do it until I get bust."

"They don't know you're eighteen?"

"Hell no." She swigged her drink. "Well, probably they do, but not officially."

"How did you meet the band?" Marcy asked.

"They were auditioning singers, I tried out."

There were guys flocking round Revel: no wonder given how she looked. A couple of them started chatting to her and Marcy, the usual kind of thing, how they liked the music, did Revel sing there often, did they work or were they at college.

The one talking more to Marcy was quite nice looking but way too old for her, he looked about twenty-eight. He would probably be even more horrified than Gray to find out she was a decade younger than him.

They talked for a while, Marcy losing track of the time. She was on her third coke when she felt someone grab her arm. She was pulled off her stool and against someone.

Before she could react, there were lips on her, fierce, crushing hers. She registered almost instantly it was Gray. He forced her mouth to open for him and was kissing her in a really possessive way.

Marcy was turned on beyond belief. She felt her insides melting just at being touched by him. Her thoughts were whirling. What was he doing? He was the one that had vowed it was all over, professional student-teacher relations only. Now he was practically devouring her.

God, how she wanted him. She just wanted to roll the clock back to last weekend, sleep with him again, then transfer to a different high school by Monday so he would have never found out.

His tongue was probing her, tasting her. His hands gripped her hips hard. She yielded to him, feeling his pelvis pressed against hers, his heat warm against her.

Abruptly he broke off. He had clearly had even more alcohol since he had spoken to her earlier. "I can't stand seeing you with those guys."

Then he turned and left. She wanted to go after him but some instinct stopped her. Over the throng she saw him swing the door open and leave alone, into the night.

Find out what happens between Marcy and her teacher Mr Grayson in Noël Cades' sexy student-teacher romance novel, French Kissing.

Made in the USA
San Bernardino, CA
25 March 2018